Without wasting a moment, she shut the door behind them.

The stranger quickly regained his balance and spun around. He opened his mouth, then snapped it shut, his gaze narrowing on her face. The furrow in his brow relaxed as his eyes dropped lower, slowly trailing past her fur-draped shoulders, lingering on the deep vee of the sequined dress. His inspection of her body skidded to a halt when it landed on the gun she had pointed right at his gut.

"That's a gun," he stated.

"A man with a brain. What a unique combination," Fallon purred.

He took a step toward her, stopping when she raised the barrel. "I don't know what your game is, lady, but . . ."

She hesitated briefly as an idea formed. "Take off your clothes."

"My wallet's in my front pocket." He flung open his suit jacket. "Take it and get out."

She raised the barrel an inch higher. "Maybe you can't hear very well. I don't want your wallet. Now strip before I get angry. Believe me, you don't want to see me mad."

The stranger's eyes narrowed and his cheeks tinged red, but he toed off one boot, then the other.

"Is this how you get your kicks?"

She raised an eyebrow. *Not a bad idea. Minus the gun, that is*. She'd file it away for future reference.

BOOK YOUR PLACE ON OUR WEBSITE AND MAKE THE READING CONNECTION!

We've created a customized website just for our very special readers, where you can get the inside scoop on everything that's going on with Zebra, Pinnacle and Kensington books.

When you come online, you'll have the exciting opportunity to:

- View covers of upcoming books
- Read sample chapters
- Learn about our future publishing schedule (listed by publication month *and author*)
- Find out when your favorite authors will be visiting a city near you
- Search for and order backlist books from our online catalog
- Check out author bios and background information
- Send e-mail to your favorite authors
- Meet the Kensington staff online
- Join us in weekly chats with authors, readers and other guests
- Get writing guidelines
- AND MUCH MORE!

**Visit our website at
http://www.kensingtonbooks.com**

SOUTHERN COMFORT

KAREN KELLEY

KENSINGTON BOOKS
KENSINGTON PUBLISHING CORP.
http://www.kensingtonbooks.com

KENSINGTON BOOKS are published by

Kensington Publishing Corp.
850 Third Avenue
New York, NY 10022

All Kensington titles, imprints and distributed lines are
available at special quantity discounts for bulk purchases for
sales promotion, premiums, fund-raising, educational or in-
stitutional use.

Special book excerpts or customized printings can also be
created to fit specific needs. For details, write or phone the
office of the Kensington Special Sales Manager: Kensington
Publishing Corp., 850 Third Avenue, New York, NY 10022.
Attn. Special Sales Department. Phone: 1-800-221-2647.

Kensington and the K logo Reg. U.S. Pat. & TM Off.

First Trade Paperback Printing: August 2004
First Mass Market Paperback Printing: May 2005
10 9 8 7 6 5 4 3 2 1

Printed in the United States of America

To my daughter, Karla Wheeler. I want to be just like you when I grow up.

Also, to Linda Bennett for believing in me. Sarah Johnson, sister of my heart. Linda Broday, for always being there. Jackye Plummer, grammar queen. Sylvie Kaye, super critique partner. Red River Romance writers, for their wonderful support. Tammy, Lisa, Connie, Ladonna, Cody—nurses rule!

And to author Lori Foster and editor Kate Duffy for making dreams come true.

Chapter 1

"*Chère*, what you think I was goin' to do when I find out you be with the DEA?" John Cavenaugh asked, his Cajun accent more pronounced, warning the three people in the penthouse suite that his explosive temper was teetering on the edge.

Fallon Hargis didn't answer; instead, she glared at the man in front of her. Hatred burned inside her even while the cold chill of death ran its bony fingers up and down her spine.

Sounding almost apologetic, he continued, "I have to kill you, sugar, or you be tryin' to take old Cavenaugh down. I can't let dat happen."

"Remember when you called me *petit chat*?" She raised her chin. "Cats have nine lives, and I'm not so easy to get rid of."

Cavenaugh chuckled without mirth. "It almost be a shame to kill you, but"—he shrugged —"business is business, *chère.*"

"Screw you."

His eyes narrowed. Reaching out, he ran a finger

down her cheek, outlining the edge of her jaw. She jerked away, but it only drew another chuckle from him.

"You be good to her, hear now? Don't mess up dat pretty face," he said to his two flunkies before he strolled out of his suite without a backward glance.

It looked like her career as an undercover drug enforcement agent was about to come to an end. The last place she expected to die was in a hotel room in Dallas, Texas.

Fuck it, she wasn't ready to die.

She pushed back the black, full-length mink and planted her hands on her hips. The slit up the side of her red, sequined gown showed more than enough leg to make dumb and dumber drool.

"Too bad we can't party first. I bet we could have a lot of fun." Her words were low and husky . . . with more than a hint of promise.

"Hey, Jack," George wiped the sweat from his upper lip. He barely paid attention where he aimed his gun. The barrel pointed more toward the floor than her. "Cavenaugh didn't say *when* we had to do it."

Jack spun the silencer onto the end of his gun. "Don't be a fool. That Cajun's meaner than a hungry gator." He nodded toward Fallon. "And she doesn't party with anyone. You should know better than most," he ground out. "We kill her, then we get rid of the body."

So maybe Jack wasn't as stupid as George. She dropped her hands to her sides and quickly glanced around the room for an alternate plan. Her gaze landed on the cart room service had brought up before Cavenaugh pronounced his death sentence. The hot coffee hadn't been touched. She inwardly smiled.

It isn't over yet, boys.

"Say your prayers, honey." Jack raised his gun.

A surge of adrenaline charged through her. She lunged for the pot. Her fingers curled around the handle.

Jack fired.

Searing pain ripped across her side.

No time to think about it.

She whirled around, flinging the steaming liquid at Jack. He screamed and grabbed his face as she slammed the pot across George's head. Stunned, George dropped his gun and fell to his knees.

"Goddamned bitch!" Jack cursed.

Scooping up George's gun, she ran out the door. *Where now? No choice. The elevator.* She stumbled inside and jabbed the button for the fourth floor. *Anywhere but the lobby.* She couldn't take a chance of running into Cavenaugh.

The doors closed.

She drew in a deep breath—then grimaced. Jeez, her side burned like someone was sticking it with a hot poker. She slipped the gun into the pocket of the mink and raised her gown.

The bullet had grazed her just above her hip. Nothing she would die from, but it hurt like a son-of-a-bitch, and it was bleeding. If she didn't do something soon she'd leave Jack and George a breadcrumb, or in this case, blood trail. Pulling a scarf from her pocket, she wadded it up and placed it against the wound, keeping pressure on it with her arm as her dress fell back in place. *That had been a close call. Too damn close.*

And she wasn't safe yet, but at least now she was armed.

She brought the gun out and pushed a button.

The clip from the nine-millimeter dropped into her palm. *Empty. Damn it!*

"Only George would carry an unloaded gun," she muttered, ramming the clip back in place.

The elevator stopped and the doors whirred open. She paused before stepping out. Except for a maintenance cart, the hall was empty. She had to find a place to hide. It would be just her luck if Cavenaugh's men stepped outside the room and saw where the elevator stopped.

Her two-inch heels didn't make a sound on the carpeted floor as she swiftly made her way to the cart. At least the maintenance person wouldn't know the gun wasn't loaded.

"I can't believe the light doesn't work," a high-pitched voice screeched.

Fallon hugged the wall and peeked around the open door. A middle-aged woman stood just outside the bathroom holding some kind of chihuahua that wasn't much bigger than a pissant. The mutt turned slightly, saw her, and began to yap. She jumped back. For a small dog it had a very irritating bark. So much for this room—too many people, and the animal would give her away.

She started to leave when her gaze fell on a roll of masking tape on the cart. Keeping watch on the open door, she laid the gun down, grabbed the tape, and tore off a piece. Cursing Jack under her breath, she jerked her gown up and stuck the tape over the scarf.

The elevator began to move.

Her heart pounded.

Five rooms down, the hall veered left. She didn't have much of a choice. Grabbing her gun and hitching up her dress, she made a run for it, gritting her teeth against the pain in her side.

Fallon heard the elevator doors open as she slipped around the corner. Leaning against the wall, she tried to stem her ragged breathing. Maybe it wasn't Cavenaugh's men. Maybe for once in her life something was actually going to go in her favor.

Staying close to the wall, she peered around the side. Jack and George stepped off. So much for wishing. They didn't look happy, either. Although she noted with satisfaction that Jack's face was a rather nice shade of red.

"Where the hell did she go? You still got that pass key? Let's start checkin' rooms."

Her options were quickly draining away. She glanced down the hallway behind her. A man stood beside a door, his back to her, as he inserted his key card. She raced toward him. He'd suddenly become her lifeline. Just as he opened the door, she shoved him inside.

"What the hell?" he growled, pitching forward and reaching for the wall as he stumbled into the room.

Without wasting a moment, she shut the door behind them.

The stranger quickly regained his balance and spun around. He opened his mouth, then snapped it shut, his gaze narrowing on her face. The furrow in his brow relaxed as his eyes dropped lower, slowly trailing past her fur-draped shoulders, lingering on the deep vee of the sequined dress. His inspection of her body skidded to a halt when it landed on the gun she had pointed right at his gut.

"That's a gun," he stated.

"A man with a brain. What a unique combination," she purred.

He took a step toward her, stopping when she

raised the barrel. "I don't know what your game is, lady, but . . ."

She hesitated briefly as an idea formed. "Take off your clothes."

"My wallet's in my front pocket." He flung open his suit jacket. "Take it and get out."

Fallon kept her eyes on the man in front of her. He still didn't understand, and she didn't have time to explain.

She raised the barrel an inch higher. "Maybe you can't hear very well. I don't want your wallet. Now strip before I get angry. Believe me, you don't want to see me mad."

Her hand trembled. She gripped the gun tighter. The burning in her side grew steadily worse.

The stranger's eyes narrowed and his cheeks tinged red, but he toed off one boot, then the other. As he reached down and yanked off his socks she glanced around, wishing a back door would materialize. There wasn't much of anything in the sparsely furnished hotel room: a large bed, two nightstands, two lamps, and a television. Her gaze drifted back to the stranger when he popped open the buttons of his shirt.

"Is this how you get your kicks?"

She raised an eyebrow. *Not a bad idea. Minus the gun, that is.* She'd file it away for future reference. Fallon had never had a man strip for her. Just the thought was enough to send shivers of anticipation over her. This man certainly had the build of a male stripper.

And the way he stood, with his feet slightly apart, like he didn't give a damn, definitely turned her on. She wet her lips when he yanked his shirt off and tossed it on the seat of the chair near the bed.

Tanned skin and the ripple of muscles. The insides of her thighs quivered.

If the situation were different, this could be interesting. He certainly had potential. She mentally shook herself. Thoughts like that would get her killed.

He faced her, his hands moving toward his pants. A question formed in his eyes.

Heat flooded her, but there was no turning back. She almost laughed. It took a lot to embarrass her, but the stranger had managed to do just that. This wouldn't be the first time she'd brazened her way out of a bad situation. She could do it this time, too. Hell, she *was* doing it. If he knew the gun wasn't loaded, she had no doubt he'd strangle her. But he didn't know. And it wasn't like she hadn't seen a man naked before. It'd just been a while. A hell of a long while.

"Everything off." There wasn't time to explain she couldn't take a chance Cavenaugh's men might catch a glimpse of his clothes while they were pretending to make love. She cleared her throat. "There's no reason to be embarrassed. I've seen it all before."

"Do I know you?" He raised a brow.

Smart-ass. He knew she hadn't meant that she'd seen *him* before. Her spine straightened. She winced.

"Men are all the same." Her words came out harsh as the enormity of her situation returned. "Only the packaging is different. Now, if you don't mind, move it. This performance isn't for my benefit."

His eyes glittered dangerously, but he shoved his pants down past snug-fitting briefs and over well-muscled thighs before kicking them off. His gaze never wavered from hers as he hooked his thumbs in the top of his white briefs and began peeling them off, his movements slow, hypnotic. It didn't help her stability that he was fully aroused. She wanted to reach forward and caress him—feel him buried deep inside her, her breasts crushed against his chest.

A door slammed. She jumped.

Damn it, she had to stay focused. They were getting closer. Soon they'd be here. The only thing she wanted Cavenaugh's men to see was a dark-haired woman supposedly making love with a man. They wouldn't suspect it was her. She'd overheard more than one comment about her blue eyes being so cold they'd shrivel a man's nuts. Her gaze moved downward. Obviously what they said about her didn't hold true with the sexy stranger.

No doubt about it, she was losing her mind. Her grip tightened on the gun. "Turn on the bedside light, pull the covers down, and get into bed."

When Cavenaugh's men didn't find her, they might assume she'd taken the stairs down. As long as the stranger cooperated, that was. She'd make damn sure he did.

Wade gritted his teeth, but flung the covers to the side. What choice did he have? The woman might have a history of insanity as long as his. . . . He glanced down. His arm.

He lay on the bed, propping his hands beneath his head and crossing his legs at the ankles. He tried to appear nonchalant as he waited for her next move—not an easy task when a woman had a gun pointed at him. One slip and he'd get the upper hand, though.

Carefully she laid the weapon on the opposite table, the grip toward her. He had no doubt she'd be able to get to it before he did.

She shrugged out of the fur and kicked off her heels.

Wade no longer thought about the gun.

Raising her hands, she unzipped the back of her dress. The scraping of metal teeth unleashing the woman was like fingernails stroking along his bare thigh.

She frowned, as if in pain. He wondered why, but his attention moved to other things when the gown eased from her shoulders, caressing her skin as it slithered to the floor, revealing high, firm breasts. He wanted to gather them in his hands and knead the soft flesh between his fingers, pull her to him so he could suck her puckered nipples.

He swallowed. Or at least he tried. The dry lump that formed at the back of his throat made it kind of hard. And that wasn't the only thing hard.

Finally he dragged his gaze away, letting it roam down her body. The makeshift bandage tinged with blood and taped just above her hip made him catch his breath.

"You're hurt." He raised up on one elbow.

She grabbed the gun and motioned for him to lie back down. "It's nothing. Only a scratch."

"Then why are you sweating?"

"Maybe you turn me on, sugar."

She smiled and for a moment he forgot he was being held at gunpoint. Her face softened. He could almost pretend she was here under different circumstances. She definitely did things to his body, but that fact was obvious.

Reaching up again, she tugged on her hair. Off came the blond wig. Ebony tresses barely reached her shoulders. Her dark hair made her skin appear more pale. Again, his gaze traveled over her.

Very slowly. An aching need began building deep inside him. His groan drew her attention.

"Don't get any ideas, buster. Just pretend you're an actor and this is a one-act play."

Then why the striptease? he wondered. Who was she? What did she want?

Her thumbs hooked inside the band of the red thong she wore.

Who cares.

She shoved the panties off and kicked her clothes under the bed, out of sight.

The door rattled. She flinched.

Grabbing the gun, the woman jumped into bed and straddled him.

He grunted, but not from pain. Her body cupped his. Sex against sex.

Taking his hand, she placed it over the bandage that covered her wound, effectively hiding it. She trembled. He could smell her fear.

"Pretend we're making love," she frantically whispered.

"Kind of difficult with a gun pointed at me."

"Better than being dead."

She had a point there. He moaned.

"Louder and with a little more imagination," she hissed.

"Sorry, I didn't realize I was being scored." He raised his hips slightly. A flash of surprise and something else, desire maybe, brightened her eyes. Okay, so maybe he'd play her game. "God, that feels good." Wade knew he wasn't lying. She felt wonderful rubbing against him. Hot and moist. Maybe she wasn't as frigid as she tried to appear. She damn sure didn't feel cold right now.

The door creaked open.

She jumped. The movement inched her forward. She lost her balance and reached out. Her palms landed on his shoulders, her breasts flattening against his chest. The gun made a soft thud when it landed on the carpet. Their gazes locked.

Her face was close to his. He wanted to kiss her lips, see if she tasted like the cinnamon he could smell on her breath. Apparently she sensed what was on his mind because she scooted downward as if he had the plague, but when she did, he slipped inside.

His surprise matched the look on her face. Neither moved as time momentarily stopped.

A noise alerted him that they were no longer alone. He covertly glanced around her. Two burly men stood in the shadowy doorway. He didn't have to be told the bulge under each of their jackets was a gun.

"Company," he breathed. They were in danger; he just didn't know why. And something told him if he didn't play the game to the end, he wouldn't see another tomorrow. If he lived through this night, he'd damn well demand an explanation from her.

"Oh, baby, don't stop," she cried in a loud, southern drawl and moved her hips.

She frowned at him.

His hips rose to meet her circular movements. He grunted with pleasure when he slipped farther inside. Wade was certain she hadn't wanted to go this far, but it was a little late now as liquid heat washed over him in waves.

She sat up, arching her back, hands resting behind her on his naked thighs. Her breasts beckoned to him. He cupped one, letting the weight rest in the palm of his hand as his thumb brushed across her hardened nipple. A moan escaped from her slightly parted lips.

Apparently they fooled the two men, who backed out of the room and closed the door behind them.

In one swift movement, he reversed their positions. Her eyes widened with surprise. He hesitated.

"Don't stop." She wiggled closer.

He didn't need any more encouragement than that and thrust deeper. Wet, moist, heat surrounded him. Grasping his buttocks, she moved to his rhythm. He rolled his hips, savoring the tight fit. *Nice. No, better than nice. Great.*

Her nipples rubbed against his chest hairs—a temptation he didn't even try to resist. Lowering his head, he swirled his tongue around the fullness of one breast, tasting the saltiness of her skin. His mouth captured the nipple and teased. She arched forward and pulled his head closer. He chuckled. *Who is in command now?*

Her hand snaked between their bodies. When she squeezed, a stab of pleasure and pain shot into his groin. She eased off, letting his testicles fill her hand. His movements slowed as she began to knead and stroke.

She might be on her back, but she'd taken command once more. Right now, he really didn't give a damn. Not as long as she didn't stop what she was doing.

He glanced down into her half-closed lids. A slight smile tweaked the corners of her mouth. She looked alone, in a world all by herself. He wondered if she realized there was a man attached to what she fondled. It seemed almost as if she was involved in the sexual experience but not the emotional one.

"Look at me." He wanted the connection to be complete. Wade didn't know why. He just did.

She moved her hand from between their bodies and he almost regretted his words. Almost.

"Look at me," he repeated. "If all you wanted was an orgasm you could use a vibrator, and honey, I'm not battery-operated."

Angry eyes glared back. She nipped his arm with her teeth, like a wild horse that resisted being tamed. Then she smiled. Seductive and sexy. Her tongue licked the tiny wound.

"Why? Isn't this enough?" Thick with passion, her words wrapped around him, drawing him closer, almost making him forget he wanted more from her.

Almost.

"I want all of you." With a will he didn't know he possessed, Wade rose above her as he began inching from her hot sheath.

Her eyes widened with surprise. "No! For God's sake don't stop."

He swiftly glided back inside. She wrapped her arms around him as if she would hold him in place.

"All or nothing," he threatened. She contracted her muscles, trying to suck him back inside as he slowly inched out.

And her tactics nearly worked.

"Look at me." He poised above her, ready to pull completely out if he had to. He wouldn't be able to walk for a month, but it was a matter of principle now.

"Damn you." Her gaze clashed with his.

He wanted her to know she wasn't alone. She could distance herself from him later, but not now. As he stared down into her angry face, he saw her capitulation. He'd won this round.

He slipped back inside, letting her fire surge around him. Her lips parted and her breath came out in little puffs, but she continued to meet his gaze. Their ragged breathing echoed through the room. He increased the pace. She met each thrust until she cried out, her fingernails biting into his flesh, her body quivering.

Wade watched her come. He didn't close his eyes until spasms shook his body.

He stood on the edge of a canyon looking into space. Mentally, his hands stretched wide as he leaned forward. His body began to fall into nothingness. Hot wind rushed past. Faster and faster he fell. Stars exploded around him—lights brighter than he'd ever seen. A pillow of softness caught him.

Then, quiet. Only the sound of trying to inhale enough air to sustain life broke through the silence.

It took him a few seconds to catch his breath. He closed his eyes, then opened them. *Jeez! What the hell happened?* He felt like a virgin who'd just experienced his first orgasm. He moved to his side and raised up on one arm, looking into the face of the woman beside him.

"Okay, lady. You owe me some answers."

"I don't owe you a damn thing." She closed her eyes as if she didn't have a care in the world, effectively dismissing him. "As soon as I catch my breath, I'll be out of here."

Swift anger flooded him. Who the hell did she think she was? He opened his mouth, then snapped it shut. Damp tendrils of hair clung to her forehead. Her skin was paler than it had been earlier. Skin like fine porcelain, shadowed by long, sooty lashes. Delicate features. She didn't look like a criminal. He gently brushed her hair away from her face before realizing what he was doing. He jerked his hand away.

If she wasn't running from the law, then why the gun? Why had those men entered the room? They hadn't been in uniform and he really didn't think they were cops. In fact, what little he'd seen had reminded him of hit men from a bad B-movie. What was she running from?

His body brushed against hers. Something wet and sticky tickled his side. He slid farther away and glanced down. The bandage covering her wound was deep crimson and so was a small area of the bed. Carefully, Wade peeled the dressing away from her body.

"Damn it! I thought you said this was a scratch. You've been shot!"

Her eyelids fluttered open. She looked annoyed that he'd interrupted her short rest. "Well, the bullet scratched like hell when it ripped through me."

Chapter 2

"It's no big deal." Damn, why had she closed her eyes, even for a minute?

"Bleed to death all over the place," the stranger grumbled. In one fluid motion he rolled out of bed and grabbed the phone.

Fallon pushed up on her elbow. "What are you doing?"

"What's it look like I'm doing? I'm calling for an ambulance."

"No, you can't!" She swung her legs out of bed and grabbed the phone, gritting her teeth against the sharp pain in her side. "They'll discover where I am and then the only way I'll leave the hotel is in a body bag." When he still hesitated, she continued. "It's nothing. I'll live. This isn't the first time I've been shot. Give me a few minutes and I'll be out of your hair." She held the scarf in place and went to the door.

"You're not planning on leaving like that are you?"

She slowly faced him. "Do you think I might be

a little conspicuous?" Damn, the man was sexy, even when he frowned—a temptation she'd be better off resisting. She continued to the door, easing it open. Nothing stirred, not even a mouse, or in this case, a couple of rats. She still couldn't relax, though. Not until she was far away from the hotel. She shut the door.

"You've lost a lot of blood," he reminded her.

"Yeah, well, shit happens. If you call an ambulance the man who shot me will do the job right next time."

He turned on his heel, showing a tantalizing glimpse of his backside before he disappeared into the bathroom.

Great ass.

Better than most.

Maybe she'd lost more blood than she'd thought. It was making her lightheaded.

When he returned carrying a couple of washcloths, her gaze swept over him. He'd slung a towel around his middle and knotted it at the hip. *Intriguing.* Just the right amount of leg and the curve of one buttock showed. Any other time she'd be tempted to break her rule and sleep with the same man twice. Maybe it was a good thing she wasn't planning on sticking around.

"Come here. Let me fix that bandage."

What do I have to lose? He'll probably do a better job than I have. She shrugged and ambled over to stand in front of him.

"We could call the authorities. I'll make sure you get a good lawyer." He gently removed the bandage and began to wash around her wound with the wet cloth.

"I *am* the law. What'd you think? That I'm the

bad guy?" She had to admit the captain had told her on more than one occasion it was almost a criminal act to let her loose on society. Maybe he'd been right. She'd really blown this assignment.

And involved a civilian. She groaned.

"Did I hurt you?"

"No," she mumbled.

"Hold this."

She held the cloth in place while he ripped one of the pillowcases. Housekeeping would be pissed.

"What do you mean, 'you're the law'?" he prodded.

How much to explain? She didn't want to spook the man and make him change his mind about calling someone. All she needed was a bunch of cops tripping over each other. Still, she hesitated. What the hell, she was already in over her head with this man. "I'm with the DEA—Drug Enforcement Agency."

"I've heard of it. And?"

"Someone blew my cover."

"At the agency?"

She bit her lip. She didn't want to think so, but there could be a lot of money involved. Enough that anyone might've taken a bribe. "Let's just say I'm not sure who to trust right now."

He nodded and knelt in front of her. His knuckles grazed her breast when he brought the strip around her waist. A flash of heat coursed through her and didn't stop until it reached the juncture between her legs.

He wasn't unaffected, either. A fine film of perspiration dotted his upper lip. Her gaze moved lower. It was flattering to know she could arouse a man so easily.

She swayed slightly, not knowing if it was from the aftershock of everything that had happened or the fact her body responded so quickly to his touch.

"Easy now."

His voice had a soothing effect. Very comforting. She wondered if he might be a doctor, or at least someone in the medical field. Curiosity got the better of her.

"Okay, we both know I'm in law enforcement. What do you do for a living?"

He didn't meet her eyes. "I'm a Catholic priest."

She coughed and sputtered. She was doomed to hell for sure. "You're what?" she croaked.

"Teasing."

When he grinned, she forgot about wanting to castrate him for cracking a joke at her expense. Not that she'd actually cut his nuts off. She was sure that would definitely be a sin.

"My"—he hesitated—"my family owns a restaurant in Two Creeks, Texas. I help out."

"You should've been a comedian."

She'd caught his slight delay between words. Maybe the place served greasy food. Not that it mattered. She wasn't planning on getting to know him.

He chuckled, his breath tickling her bare breasts. "The next time you hold a man at gunpoint and order him to strip, you might want to ask. By the way, my name's Wade. Wade Tanner."

When he paused, she knew he wanted to know hers. Fallon supposed since they'd been intimate she could at least tell him her name. But which one? Sometimes she didn't remember.

At fourteen she'd run away from the only home she'd ever known and lost herself in another town, another place. Fallon discovered she could be anyone she wanted.

And someone no one wanted.

As a drug enforcement agent she continued the charade. Each new assignment gave her another identity. Somewhere in the midst of all the different personalities, she'd lost herself.

"You *do* have a name?" Wade looked up at her.

She took a deep breath and swallowed. Sometimes it was a good thing to forget. "Fallon Hargis."

He tied off the loose ends. "So, who shot you, Fallon Hargis?"

"The bad guys."

"Why?" He stood.

"Because I knew too much. Sometimes it's safer if you don't ask too many questions."

"Is that a warning?"

She shrugged. He could take her words however he wanted.

It was his turn to frown. "Sit," he ordered, placing both hands on her shoulders and pressing her to the bed. "I'm going to dress. Don't run away." Scooping up his clothes, he went into the bathroom.

For a long minute, she stared at the closed door. He acted the perfect gentleman even though he didn't know her from Eve. Just like they hadn't had sex a few minutes ago. Just like she hadn't been shot.

Why the hell did she have to pick this room? That was easily answered. Wade Tanner had been the only person standing in front of his door about to insert his key.

That should've been the only thing he'd inserted.

The situation had become complicated. She had more problems than she wanted to deal with right now. Lean, sinewy, muscled maleness had not been on her menu for tonight.

In all her thirty-three years she'd never screwed up as bad as she had tonight. Literally.

Wade leaned against the bathroom door and closed his eyes while he tried to catch his breath. Tantalizing images of Fallon's naked body filled his thoughts. He wanted her again. She'd been shot, was bleeding and possibly on the verge of passing out, and all he could think about was fucking her again.

He pushed away from the door.

So what did that make him? A pervert? A sexual deviant?

Or only human. She did have one incredible body.

Wade tugged on the knotted towel and let the white terry cloth drop to the floor before grabbing a hand towel and washing.

By the time he'd pulled on jeans and a T-shirt, his ardor was somewhat under control. That put his brain back where it should've stayed—in his head.

Now he only had one problem that he could see. What was he going to do with her? She'd been right about her wound being a graze. It was deep and nasty, but she probably wouldn't die unless an infection set in.

Men were still chasing her, though. He couldn't very well leave her on her own to go up against two gun-toting thugs. She couldn't travel by herself, either. Alone, she'd be damn lucky if she made it out of the hotel. He had one choice—take her with him. It was the only logical solution to her survival. He just wasn't sure if his small Texas town could survive Fallon.

Or maybe it was himself he worried about more. He'd quit the city, and in return gained a peaceful, quiet existence. At least until Fallon barged into his life.

He opened the bathroom door . . . and stopped in his tracks. She wasn't sitting on the bed. His heart thumped loudly in his chest. Did the little fool think she could get away from the hotel on her own?

As soon as he stepped from the bathroom, she came into his line of vision in front of the open closet. "What are you doing?"

She turned from rummaging through the clothes he'd hung up yesterday, tugging a blue shirt from a wooden hanger as she did. "Borrowing a shirt. Do you mind?" Holding it by one crooked finger, she raised her eyebrows.

Had he ever met a woman so unconcerned with her own nudity? Wade didn't think so. Not that he minded. She was damn easy on the eyes.

When he thought about it, she wasn't completely naked, either. Not if you counted the tattoo of a tiger on the left cheek of that sexy little bottom. Damn, the woman gave him a constant hard-on.

He glanced at his shirt. "Would it matter if I did?"

"Not really. Mind if I use the bathroom?" Without waiting for his answer, she sauntered past and closed the door behind her.

Bold, brassy, and beautiful. He could think of a lot of other words to describe her. Stubborn, ill-tempered, and obstinate. Sexy, sultry, and exciting.

Water splashed from the other room. His attention was riveted on the closed door as he imagined her running a wet cloth over her naked body, droplets of water sliding between her breasts. Abruptly, he turned and strode to his suitcase. He tossed it on the luggage rack and flipped it open.

What the hell would he do with her once he got her home? He raked his hand through his hair and began dumping clothes inside the bag. With more effort than he needed, Wade slammed the lid and yanked the zipper on the suitcase.

Fallon placed the palms of her hands on the counter and waited for the wave of dizziness to pass. She felt like warmed-over death. She really had to quit skipping meals . . . and getting shot.

A half-cocked grin lifted one side of her mouth. Slipping into Wade Tanner's room had gotten rid of a lot of pent-up tension, though. Sex with him had been damn good.

But she had his type pegged: a protector. As soon as he'd offered to get her a lawyer when he didn't even know on which side of the law she walked, she'd labeled him. And Fallon didn't need him, or anyone else, taking care of her.

Now she had to figure out how the hell she was going to slip undetected from the hotel. She glanced at the shirt, her new attire, before slipping her arms inside, being careful to lean toward her injury. The last thing she wanted to do was start her wound bleeding again.

She stared at her reflection. The sleeves dangled over her wrists. She rolled them up enough so they'd be out of her way and buttoned the front. This wouldn't work. She looked like a woman in a man's shirt. Her gaze roamed the bathroom.

"Hey, Tanner," she called out. "You got a knife?"

"Why, are you planning on holding me at knife point this time?"

She opened the bathroom door and casually leaned against the frame. "Would it bother you if I did?" she drawled.

His gaze lingered on her before he shoved his hand inside his pants pocket. "Here," he spoke gruffly and handed her a small penknife.

"Thanks." She grinned and shut the door.

She had no earthly idea why she enjoyed teasing him so much. Something about him made her want to hang around longer than she should. All the more reason for her to leave as soon as possible.

"By the way, your gun isn't loaded," he spoke from the bedroom.

"Yeah, I know." She stepped on top of the closed toilet lid.

"Don't you think it would've been kind of hard to shoot me without any bullets?"

Fallon smiled as she braced one foot on the side of the tub and reached toward the blue-flowered shower curtain. This guy could grow on her. She liked a man with a sense of humor.

"But you didn't know it was empty." Neither had she when she grabbed it and fled Cavenaugh's room.

She sliced across the top and down the side of the vinyl. When she had her feet firmly on the floor again, she cut two strips, leaving a wider rectangle. One strip she used to hold the makeshift miniskirt in place. Then, leaving her shirttail on the outside, she used the other strip as a belt around her waist.

"You still alive in there?"

"I'm fine. I'll be out in a second." She surveyed the results in the mirror. Not bad. Who knows, she might even start a new fashion trend.

She wet her hair and used his comb to slick it back. Her gaze swept the counter. The hotel had left a complimentary packet of matches in an ashtray. She lit one and blew out the flame. She waited a few seconds for the end to cool before crumbling the match head into a fine, dark powder. She applied it to her eyelids in a sweeping arch. Again, she inspected her handiwork. Not bad. At least she resembled Elvira more than the blonde she'd been earlier.

Wade stood up from the bed when she opened the door. *The perfect gentleman.* She sighed and watched his eyes widen, then narrow.

"Isn't that the shower curtain?"

"Was. Now it's my ticket out of here. Makes a great miniskirt."

"And the eyelids?"

"Trade secret."

"You won't get far."

"I've made it out of tighter jams than this."

"Where will you go?"

"I'll figure that out when the time comes." If only to herself, she admitted she was worried. When she'd run away from the two men all she had were the clothes she wore and the disk she'd slipped into a quickie, makeshift pocket on the inside of her dress before Cavenaugh insisted she go to Dallas with him. She hoped the evidence would put him away for a long time.

But as soon as the drug lord discovered she was still alive and might have enough proof to indict him on his criminal activities, there'd be an all-out search.

"I'll manage." She didn't need this man's pity or concern. She pulled her clothes and wig from under the bed. "My gun, please," she said as she straightened.

"You're right. You *might* make it out the front door by yourself. Then what? Sleep under a bridge? How are you going to find the traitor that way?" He scowled.

She looked into his eyes and wondered if her wound caused her to tremble, or the man standing in front of her. How could one man be so devilishly handsome? Ah well, he'd been a nice diversion.

"You have a better idea?" she asked.

"Yeah. I'm taking you home with me."

Chapter 3

"We're here."

Fallon roused and peered through sleep-laden eyes. "Where's the town?" she mumbled past a yawn.

"This is it. The main street of Two Creeks. One grocery, a post office, various stores and offices." He pointed to a limestone building in the center of the square. "That's the courthouse. Built in 1875."

"I suppose you've lived here all your life." She eased into a straighter position.

"Something like that."

This was worse than she could've imagined. The town wasn't big enough for her to lose herself. If Cavenaugh figured out where she'd gone, it wouldn't take him long to find her in this rinky-dink place. Right now, she didn't have much of a choice. She'd stay here until she regrouped, but after that, she'd be gone so fast all anyone would see was a trail of dust. And she wouldn't look back. She didn't need anyone taking care of her.

He turned the corner and went a couple of blocks

before pulling into the driveway of a small, white frame house with yellow trim. *Cozy.* A sudden thought occurred to her. "You're not married, are you?"

He laughed—a deep, resonating sound that filled the interior of the vehicle. "It's a little late to think about that now. You did hold me at gunpoint while you had your way."

"I didn't," she snapped, coming straight up in her seat, wincing when the flesh at her wound pulled taut.

He turned the key and faced her. "Oh, what would you call it?"

"I didn't mean for it to happen. Not the sex part."

"Are you sorry it did?"

His question threw her. She didn't want to dwell on why it had seemed different with him. She'd always used sex as a way of releasing bottled-up tension, and always with someone she knew she'd never see again. She pushed her thoughts to the back of her mind and looked across the short expanse of leather. "Sorry about the sex?" She shrugged. "Not really. Just don't get any ideas because it won't happen again. It was an accident."

"Are you sure?"

"That it was an accident?"

"No, that it won't happen again."

"Quite sure. Now, if you don't mind, my side feels like hell during a heat wave. I need some aspirin."

He grabbed the keys, sticking them in his pocket as he climbed out of the vehicle. When she started to open her door, he said, "Wait, I'll help."

"I don't need your help," she told him, but he was already hurrying around to her side. She should've known he wouldn't listen—the man had a stubborn streak.

Not waiting, she stepped from the SUV, but her legs were stiff and she stumbled. Wade caught her, the heat from his body searing her skin.

Fallon glanced up; their gazes locked. The sudden flare of passion reflected in his eyes should've warned her to move away, but her feet wouldn't budge as he leaned down, his lips stealing over hers. The taste of him almost took her breath away. The moment was brief, but it lasted long enough for her to know she'd lost control once again.

She balled her fists. She wouldn't let any man have that kind of power over her. "Kiss me again and I'll spill your guts all over the sidewalk."

He arched an eyebrow. "Did anyone ever tell you that you have a nasty temper?"

She grimaced. "Yeah, the last guy I splattered all over a sidewalk." Instead of taking the hint, he chuckled and aimed her toward the front door. She shook off his helping hand. "I can manage by myself. It's only . . ."

". . . a graze. I know, it's not the first time you've told me." Wade let go and walked slightly ahead of her down the sidewalk. When he got to the front door, he opened it and casually strolled inside.

She halted on the front porch, her senses suddenly alert.

No trampled bushes. Not that the porch light cast much of a beam. Her eyes scanned the area. Did a curtain flutter in the window next door? Gritting her teeth against a sudden stab of pain, she slipped the gun from the waistband of her makeshift miniskirt.

He turned back around. "Now what are you planning to do with the gun?"

"Shh, your door wasn't locked. The intruder could still be inside."

"I never lock . . ."

"Shh . . ."

"Fallon, I never lock my door."

"Are you crazy, or what?" She lowered the gun. If Cavenaugh and his goons did show up in town Wade would probably give them directions to his house. No one left his door unlocked. It just wasn't done.

A clatter drew their attention to the kitchen. She brought the gun up once more and slipped past him toward the noise.

"Now what?"

"Someone's in your kitchen," she whispered as she slunk toward the other room. "The gun might scare them off."

"It's just my cat." He'd never realized there were undercover agents this high-strung. He casually walked past her, went through the small dining room, and into the kitchen. Besides, with Ms. Johnson next door a would-be burglar wouldn't make it into the house. She'd clobber him with an iron skillet before he opened the door.

Wade switched on the light and glanced around. "Hello, baby." He strolled to the cabinet and picked up the plump tabby. "What'd Callie feed you? Huh? You feel a few pounds heavier."

He returned to the living room. Fallon still had her gun in her hand, ready to shoot the bad guy.

"Cleopatra, this is Fallon. If you purr real nice maybe she won't splatter your guts all over the sidewalk next to mine."

"Very funny." She stared at the cat, a frown bunching her forehead. "That has to be the ugliest creature I've ever seen. Are you sure it's even a cat?"

He looked at Cleo. Fallon was right about the cat being . . . well, sort of odd-looking. He'd rescued her from the river one hot afternoon a few years ago. Someone had put the kitten in a sack and tossed it in the water, but the sack had snagged on a log instead of sinking.

When Wade looked inside, he wondered if he was doing the right thing. The yellow-and-white kitten only had one eye, three legs, and it looked like her ear was chewed half off. Something about her tugged at his heart, though, and he'd brought her home, much to the amusement of his family. Now she weighed a good fifteen pounds.

"I mean—" Fallon continued "—it won't bite or anything, will it?"

"She might scratch if you corner her." He rubbed the cat behind the ear, but looked at Fallon when he spoke. "A gentle hand usually calms her down." Cleo began to purr as if confirming his words.

"If you say so." She shrugged. "You mind if I crash for a while?"

Why hadn't he seen what was right in front of him? Fallon's tough exterior was starting to crumble. They'd only been driving for a little over an hour, and she hadn't fallen asleep until the last twenty minutes. He didn't know how long she'd been up before that.

He let the cat jump to the floor and scooped Fallon into his arms before she collapsed.

"I can walk. You don't have to carry me."

"Just putting you to bed like a good host." Besides, she felt nice in his arms. It had taken a strong effort on his part to keep his hands off her this long. The kiss had only whetted his appetite.

"Don't get your hopes up. You're not going to park your boots next to my bed."

"Hey, you're the one who forced me."

"You were a prop in a play. Don't take it too personally."

But he did, and he couldn't wait for act two. Wade knew there'd be an encore performance. Fallon had enjoyed the sex too much. He wouldn't push her right now, though. There'd be plenty of time later, after she rested.

The door to the bedroom was open. He set her on her feet next to the bed, sliding his hands up over her hips to rest lightly around her slim waist, careful not to get near her injury. Her pupils dilated and her tongue darted out to lick her lips. He leaned forward, heard her sigh, but instead of covering her mouth with his, he kissed her lightly on the forehead.

"Sweet dreams." Taking the gun from her, he stashed it in the drawer of the nightstand before strolling out of the room.

"Asshole," she muttered.

Wade smiled. She could deny her passion all she wanted, but he knew differently.

He went to the kitchen and grabbed a filter and the coffee. As he did, realization of what he was letting himself in for hit him like a spray of cold water.

Sex should be the furthest thing from his mind. Hell, there were men hunting her. Bringing her here might be more dangerous. How could he protect her? Not that she looked like she'd need a lot of help. But there was only one of her, and they wanted her dead. This wasn't how he'd envisioned his future. His life was supposed to be peaceful, unlike the chaos of the big city.

He sloshed water over the top of the coffee machine. Swearing softly under his breath, he grabbed a towel and cleaned up the splotches before flipping the switch on.

While the coffee brewed, he stepped out the back door and deeply inhaled the crisp morning air. The sun was starting to rise in the east. Calm stole over him. It wouldn't be long before the fruit trees began to bloom, maybe in another couple of weeks.

Wade glanced toward the window of the room where Fallon slept. She'd been right to guess he'd lived here most of his life. He wondered what her story was. He doubted she stayed in one place for very long. There was something about her he didn't see very often in a female—a hard edge.

He glanced at the clock as he ambled back inside. Ten minutes until six. Doc should be up. He grabbed the cordless, poured himself a cup of coffee, and took it to the table, sitting in one of the cane-back chairs. After punching in the number, he leaned back, blowing on the hot liquid before taking a scalding sip while he waited for Doc to answer.

"Hello."

Not a question. More of a gruff demand. Wade sometimes wondered why Doc Canton felt the need to become a doctor. He seemed to dislike people immensely.

"Doc, it's Wade."

"I thought you went to Dallas." He said the city's name like the word soured in his mouth.

"I did, but I came back early."

"Ha! I knew you wouldn't stay. Too damn much traffic. When a person tells you it's across town it takes you half a damn day to get there. Craziest thing I ever heard."

"That's not the reason I came back early. I've

got a problem." He took another sip of coffee while he thought about how he would explain he had a wounded female in his guestroom.

"You didn't let some city gal give you the clap, did you?"

Wade blew coffee across the table.

"I told you young kids that you have to wear protection nowadays. Not a one of you ever listens."

"No, Doc. It isn't that at all." At least he hoped he didn't have to go to Doc Canton with a disease. Fallon didn't seem like the type who slept around. Hell, she was too mean-mouthed. A looker, though. *A damn fine looker.*

"Haven't got all day. If you don't have the clap, then what's wrong?"

"I brought a woman home with me."

"She got the clap?"

Wade rolled his eyes heavenward. "No, she has a bullet wound."

Silence. "Is she dead?" His tone was suddenly serious.

"She wasn't the last time I checked on her."

"Did you shoot her?"

"Now, Doc, what do you think?"

"Yeah, I guess not. Your daddy raised you better than that."

"It's a graze, but deep. Her right side. Probably needs stitches."

"What I'm wonderin' is why you didn't take her straight to the emergency room."

Wade hesitated. He knew he was about to ask a lot, but it couldn't be helped. If he took her to the hospital, it could cost Fallon her life. He took a deep breath. "This has to be kept quiet."

"It's like that, is it."

"Yeah."

There was a brief hesitation. "I'll get dressed and stop by the clinic and pick up a few things. As far as anyone knows, she has a bad stomach virus."

"Thanks, Doc."

After clicking the phone off, Wade leaned back in his chair. Doc wouldn't tell a soul. Fallon would be safe. He glanced toward the bedroom, wondering why he should care.

There was something about her. She seemed tough enough. Like she didn't need anyone. Maybe that was it. Everyone needed someone. He doubted she had anyone in her life. He wondered if she ever had.

The front legs of his chair slapped the linoleum as he stood. He strolled into the bedroom and glanced down at the sleeping figure. Fully dressed, Fallon had pulled one corner of the bedspread over her legs, as if she was afraid of getting too comfortable.

Cleopatra was curled beside her, her head resting on Fallon's arm. The cat opened her eye, saw it was only him, and went back to sleep. It was almost like the cat was watching over her, too.

He studied Fallon as the sun began to rise beyond the bedroom window. She looked vulnerable in sleep. The harsh contours of her face softened. Did she need watching over? He rather thought she did.

Seeing what lay beneath the tough exterior would be interesting. What kind of person was she hiding from the world? Not that it really mattered to him that much. He was only curious. That's all. He turned and left the bedroom.

* * *

The sound of voices roused Fallon from her sleep. Without moving, she barely opened her eyes. They were in the other room. Where was her gun? She vaguely remembered Wade placing it in the drawer next to the bed.

She started for it, but something warm and soft was curled next to her. She glanced down. The cat raised her furry head and looked at Fallon.

Frowning, Fallon glared at the creature. "Scat before I make a pair of earmuffs out of you."

The cat stretched lazily and jumped from the bed.

The voices got louder. She winced as she rolled onto her side and opened the drawer. An older man stepped into the room at the same time she grabbed the gun and aimed it toward him.

"Blast it!" He jumped. The cup he held fell from his hand, thudding to the carpet and spilling coffee everywhere. "Now look what you made me do."

"Just stop right there," Fallon threatened the stranger.

The old man glared over his shoulder. "You didn't say she had no manners. You could've at least warned me."

"I figured you'd discover it for yourself soon enough." Wade stepped around the other man and picked up the cup.

"Smart aleck." The older man pulled a handkerchief from his front pocket and began mopping at his suit jacket. "Get me out of my bed at this unholy hour and what thanks do I get but to have a gun pulled on me."

"I thought doctors were used to getting up at all hours?"

"Are you having a baby?" He looked at Wade.

"No."

"That's the only reason to wander the town this early. I could be at home drinking my own coffee. Which is a sight better than yours."

Fallon looked from Wade to the older man then back to Wade. "What's he doing here?"

"He's going to examine your wound."

"I told you not to call anyone." She rested against the pillows, her strength draining. The last couple of days were catching up with her. She might outrun Cavenaugh, but she couldn't escape exhaustion.

"You gonna shoot me or let me look at that wound?"

The doctor seemed harmless enough. Not that she had much of a choice.

"You're here so you might as well, but it's just a graze."

"You got a license to treat people?" he asked as he took a black bag from Wade.

"No," she said.

"Then let me be the judge."

Now who was the smart aleck? *Crusty old geezer.* He tramped to the side of the bed, set his case on a nearby chair, and turned to Wade.

"You a nurse?"

Wade looked confused. "You know I'm not."

Doc took off his glasses and began to clean them. "Then shut the door on your way out." He flipped on the bedside light and inspected the lenses. Satisfied, he replaced them on his nose.

"But I . . ."

"You need me to examine your ears?" He didn't look up, just expected his orders to be carried out.

Mumbling to himself about grumpy old men, Wade closed the door behind him.

"Now, let's look at that wound."

His demeanor rapidly changed. His voice became soft and gentle. Fallon found herself turning on her side and raising her shirt.

The doctor pulled on a pair of latex gloves and leaned close. Using a pair of scissors he unearthed from the bottom of his bag, he cut the binding and carefully pulled away the bandage.

"Still seeping blood. It's probably closing, but when you move, it opens right back up. Another quarter of an inch and it wouldn't be a graze."

"Can you stitch it?"

"Only if you'll agree to stay in bed a couple of days so it'll have time to heal and not bust open."

"You're joking." She couldn't stay in bed. There was too much to do. She needed to find out if someone at the agency had betrayed her. She had to see if it was safe to go in.

"I'll have your word or I won't so much as slap a Band-Aid on it."

"That's blackmail. You're a doctor. You took an oath."

"I had my fingers crossed. Now, what's it to be?"

"Okay, you win," she grumbled. *What is it with these people?*

"Are you allergic to anything?" The doctor asked as he reached inside his black bag and pulled out a small bottle of clear liquid and a syringe.

"No." She eyed the needle warily. "What's that for?" she finally got up the nerve to ask while he drew out some of the medicine.

"Just something to deaden the area. It'll sting a little, but not for long."

"Good." She relaxed. She could handle that.

"The shot comes later," he said easily, recapping the needle and gathering the rest of his supplies.

She frowned. "Thanks a lot for reassuring me." When he began to take care of the wound, she turned her head and tried to concentrate on something else.

He inserted the needle filled with the pain-numbing medicine into the wound. She gritted her teeth and focused on the back window, past the lace panels and into the backyard. There was a tug as the doctor pulled her skin together to make the first stitch.

Wade walked outside and leaned against the porch rail. She turned her attention on him. What kind of man took a gunshot stranger into his home with little explanation? What kind of person did that?

There was another tug on her flesh as the next stitch went in.

Does he have a girlfriend? Or maybe a fiancée? No, she didn't think so. He'd laughed when she asked if he was married. Not that she cared one way or the other. She didn't need anyone . . . never would.

Three more stitches later, Wade straightened, moving out of her line of vision.

"Well, that ought to do it."

Fallon glanced at the old man. For a moment she felt disorientated. Then her eyes focused.

Reaching in his bag, he brought out some ointment and applied it to the wound before bandaging it. He turned and dropped the tape back into his bag and pulled out a pre-filled syringe. "Tetanus," he said.

Before she had time to react, he'd removed the needle and was dabbing her arm with an alcohol swab.

He began to collect his equipment, but paused for a moment to glance at her with narrowed eyes. "You move around much and those stitches are going to break loose. I saw a couple of other scars that didn't look like you got them from tripping and falling down. Take care of yourself, little girl." His wise old eyes seemed to look right through her. "Maybe it's time you stopped running from yourself."

She opened her mouth, then snapped it closed. He didn't know her. The doctor was only guessing and not doing a very good job of it. She wasn't running from herself, but from Cavenaugh and his goons. Why would she run from herself? There wasn't anything she was afraid to face. A little voice inside her began to laugh. *Are you sure?*

Wade glanced up from washing his cup when Doc entered the kitchen. "You get her all stitched up?" He shook the water off and placed the cup in the drainer.

"I got her fixed. If she'll stay in bed, that is."

"Want another cup?" Wade nodded toward the pot.

"About half." He looked at his watch. "Got Skip Yates coming in early this morning."

"Going to get his cast off?" Wade got a clean cup from the cabinet, poured the coffee, then handed it to Doc.

"You make coffee just like your mama—too damn strong," he said after taking a sip, then continued before Wade could comment. "Skip can't afford to miss any more work. He was off for a week after that mare kicked him. I told him if he dropped by before work this morning I'd remove it."

Even with all his complaining, Wade liked the old man. "You're a good person, Doc."

"So are you." He blew on his coffee and took another sip. "But what about that gal? If I'm not mistaken, you left the city because of all the problems. Looks to me like you're starting to bring them home with you." He didn't look at Wade. "Most people don't get bullet wounds for no reason."

Ah hell, Doc was right. He'd probably brought more trouble home with him than he wanted to tackle. But it was only for a couple of days. What harm could she cause in that short a time?

Doc raised his head and stared pointedly at him. He knew the older man wanted to hear Fallon's story, but Wade had promised not to reveal the fact she was with the DEA. Doc did have a right to know, though. He'd put his license on the line. Still, he hesitated.

Fallon spoke from the doorway. "I'm with the Drug Enforcement Agency and I'd just as soon that didn't become public knowledge."

Both turned to face her.

Doc frowned. "You promised not to get out of bed."

"I had my fingers crossed," she fired back. "Besides, I wouldn't have if someone had brought me a cup of coffee."

"Sit," Wade ordered. "I'll get you some."

Doc swallowed the last of his coffee, stood, and placed his cup in the sink. "I'll come by tomorrow. If you break those stitches open before then, buy some Super Glue." He reached inside his bag and slapped a packet of pills on the table. "Antibiotics. One every six hours. I'm going to the office." He left muttering something about ornery women and mule-headed mares.

"He's right, you know. You should be in bed letting that heal." The mutinous expression on her face told him he probably should've kept his mouth shut. He handed her a cup of coffee and sat across from her.

"There's too much to do. I have to find out if someone at the agency betrayed me. Right now, I don't know who I can trust."

"You're safe here. The man who's after you will eventually stop looking." Fallon refused to meet his gaze, blowing on her coffee before taking a drink. She was hiding something. "What haven't you told me?" he asked.

Carefully she set her cup down and looked across the table. He didn't back down. She dropped her gaze, running her finger over the rim of her coffee cup before meeting his eyes again. "They might not give up quite so easily when they discover I downloaded some stuff from Cavenaugh's computer."

"What kind of stuff?"

"Incriminating stuff."

Wade had a sneaking suspicion this was one time he should've just said no when it came to strays. Why didn't he listen to his gut instinct? Hell, he'd have to be blind not to know she was going to be trouble.

She took a drink and set her cup down, wearing a thoughtful frown on her face. "Aren't doctors supposed to report gunshot wounds?" she changed the subject.

Even though Wade wanted to know more, he didn't think she was ready to divulge anything quite yet. It didn't matter. He'd find out soon enough. If she wanted to talk about something else, that was fine with him. "Doc did report your gunshot wound."

She clenched her hands together. "To who!"

"Me." He crossed his feet at his ankles and leaned back in his chair. "I *am* the law. What'd you think? That I was the bad guy?"

Chapter 4

Fallon's eyes narrowed. "What do you mean, 'you are the law'? I thought you said you were in the restaurant business?"

He shook his head. "No, what I actually said was my family has a restaurant, and I help out."

But he'd implied he worked in a restaurant, not law enforcement. Why hadn't he told her the truth—unless he didn't buy her story. He suddenly became dangerous. And if he wasn't careful, he could get her killed. "Don't even think about calling the DEA office. As soon as you start asking questions, Cavenaugh will be hot on my trail."

"Then don't give me a reason to call them," Wade warned.

She gripped the handle of the coffee mug so tight she wondered why it didn't shatter. "What do you mean by that?"

He sat forward in his chair. She had a sudden urge to lean back . . . to stay out of arm's reach.

"Just that I *am* the law in Two Creeks. This is my town. I'll give you refuge, but I don't want any problems. This is a quiet place, and I plan to keep it that way." He stood and walked to the drainer beside the sink to retrieve a cup before pouring himself some of the dark, rich coffee.

"You're giving me orders?"

"While you're under my roof, I am."

Ha! Wade spoke like he actually believed she'd obey his commands. When had she ever followed protocol? She could tell him he might want to talk to the captain about her and rules, but she wasn't completely sure she could trust King, either. Besides, why warn Wade that she didn't always go by the book? It wasn't like she owed him anything.

A sudden image of the two of them wrapped in each other's arms, their naked bodies straining toward fulfillment, clouded her vision. Sex with him *had* been pretty fantastic. Maybe she did owe him something. A flash of heat stole over her body. She clamped her legs together, but that only increased the small spasms that swept through her.

Her gaze flew to him as he brought his coffee back to the table. Once more, he sat across from her. She watched him spoon in sugar, remembering how his fingers had teased her body, gliding over the surface of her skin, barely touching as they skimmed across the sensitive areas.

An unexpected impulse came over her to unbutton the borrowed shirt she wore. Let it slip from her shoulders and drift down her arms. She wanted to feel his thumbs brushing across her nipples, his mouth sucking at her breasts, his teeth pulling on the tender nubs.

"And my rules aren't made to be broken," he said, successfully shoving his way past her fantasies.

She closed her eyes for a couple of heartbeats.

When she opened them once more, she'd regained a little of her composure.

If he wanted to enforce a certain standard for her to follow, then so be it. Her rules weren't made to be broken, either; she never slept with the same man twice.

Fallon knew he waited for her to agree to his terms. Setting her cup back in the saucer, she met his gaze unflinchingly. "I won't cause any problems, but I have a few conditions of my own." She crossed her arms in front of her and almost moaned aloud when the material pulled taut across her sensitive nipples. "No touching. No kissing. No sex." Her words lacked the conviction she wanted while at the same time her mind screamed those were really stupid conditions.

After all, she was only going to be here a few days. What would it hurt to catch up on some of the pleasures life threw her way? Instinctively she knew it would be different with Wade. She couldn't afford to let him get too close when she knew the relationship would be doomed from the start—just like the other ones littering her past.

"Anyone home?" a voice called from the other room.

Fallon jerked her head around and automatically reached for her gun, but it was in the bedroom.

"I'm in the kitchen," he called back and then, in a quieter voice, spoke to Fallon. "When I was in Dallas I met an old friend named Josh. You're his cousin who's applying for the opening at the sheriff's office, except you came down with a sudden bout of stomach flu." Wade stood as a tall, lanky blonde strolled into the kitchen. "Hi, Sis. I'll put on a fresh pot if you can stay."

"Well no, I'm in a hurr . . . ." her words trailed off and her eyebrows rose when she noticed Fallon. "Maybe just one cup."

"Fallon, this is my younger sister, Bailey." He went to the counter, removed the filter from the coffeepot, and dumped the used one in the trash under the sink. "Fallon is Josh's cousin. She's applying for the records job at the sheriff's office."

It was Fallon's turn to raise her eyebrows. How easily the lies slipped from his lips. Okay, he'd impressed her—a little. She certainly wasn't this Josh's cousin. And going to work in records? Her? Hell, she could barely keep her reports straight.

"How nice," Bailey murmured.

He glanced over his shoulder. "Don't get too close," he warned when she pulled out the nearest chair. "Fallon has the stomach flu. Doc just left and doesn't think anyone should be around her."

Bailey moved to a chair on the opposite side of the table. "Nice to meet you," she murmured, then looked at her brother and added, "Doc isn't afraid you'll get it?"

"I guess since he's already been exposed it didn't matter," Fallon replied sweetly. "I do feel like I've been so much trouble. I didn't even realize I was ill until late last night, but by then we were on our way here. Wade wouldn't hear of me staying at the motel as I'd planned." She suddenly grimaced. "I wonder if this awful churning will ever stop."

Her gaze momentarily locked with Wade's. His face showed surprise. She had to admit she was rather good at deception. She'd certainly fooled Cavenaugh for a few months while she gathered information. Trouble was, the only hard evidence happened to be on the disk. She hoped it would be enough to lock him away.

"I hate being sick. I'm a terrible patient," Bailey said, capturing her attention again. "What'd you think of Doc Canton?"

Against her will, Fallon smiled. "He's a little on the crusty side, don't you think?"

Bailey grinned. "But if you trim away the hard edge, you'll find a tender and compassionate man."

"Is this the same Doc Canton that I know?" Wade asked as the coffee began dripping into the glass pot.

"The one and only, and you know as well as I do the man has a heart of gold."

"He's certainly fooled me."

Bailey tossed her blond curls over her shoulder and grinned. "Now, you know you love him as much as I do. He's certainly bandaged enough of your scrapes, and he didn't tell Mom where you got some of them. If he had, you'd still be grounded."

"All right," Wade smiled and brought his sister a cup of coffee, setting it in front of her before he took the chair beside her. "Maybe he isn't quite that bad."

Fallon watched the exchange from the sidelines. A deep, painful yearning rose within her that left her shaking on the inside. A vague picture formed in her mind of what her life could've been like. It would never happen, though. The image faded.

Bailey abruptly turned toward Fallon. "I thought I'd heard about or met all of Josh's cousins. He and Wade were inseparable during high school."

She's good, Fallon thought. *Hit when a person isn't expecting it.* "And I'm the best of the bunch," Fallon easily responded with light banter. "Shame on him. Are you sure Josh hasn't mentioned me even once?"

Bailey shook her head. "You have an unusual name. I think I would've remembered it."

"I'll have a talk with him. But then, I guess I can't fault him too much. I was away most of the time. You see, I'm actually a second cousin. His Uncle Bob's wife's oldest daughter's daughter. That's on his father's side, of course. We moved around a lot. My dad was in the Air Force." By the look of confusion on Bailey's face, Fallon knew she'd put in enough relations so the girl probably bought her story. And everyone in Texas had an Uncle Bob in the family. At the very least, by the time the girl unraveled the relatives, Fallon would be history and it wouldn't matter.

Bailey finally nodded before glancing pointedly down at Fallon's hand. "Oh, you're not married, either." Her innocent eyes turned to look at her brother.

"Doc was pretty adamant that you don't overtax yourself," Wade quickly changed the subject.

"You're right, and I'm starting to feel a bit queasy. I think I'll lie down again." She was relieved she didn't have to sidestep any more of his sister's questions. "If you'll excuse me."

"Oh, cute skirt," Bailey commented as Fallon stood.

"Thanks. I got it right off the rack."

A fit of coughing overcame Wade.

Bailey cast a cautious look in her brother's direction. "Maybe I should leave, too. I'd hate to get sick." She looked back to Fallon. "It was nice meeting you. I hope you feel better soon."

"Thanks." Fallon held her stomach as she made her way to the guest bedroom. She hadn't really stretched the truth that much. The room had started to close in on her, getting smaller and smaller. People always made her nervous, and there were two too many in the kitchen. Fallon had never been much on socializing. The sooner she got the hell out of Dodge—or Two Creeks, to be exact—the better.

Once she was back in her room, the knots in her stomach lessened. She eased down to the side of the bed. Cleopatra joined her.

"I certainly don't need your company, either."

The cat didn't seem aware of her indifference. She purred softly and nudged Fallon's hip with her head.

"You're butt-ugly, you know." She didn't even like cats. They shed everywhere and sharpened their claws on whatever was handy. A nuisance, that's what they were. She scooted away from the mangy beast.

What was she doing here? Fear coursed its way through her. She knew her apprehension didn't stem from the fact she thought Cavenaugh or his men would discover her whereabouts before she had time to regroup. At least, not this quickly. No, it was something much worse. Wade, and those around him, represented everything she tried to avoid.

Caring about other people.

During her seven years with the DEA, she'd always worked alone or kept to herself. If she had the misfortune of having a partner, she didn't let herself get drawn into his private life. What did she care if everyone thought she was a cold-hearted bitch? She was a damn good agent, and that's all that mattered.

And she didn't have to care. She didn't have to feel. She didn't have to risk ever being hurt again.

"You're pretty good," Wade spoke.

Her head jerked up. He casually leaned against the door frame, his arms crossed in front of him.

She tamped down the flutter of excitement that rose inside her. "What do you mean?"

"If you can fool Bailey, then you can fool anyone. She can usually spot a fraud."

Her brows drew together. She wasn't sure she liked his implication.

Realizing she was also petting the dumb cat, Fallon drew her hand quickly to her lap. Cleopatra jumped to the carpeted floor, going straight to Wade and rubbing her body against his leg. Deep purrs came from the animal. Fallon couldn't blame the feline. Wade had gotten the same reaction from her.

Not caring for the direction her thoughts had taken, she instead concentrated on his comment about her acting ability. "It's my job to fool people. I wouldn't have lasted this long if I couldn't play whatever role the agency threw in my direction."

He straightened and ambled farther into the bedroom. Wade moved with the stealth of a predator locked on his prey, his gaze never wavering. "Maybe that's your problem," his words softly caressed her soul.

"What do you mean?" She swallowed past the sudden lump in her throat.

"Just that it might be time to stop acting." He paused a few feet from the bed. "When we made love, I think the real you emerged for a moment. How long has it been since you let her out of the hard shell you've built around yourself?"

She stood, then wished she'd kept her seat. Instead of putting herself in a less vulnerable position, she was more aware of his body. Only a foot separated them: close enough to feel the heat radiating from his body, but still far enough away for her to yearn to step closer. Maybe she did lean forward a little because his breath fanned her face with a light, sensuous touch.

Transfixed, she watched silently as his gaze slid down her length, then slowly began the journey back up, lingering on her breasts until her nipples hardened. When he raised his head there was a knowing look in his eyes.

"You're playing with fire, Wade. Careful, or you'll get burned." Or was she more afraid the warmth emanating from him would draw her too close . . . close enough to incinerate her. Even now, if she leaned forward a fraction more, their lips would touch. A yearning swept through her to make the move and taste what she knew he offered.

"Maybe I don't mind the fire." He took the initiative and closed the distance, his breath tickling her ear when he whispered, "Can you make it hot enough to scorch me?"

Ah, so that was his game. He was teasing her, handing her the apple from the tree in the Garden of Eden to see if she would cave in and take a bite. Two could play this game of temptation. Turning slightly until her lips grazed his ear, she whispered, "Baby, I could put you in the intensive care unit of the burn ward." She felt the shudder sweep over him. "What we did last night was only a small sample. You have no idea what I could do. In this line of business, you see more than you want." Her words were low and husky. "There are ways to have an orgasm that you probably would never imagine. Are you scared of heights? I could take you higher than you've ever dreamed possible."

It took all her willpower to step away from him and saunter to the window. Not only had she probably conjured fantasies in his mind, but her own thoughts would make a porn director blush.

When she faced him, she wasn't even close to having herself under control. He didn't look much better off. Maybe he'd be able to see the games had to stop . . . right here, and right now.

"Remember my rules, Wade. No touching, no kissing, no sex."

He drew in a deep breath. "Where's the harm? It's not like we haven't made love before." A lock of his hair fell across his forehead as he took a step toward her; when he grinned, her insides tumbled like loaded dice across a crap table. If she had to confront much more of his charm, she'd be leading *him* to the bed. Hell, she'd be dragging him.

She held up her hand, breathing a sigh of relief when he stopped. Even a couple of feet was too damn close.

"I never sleep with the same man twice," she told him.

His eyebrows rose. "You're joking."

She shook her head. "Too many complications."

"But you won't be here that long." Wade couldn't believe what she was telling him. A woman as sexual as Fallon, as tempting as Fallon, and she was saying she'd never sleep with him again. She'd leave him with a taste of her body and nothing more? That was downright cruel—and a challenge if ever he heard one.

They might have been playing by her rules before, but now it was time they began playing by his.

He sauntered toward her, closing the distance between them, stopping just short of his body brushing against hers. "Are you so sure you'll never sleep with me again?" He slipped behind her, his breath fanning the back of her hair, but he drew no closer than that. "Are you sure you don't want me touching you? Sliding deep inside the moist heat of your body?"

"Positive."

He wasn't convinced she meant it. Her words might say one thing, but her eyes told him a different story.

"I'll take you where you've never been before. You were right when you said this line of work can lead you down paths of wickedness and sexual delights most people would never imagine."

"A small-town sheriff?" she scoffed. "I doubt it."

"I haven't always been the sheriff here. I worked for the Dallas police force before switching to undercover work. Have you ever heard of The Pit?"

Her shoulders stiffened. Only slightly, but enough that he saw her reaction.

"Of course I've heard of it. Anyone in law enforcement has. You're not going to tell me you've actually been there. Only a handful of cops have . . . and lived to tell about it."

Their shoulders lightly brushed when he faced her. Hers were stiff, unyielding. Skepticism narrowed her eyes. He didn't think she'd believe him. Hell, it was hard for him to believe he'd once lived that close to the edge. He'd been to hell and back, and survived. It was a trip he vowed he'd never make again.

"I was undercover there for almost five months," he continued. "Can you even imagine what it was like? Every vice known to man, every temptation, every sexual appetite you can conceive—and some you can't. Every need met."

"You're lying."

"Am I?" He slipped his hands behind her neck and lightly massaged.

"No touching." She jutted her chin forward.

"Did I promise not to touch you? I don't remember agreeing to your rules." He noticed she didn't move away, though. He'd been right about her passionate side. She enjoyed sex too much to adhere to the standards she'd set for herself.

"You're not playing fair."

"But then, I never have." He lowered his mouth to the fullness of her lips and sucked gently on the lower one before delving inside the sweetness of her mouth.

At first she didn't respond to his searching tongue. He sensed she held back—to prove she would keep her vow. That didn't really worry him.

He kept the rhythm of his kiss slow and sensual, with a light touch while his hand moved to her ear. He ran his fingers over her tender lobe, gently massaging.

His willpower was stretched to the limit, but he kept himself in check. Never had proving a point been so damn hard. He stroked her tongue one last time before ending his self-inflicted torture.

"No kissing?" he asked.

"Screw you, Tanner. We kissed, so what." Her breathing was ragged, though.

He didn't buy her act that his kiss meant nothing to her. He continued with the game.

"And you said no touching, either, right? But if I just undid the buttons on your shirt, that wouldn't really be touching, would it?" He slid one button from the hole. "I mean, I am only touching the shirt and not you." He slipped another button through and then another. "After all, it is technically my shirt."

"But I'm the one who's wearing it."

"You'll like how I make you feel, trust me."

"Trusting you would be like walking across shards of glass and not expecting to get cut."

Still, she didn't pull away. He knew she wasn't going to. "You have to admit, your rules weren't going to last."

Very slowly, she let her gaze slide over his body, as if trying to decide if he was worth getting sweaty over. "Maybe I'll make an exception, but . . . it's only sex. A means to an end."

"Don't worry," Wade tugged her closer. "I won't expect you to marry me afterwards."

"I wouldn't ask," she crooned. Pulling out of his arms, she trailed her fingers across his chest before circling around to his back. For a moment he was lost in the fantasy of her touching other parts of his body. Facing him again, she lightly ran her fingertips over the zipper of his jeans.

He sucked in a shallow breath. Jeez, she was driving him to the edge of madness. He'd sensed the trouble she would cause him, but even now, he couldn't stop himself. She was an addiction he couldn't fight . . . so why try?

Running the tip of his finger down the center of her chest, he exposed a strip of creamy skin. He wanted to draw his tongue down her silky flesh, taste the woman she was.

Instead he pulled his gaze toward her glazed, heavy-lidded eyes before opening the shirt more to reveal one of her breasts. She was beautiful. Almost too perfect. He cupped her breast in his hand, rubbing his thumb against the hardened nipple. She arched toward him.

He slipped back the other side of her shirt, exposing her other breast. He cupped it in his hand while rubbing his thumb over her nipple. She moaned and leaned her head back. When she did, he caught the sudden flash of pain on her face.

Damn, for a moment he'd forgotten she was wounded. What the hell was he thinking? Regretfully, he pulled her shirt closed and stepped back.

"What are you doing?" she asked, her voice filled with frustration.

"Your injury."

"Fuck the injury. You started the game this time, and we're damn well going to finish it."

Wade hesitated. The ache in his crotch grew stronger. He wanted Fallon more than he could remember ever wanting any woman. He closed his eyes against the temptation she represented and tried to bring himself back under some semblance of control.

Closing his eyes around a seductress wasn't the smartest thing he'd ever done. When she massaged the front of his jeans, he realized Fallon didn't give up quite so easily. His already rock-hard dick quivered beneath her touch.

Crap! She didn't play fair, either.

Chapter 5

Grabbing Wade's crotch had been a stroke of pure genius—and Fallon planned to keep stroking until he satisfied the hunger within her. She wasn't about to let him leave her trembling and so damn horny her eyes were almost crossing. Every one of her nerve endings screamed for gratification.

When he groaned, she smiled triumphantly. *Mission accomplished.*

Okay, so maybe she hadn't planned on sleeping with him again. Things didn't always work out the way she wanted, and if she could break every other rule, then why not her own? She was still in control, still in charge of the situation.

And still calling the shots.

She let go of him long enough to lose her shirt and shower-curtain skirt. "So—" she purred "—do you really want to stop?"

His hungry gaze devoured her naked body, causing tingles of pleasure to spread to the juncture between her legs. She wanted to feel him buried deep inside her, but when she reached forward, he stayed her hand. From the moisture dotting his upper lip, she knew how much his action cost him.

Did he really think she would let it end here?

She wiggled her hand loose and yanked his shirt from his jeans, then jerked the ends apart. She gritted her teeth against the sudden stab of pain in her side as buttons popped and scattered to the carpet.

Her discomfit was quickly forgotten as her gaze became transfixed on the man before her. She drew in a sharp breath. "God, you're beautiful." Smooth, tanned muscles rippled when she scraped her fingertips from the top of his sternum down to his belly button.

She kissed his chest, letting her lips linger on one taut nipple before swirling her tongue around the darkened areola and tasting the salt of his body. "I want you." The palms of her hands began to itch with the need to feel all of him. She slipped her fingers inside the waistband of his pants and undid the top button.

"Easy, babe. Slow down." He cupped both her breasts, lightly pinching the nipples.

Her fingers curled into the denim as liquid heat spiraled to the cortex of her being.

"We've got all the time in the world," he murmured.

Fallon knew better than anyone that time could be snatched away in the beat of a heart. She raised her head and met his gaze. "But I want you right now." She tugged his zipper down, freeing the man within. He sucked in a shallow breath, but quickly recovered—then retaliated.

"You mean something like this?" He trailed his hand over her stomach and didn't stop until he came to the vee of her legs, tangling his fingers in her curls and rubbing against her clitoris.

An orgasm swept over her, rocking the ground beneath her, buckling her knees. She clung to him, moaning into his shoulder. "Ahh, that feels nice."

"Just nice?"

He spun her around until her back was snuggled against his chest, her buttocks cupping him. She wanted to caress him, but he'd made it impossible. Fallon could only cling to his thighs, and that wasn't enough to satisfy her need to feel all of him.

But when Wade danced his hands in a slow waltz over her body, lingering on the fullness of her breasts, wandering across her stomach, her thought process malfunctioned. She arched her back, not caring about anything but what she felt right now. Her eyelids fluttered closed while she indulged in the sensations rippling over her body.

He eased her a little more to the left and whispered into her ear. "Open your eyes."

She did . . . and saw they faced the full-length mirror. Her mouth went suddenly dry as she watched, mesmerized, while his callused palms kneaded her breasts. Heat coursed through her when he flicked his fingers across her hardened nipples. The moan she'd tried to stifle burst forth.

"It feels good, doesn't it?" he murmured, the heat of his breath fanning her cheek.

She groaned.

"No, don't close your eyes. See what I'm doing. Watch it all."

She dragged her heavy lids upward.

He splayed his fingers over her flat stomach, sliding them down her hips. Leaning into her, he trailed his fingers up and down the tops of her legs. She held her breath when he moved his hands to her inner thighs, his featherlight strokes started a slow burn deep inside her.

"Ahh . . . don't stop. . . ."

"What? This?" His finger tangled in her curls, scraping across the sensitive nub, locking her in a hazy mist of pleasure.

Entranced, she kept her eyes open as he touched her, spreading her labia, exposing her to his view. It almost felt like she was watching a very tantalizing, sensuous movie, except for the quivers of pleasure running up and down and around her. She leaned against him, drawing from his strength, and just experiencing the sweet ache he'd started.

"Do you like me touching you?"

"Umm . . ." She didn't want him to stop. His butterfly touch only stoked the fire, and she didn't really care if the heat turned her body to ashes. Living in the moment, that's what mattered . . . the only thing that mattered.

She barely realized when he brought her hand to his lips and began to suck her fingers, one by one while his other hand continued an assault all its own. For once in her life, she surrendered her body completely to a man's manipulations. He removed her fingers from his mouth.

"Now . . . pl—now. Just fuck me."

"Not yet." He took her hand and slid her still wet fingers over her sex.

Her knees buckled, but he caught her against his body at the same time, slipping his finger inside her.

"Don't stop touching yourself," he told her.

She couldn't even if she'd wanted. There was

something highly erotic about watching herself stroke the most intimate places on her body while he slid his finger in and out of her . . . and knowing he watched, too. Knowing he was just as turned on. Knowing that his ragged breathing matched her own.

She gritted her teeth as spasms of pleasure swept over her. Before even one whimper escaped past her lips, he lowered her body to the plush carpet and entered her.

"Don't stop looking," he told her.

She turned her head and watched as he eased from her, sliding inside her moist heat. She rose to meet his thrust. He turned his head toward the mirror, met her gaze, and plunged deeper still. She tossed her head back, but couldn't take her eyes off the naked couple in the mirror. Again and again their bodies merged, then pulled back. She wrapped her legs around his middle, bringing him even closer, and reveled in the pleasure on Wade's face, intensifying her own gratification. Sweet release came in waves that crashed over her, shaking her to the very core of her womanhood.

Wade groaned, his body stiffened . . . and she watched it all through half-veiled eyes.

In the space of a few moments something passed between them . . . something that terrified her. How could she have let it go so far? She'd let him take control of her body, and worse, she'd enjoyed every minute.

Wade rolled onto his side, and the silence stretched, their ragged breathing the only sound in an otherwise silent room. It didn't matter. She wasn't ready to talk about what had happened.

She wasn't supposed to feel like this . . . so damn

satisfied. So damn warm on the inside . . . almost as if she should care about him. She couldn't afford to care for anyone. The price was too high.

Hadn't she learned anything over the years? She couldn't let her guard down—especially to a man who made her forget her past. And, for a little while, Wade had made her do just that.

It was time to end it. She turned onto her good side and stood. Stiffening her spine, she gazed down at the magnificent male stretched out in all his glory on the beige carpet. "Not bad, Tanner. Mind if I use your shower?"

Wade opened his eyes. He'd known the minute she closed herself off from him. Her armor had come up, effectively dismissing what they'd just shared.

Son-of-a-bitch, she could go from so hot she nearly melted his body when she rubbed against him, to so cold he could almost see a layer of ice crystals forming on her body.

"It's down the hall," he growled, unable to keep the frustration from his voice. As she sashayed from the room, he called after her, "And I happen to like my shower curtain."

Damn it, he'd known what he was getting himself into from the very start. Hell, it would be kind of hard to miss since she'd pointed a gun at him and ordered him to strip. But he'd brought her home with him anyway.

He jerked to a sitting position and ran a hand through his tousled hair. Now she acted like the only reason she tolerated him was for a safe haven, and an occasional quickie.

His bad humor suddenly faded and a smile curved his lips. Okay, maybe more than a quickie. His glance landed on the mirror, but instead of his reflection looking back at him, he saw Fallon—touching herself . . . his hands intertwining with hers . . . their bodies becoming one.

He groaned and jumped to his feet. Jeez, she was right. There wasn't a damn thing between them except sex—admittedly the best he'd ever experienced—but it was still just sex. And in a day or two she would leave and his life would return to normal.

Grabbing his clothes, he left the room, pausing outside the bathroom door to listen. The spray of water hit the deep green plastic liner like raindrops on a tin roof. Was she washing him off her body? Wiping away the stain of what they'd just shared? Removing his brand? She'd enjoyed it too much for her to obliterate the memory, though.

He continued to his bedroom. Maybe it was a good thing the master suite was on the other side of the house. Less temptation. He snorted. Like that would be a hindrance. He'd already proven it didn't matter where Fallon slept.

He tossed his clothes on the bed and went into the small bathroom connected to his room. What was it about her that made him want to draw closer? Whatever the hell it was, he'd better get her out of his system damn fast. He knew her type. She wouldn't hang around long. Once it was safe for her to go back to the agency, she'd leave. Her kind never stayed in one place for any length of time.

He turned on the water and stepped under the stinging spray, sucking in a deep breath. It wasn't enough that Fallon turned him inside out, but she'd used almost all the hot water. Not that it mattered. He needed something to dampen his ardor. Just thinking about her again made him hard. A fortune-teller would probably warn him there'd be a lot of cold showers in his future if he wanted to keep from making love to her again.

In less than twenty-four hours she'd taken him from his comfort zone, where the only thrill he'd had in the last two years was when Ronnie Bishop had glued *Playboy* pictures to Reverend Benton's house. The poor man nearly had a coronary. Trouble was, Wade couldn't be sure if it was from anger . . . or excitement.

Now Fallon had stormed into his life and turned it inside out. He'd left undercover work because each day had blended into the next. For every scumbag he put behind bars, there were ten more to take his place.

He was through with all that now. Living on the edge was in his past, and Fallon would be, too, once it was safe for her to leave.

Two Creeks was a nice little town. He planned to keep it that way. He wouldn't let her disrupt his quiet, calm existence. They'd enjoy each other's company, and when it was time for her to leave, they'd part and never look back. Which was as it should be.

After drying off, Fallon replaced the bandage that had covered her injury. Her wound seeped blood. Troublesome, but nothing she couldn't live with. Dr. Canton wouldn't be a happy camper, though, when he saw she'd busted one of the stitches.

Had sex with Wade been worth all the problems cropping up in her life? Damn it, she wasn't sure. Nothing was going right. She should be focused on bringing Cavenaugh to justice.

She closed her eyes, trying to concentrate her

energies on what was important, but instead of Cavenaugh, the memory of Wade's hands stroking her body filled her mind. Frowning, she shook off the vision her thoughts conjured and leaned against the counter, absently tossing the damp towel to the floor.

Making love with Wade should be tops on her list of things to avoid. She opened the cabinet and grabbed a yellow towel.

Really though, what would be the harm of a little sexual fun?

Cripes, she did need sleep if she was going to start thinking like that. Cavenaugh was the only man she needed to be thinking about right now.

Still, her life had centered on bringing him to justice for as long as she could remember. She hadn't even taken a vacation in three years, and never much of one before that. If she weren't searching for Cavenaugh, then King would have something *really* important he wanted her to do—and invariably would swear she could take a break after the assignment. Another case usually dropped in her lap, preventing her from taking time off.

Maybe a few days R & R were in order. Wade would certainly make the time enjoyable and take the edge off. And it wasn't like she could do anything until Cavenaugh resurfaced. She wrapped the towel around her body, tucking the end between her breasts. And she *was* stuck here for the moment.

Sleep, she needed sleep. Why else would she even be considering having sex with Wade again. It was bad enough she'd broken her own damn rule and slept with him the second time. Maybe after she rested she could get her mind off him and remember what her priorities were.

She sauntered out of the bathroom.

"As much as I enjoy the view, we might want to find you something to wear other than a towel or shower curtain."

She looked up.

His gaze lazily drifted over her. She was unable to stop the tingles of pleasure that ran up and down her spine. Crap, he was doing it to her again. Did he have magical powers or something?

Against her will, her gaze slid over him. He'd showered and pulled on a pair of faded jeans and a black T-shirt. Damned if he didn't have her wanting him again. What was it about Wade that was so different from other men she'd had sex with?

"If you don't stop looking at me like that I'm going to carry you to bed."

She regarded him with slow appraisal. "Are you sure you'd be *up* for the exercise?"

Instead of taking offense at her smart remark, he chuckled. "I think I could *rise* to the occasion."

Flames licked her insides. She cocked her head and eyed him. The man was much too sure of himself and needed to be brought down a peg. She opened her mouth to do just that, but he began talking before she could utter a word.

"Come on, I think I have a few of Bailey's things you can borrow until we get you some clothes of your own. Unless, of course, you'd rather try out the bed. It's a lot softer than the floor." His eyebrows rose in question.

Not a bad idea. But her body throbbed from the exertion she'd already put it through. Making up for months of celibacy in twenty-four hours wasn't a smart move. Especially when she suffered from sleep deprivation. She was too susceptible, and

Wade was too sexy for his own good. But damn it, she *was* tempted.

"Never mind." He grinned, as if he sensed her indecision. "Clothes . . . then rest, before you fall over."

Fifteen minutes later, he'd found her a pair of jeans and a midriff-showing, blue knit shirt. He also tossed in a pair of lacy panties and a pair of plaid pajamas, mumbling something about having to do not only his laundry, but Bailey's as well. When he abruptly turned, he caught her stifling a yawn.

"Why don't you catch a few zzzs."

She started to argue but realized the futility as a wave of exhaustion drained away the last of her reserves. Wade was right. If she didn't sleep, she'd be prone to mistakes. As if she hadn't already made enough.

She nodded, but instead of leading the way to the guestroom, he turned and went into the kitchen.

Once there, he handed her a white tablet from the packet on the table. "Antibiotic. You don't want to get an infection. It would really piss off the doc."

He would be, anyway, when he saw she'd busted one of the stitches. But she didn't want to make matters worse.

After swallowing one of the pills, she aimed for the guestroom, but at the entrance to the hallway, she stopped and turned. Wade's eyebrows rose.

Did he realize what he could be letting himself in for? "Cavenaugh is bad news," she warned. "He'll kill anyone who gets in his way."

"Yeah, I kind of figured that out already."

Wade was a cop. If he'd been undercover like he

said, and survived The Pit, then he would be well aware of the risks he had taken bringing her to his home. She just didn't like involving anyone in her mess.

"It's okay," he quietly told her. "He doesn't know you're here."

She nodded and left the room. Wade didn't think she quite believed everything he'd told her about his being undercover.

He continued to watch until there was no reason to stand in the middle of the living room. She wasn't very trusting, but that could be from her line of work.

Hell, he'd been about as hard-edged as they came when he'd worked in the city. Taking risks he knew were dangerous. Living life in the fast lane.

And no emotional entanglements.

He had a suspicion no one would crack Fallon. He sensed she'd stopped feeling anything long before going to work at the agency. *A shame.*

He went into the kitchen and picked up the phone. She wouldn't like him asking questions, but there was one person from his old life he knew he could trust. If anyone could ferret out information about Cavenaugh, Josh could. The sooner this guy was captured, the sooner Wade's life would return to normal.

Chapter 6

Fallon's hand encountered something soft and furry when she yawned and stretched. She opened one eye and glared at the cat. "Mangy beast. Find another bed to sleep in besides mine." She scratched the animal on top of the head before nudging her out of the way.

"Dumbest animals on God's green earth," she mumbled as she rolled over and sat on the side of the bed.

Ugh. She couldn't feel worse if she'd been run over by an armored truck. Her gaze swept the dark room. *What time was it anyway?* And how long had she slept?

She glanced at the clock on the bedside table. The bright red numbers told her it was after nine. She glanced out the window. In the evening.

Her stomach rumbled. She sniffed. Grilled steaks? Had she died and gone to heaven? *Ha!* As if St. Peter would let her past the pearly gates. Not that she cared.

She stood, her gaze searching the room until it

landed on the nightclothes she'd tossed on the floor before crawling naked into bed. Sleeping in clothes would be like taking a shower in a bathing suit, but she didn't bother explaining that to Wade when he'd given her the plaid tops and bottoms.

She'd needed the kind of mind-numbing sleep she could only get when she was comfortable. Maybe deep down she'd sensed nothing would happen, that she was safe from Cavenaugh—for the moment, anyway.

The pj's would come in handy around the house, she supposed, as she slipped them on. Maybe they would keep her mind off sex.

Damn. Just thinking about Wade made her nipples tight. What was her life coming to? Lusting after the first man who offered her sanctuary. Okay, so if he'd looked like Barney Fife maybe she wouldn't have jumped into the sack with quite as much eagerness. And apparently she needed a lot more sleep than she'd gotten if she was already thinking about him sexually.

She shook her head and caught her reflection in the mirror. Tousled hair, eyes heavy from sleep.

Good, she was safe from his advances. The way she looked right now Fallon doubted she'd inspire anyone to have thoughts of hot, wild sex. She scraped her hand through her black hair, buttoned her top, and left the room.

Following her nose, she headed for the kitchen with the darn cat trailing beside her. As she walked through the doorway, Wade came in from outside carrying a platter with two large steaks. They both stopped . . . and stared.

She drank in the sight of him as if they'd been separated for months, rather than hours. Wind-blown hair fell across his forehead. She'd almost forgotten how intensely green his eyes were.

Her gaze lowered, drifting over wide shoulders and a strong chest, past his slim waist and down muscled thighs. She couldn't help remembering what he looked like underneath the black T-shirt and low-riding jeans he wore.

Fallon forced herself to think about her priorities, but all her good intentions faded when she saw he returned her blatant appraisal.

The blood pounded through her veins. Time stood still. Between them the air sizzled and crackled. Each one waited for the other to make the first move.

A sudden breeze swirled past them and whisked through the kitchen, creating a chill and effectively extinguishing any fires that had begun to build.

She rubbed her arms to rid herself of the goose bumps. "Isn't it a little cool to be grilling out?" Not that she'd care if he froze his buns. On second thought, he really did have a nice ass. Okay, so maybe she didn't want that particular part of his anatomy to freeze. She could think of other places she wouldn't mind being frozen solid and rock hard, though.

He shrugged and closed the door after letting Cleo out. "I just slap the meat on the grill and let the coals do the rest. No big deal." He set the platter in the center of the table and gave her another slow appraisal. "I see you decided to wear the pj's. I kind of wondered what you'd put on when you got up." A rakish grin lifted one side of his mouth. "I've noticed you have an aversion for clothes."

"You watched me while I slept?" The thought

didn't bother her in the way he might think. Rather, it sent naughty tremors up and down her spine. She had a tendency to toss and turn in her sleep, flinging the covers off one minute and snuggling under them the next.

How much of her body had been exposed to his view? And had he wanted her as much as she wanted him right now? She didn't doubt he'd looked his fill—and remembered the sexual experience they'd shared.

"Do you mind that I did?" he drawled.

His words sent waves of sensuous pleasure over her, evoking images of her lying on the bed with only a strip of the sheet covering her stomach . . . her bare breasts enticing him to do more than look . . . begging him to come closer and taste the tender flesh, to suckle her nipples.

She swallowed past the lump in her throat. Had she inadvertently opened her legs to him, maybe sensing his presence even in her sleep? Her stomach tightened at the thought before rumbling loudly, dispelling her erotic thoughts and dumping her back into reality. Lack of food had made her lightheaded.

Yeah, right. It wasn't her need to fill her gut that made her itch to jump Wade's bones.

She abruptly turned and went to the counter. "I'm starving." She grabbed a crusty roll from a cloth-covered basket and bit into it. Hot from the oven, the bread tasted mouth-wateringly good and gave her something else to think about.

"You'll ruin your dinner."

"Doubtful." She wasn't a lady when it came to eating. Hell, she wasn't a lady when it came to any-thing—no role models. She took another bite, absently brushing the crumbs off her pajama top.

And she could outeat any man. Most of the time she snatched food on the run, but every couple of weeks or so her body binged. Someone once told her she was like a bear getting ready for winter. She hadn't mentioned it was an acquired trait. They wouldn't have understood.

"I have a salad in the fridge and I'm nuking potatoes. That okay?" As if to affirm his words, the microwave beeped.

"You're quite the cook." In fact, she could picture him in a chef's apron . . . and nothing underneath. She boosted herself onto the counter and crossed her legs.

"Like I said, my family has a restaurant." He walked to the microwave and removed two potatoes, dropping them into a yellow bowl before taking them to the table. "If you're that hungry, make yourself useful and grab the salad."

"A man who knows how to give orders," she purred. "Umm, it brings out the cave girl in me."

"I'll remember that if we ever find ourselves alone in a cave." He sauntered to the cabinet, not stopping until he stood in front of her. "I can dream up a number of things I'd love to see you do on demand. You might even enjoy a couple of them yourself." His fingers trailed lightly over the cotton sleeve of her pajamas.

His words were filled with a promise she knew he wouldn't have trouble keeping, while his touch sent excited quivers up her thighs.

She'd had more sexually explicit mental images in the last few hours than in the last two years. Maybe it was time she tuned them out, and tuned

in to what was going on in the real world. She had
a criminal to put behind bars, and a weasel to cage.

But before she could concentrate on that, she
had to have food. "Can we eat?"

"That's exactly what was on my mind." His rogu-
ish grin had her quickly scooting away from him
and off the cabinet, before going to the refrigerator. She grabbed a clear, glass bowl with lettuce in
it, and after depositing it none too gently on the
table, yanked out a chair and plopped down.

Wade found he enjoyed baiting her. And why
not? She had an aura about her that drew him
nearer. He couldn't quite figure out what it was
about Fallon that made him throb.

She wasn't what he'd call beautiful, at least not
in the conventional way. Her velvety dark hair
brushed her shoulders in a slightly uneven haircut.
With today's styles, he wasn't sure if it was intentional
or not. But it looked kind of sexy on her, fitting with
her unconventional personality. No, there was something else about her that he couldn't quite see, but
he damn sure felt it.

Maybe it was seeing her struggle as she tried to
fight the attraction between them. *A losing battle.*
While she'd slept he'd decided to go with the flow.
Hell, she wouldn't hang around that long. They
might as well both enjoy each other's company.

"Excuse me, we *are* going to eat today, aren't
we?"

He turned from his musings. "I'd thought about
it. What do you want to drink? Beer?"

Her whole demeanor changed in an instant. She
sat straighter in the chair, her hand fluttering close
to her neck.

"What, no Chablis?" she asked in perfectly enun-
ciated English. Her brow wrinkled and her bottom

lip pouted. "I had so hoped we might enjoy a glass of fine wine."

He opened his mouth, then snapped it shut. Had he been caught in a time warp and transported to a glitzy restaurant, with Fallon a debutante and him the lowly waiter who'd created a major *faux pas?*

Fallon chuckled, stabbed one of the steaks with her knife, and dropped it onto her plate. "A beer will be fine, Tanner."

He frowned. "For a moment I forgot you were such a consummate actress, but then, you did say that's what made you a good agent. I guess you can adapt to any situation." He whirled around and went to the refrigerator. After grabbing two beers, he returned and clunked one down in front of her before dropping into his chair.

"Oh, I have lots of hidden talents." A slow, sexy smile crossed her lips as she twisted the beer cap off and maneuvered it between her thumb and middle finger. She looked at the cap, glanced at the trash can, then back at him. A challenge sparkled in her cool, blue eyes.

His eyes narrowed. "You'll miss."

"Want to wager?"

He judged the distance from the table to the trash can. It was a good six feet. She'd never hit it.

Hell, he used to play this game when he was a teenager. The person who could snap a cap between his thumb and middle finger and get the closest to a bucket won the money in the pot. Usually the winnings were not more than five dollars, but it was the principle that counted. Josh had actually hit inside the can a couple of times, but Wade suspected it was by pure accident. He doubted Fallon would even get close.

He studied her with a skeptical eye. She fidgeted with her fork, rearranging the placement beside her plate before meeting his gaze.

Maybe she thought he'd back down and then she could gloat without ever having tried to hit the blasted can. *That was it.* She was trying to bluff him. "You're on. What's the bet?"

"Make it easy on yourself."

He leaned forward. "One hour where the loser does whatever the winner wants." *Let her chew on that. She'll think twice before . . .*

"You're on." She glanced toward the trash can, snapped her fingers, then casually returned to the process of cutting her steak.

The cap sailed easily toward the can and landed inside. When he glanced her way, she was concentrating on eating. She hadn't even bothered to see if she'd made the shot.

He'd been hustled.

She took a bite and closed her eyes as she savored the taste. "Damn, this is really good. What the hell did you put on the meat?"

"Seasoning." His eyes narrowed. "You knew you wouldn't miss, didn't you?"

"Of course. I only bet on sure things." She put another piece of meat in her mouth and chewed. "So, what kind of seasoning? Never mind, it doesn't matter. I'll never be Suzy Homemaker."

He sawed across his steak like it was boot leather rather than a tender cut of beef. "Really? For some odd reason I can easily picture you cooking up a feast in the kitchen." He didn't try to hide his sarcasm. "It must be your sweet, down-home nature that shines through."

"Yeah, I bet it's the first thing people notice." She spoke around a mouthful of steak, swallowed, then downed half her beer before looking at him and grinning.

Sweet Jesus! Her eyes twinkled at him, while the fullness of her lips beckoned him to lean forward and kiss her.

Wade grabbed his beer and took a long swig. He had to think about something else before he completely lost control and lunged across the table.

Cavenaugh was the first thing that popped into his mind. "So, what are your plans?" The more she told him, the better off he'd be. He didn't like surprises.

She carefully laid her fork and knife on the table. His gaze fastened on her tongue as it came out to temptingly lick the steak juice off her lips. His mouth went dry at the thought of what her tongue could do to him.

"I'm not exactly sure. You did say a whole hour, right? Anything I . . . um . . . want? That could lead to some interesting possibilities. I might have to think on it a while."

He covered his groan with a cough. "I wasn't talking about the bet. I was talking about Cavenaugh."

"Oh, now that's a different matter."

She grabbed her utensils again and cut off another piece of meat as if she hadn't just given him a hard-on that could hammer a six-penny nail into a concrete wall.

"I guess I'll open the disk and see exactly how much evidence I have against him."

"You don't know?"

She furrowed her brow. "Cavenaugh didn't give me much time before he insisted I go with him to Dallas." She snorted. "He said he might need me to take notes. I knew something was going down, but I didn't think it would be me." She cut viciously across the tender steak. "I was so friggin' close, and all I have to show for months of work is one blasted disk." She slammed her knife down, pushed away from the table, jumped to her feet, and paced across the tile floor.

"It's okay. If you don't get him, someone else will. His kind always screws up sooner or later."

She whirled around and faced him. "But I want to be the one to put him away. Cavenaugh is mine." Her eyes spit fire.

His instincts kicked into high gear. Why did getting Cavenaugh mean so much to her? She should know when someone did catch the drug lord, another would take his place. That was one reason why he'd quit the city and moved back home. There never seemed to be an end.

"Why is this one so important?"

She hesitated briefly before shrugging her pretty shoulders. "It doesn't matter. You're right. He's just another drug dealer, no better than the ones on the street. He just has a little more area to cover, and makes a lot more money."

Before she took another breath, her manner quickly changed and she presented him with a cocky grin. "Like I said, I don't like losing. And I don't want to spoil my appetite with talk about Cavenaugh. Got another beer?"

He nodded toward the refrigerator. She pulled a cold one out of the box and went back to her chair as if she hadn't lost her temper. He thoughtfully chewed his salad and continued to study her.

Had she told the truth when she said there was nothing special about Cavenaugh? Maybe. Fallon was a passionate woman, but he already knew that. Passionate during sex, where each touch of his hands drew a moan from her. Passionate about food, where each bite put a look of sensuous pleasure on her face. Passionate about her convictions, where the thought of someone poisoning people with drugs brought out her fury.

Could there be nothing more to it than she wanted the man off the street? He doubted it was as simple as that.

"What?" Fallon stared across the table. Wade was too deep in thought, and it made her uncomfortable. She didn't want him questioning her motives. Cavenaugh was hers to bring in. That's all he needed to know. "It might be better if I did get a motel room." She'd have a hell of a lot fewer problems.

He shook his head. "Not a good idea. Bailey would only make you stay with her since she thinks you and Josh are cousins. We're practically related now. Josh is like a brother."

She damn well didn't feel like Wade's sister. And staying with Bailey would be out of the question. She didn't want anyone else involved in her mess.

Okay, so she was stuck here—at least for the moment. She'd be more careful in the future about letting her feelings show. She didn't want Wade to know the real reason putting Cavenaugh behind bars was so important to her. Her motivation went deeper than the fact that he was breaking the law.

Much deeper.

Chapter 7

Tension filled the room as they sat in front of Wade's computer. They'd retrieved the disk out of his suitcase and now Fallon pushed it into the slot.

Wade had to admit he was curious about this Cavenaugh. There was more to the story than she was telling. Not that she'd reveal what it was, though. But something more was going on other than the fact this man was a drug dealer.

He watched her from the corner of his eye. Her lips were set in a grim line, her muscles tense. Had she reached the point where she'd become obsessed?

"He's just one man, and he makes mistakes like everyone else. You *will* get him."

She turned questioning eyes toward him. "Will I? You don't know him like I do. The man has bribed more city officials than I can count, and probably some at the state and federal level."

"But he isn't invincible."

"Sometimes I wonder." She shook her head.

"He's cautious. It took months to get what little I have, but a few days ago I stumbled onto something."

"What?"

Fallon didn't answer right away. He suspected that although she knew he was a cop, it didn't keep her from being careful how much she told him.

"Another office," she admitted.

He doubted she let her guard down with many people, but then, maybe it *was* because of his background. With his knowledge, she could just be using him as a stepping-stone to nab a criminal.

"What kind of office?" he prodded.

"Even King doesn't know what I found. I didn't have time to notify him."

He could see she was deliberating whether to tell him or not. But he was a patient man.

Finally she took a deep breath and began to speak. "The office was concealed behind a panel. I found it by accident a couple of days ago, but I didn't have a chance to look through anything until the night before we left, and then I only had a few hours. It took me almost that long to figure out the password to open his files. I downloaded as many as I could onto the disk."

"So, you might have nothing at all."

"Or I might have a lot. I won't know until I look at it."

"Then let's see what it is you have." His gaze moved to the computer screen when she picked a file and clicked on OPEN. Names and numbers began to flash in front of him as Fallon scrolled down.

"Holy shit," she breathed. "I think they're bank accounts."

"Money laundering?" He leaned closer. "It makes sense. He'd have to clean the drug money."

"It looks like he's distributing his cash into these smaller, less conspicuous accounts." She scrolled down. "Jeez, there must be close to a hundred."

Wade studied the list. "Whoa, wait a second. Scroll back up." His gaze skimmed across the numbers. "Look at the last four digits of the accounts in that group. The ones with PH in front of them. He's listing the zip codes. I recognize a couple."

"And?"

He pointed toward several with the same last four numbers. "Those are in the Philippines. They only use four numbers in their zip codes. He's distancing his money from its illegal source. If I remember correctly, the Philippines aren't very cooperative in money-laundering investigations."

"A layering effect," she murmured. "He's wiring the money through a series of banks, then integrating them back into the country."

"And he comes out smelling as sweet as a dryer sheet."

"Almost. The agency has been monitoring his activities for a long time. We just haven't had any concrete evidence."

"Until now."

"I've nailed the bastard."

"All you have to do is turn the disk over . . ."

"No." She jumped to her feet. "Are you forgetting someone told Cavenaugh I was undercover? If that same person gets hold of the evidence, believe me, it will come up missing."

He didn't want to be pulled into her problems—at least not this much. Giving her a place to stay for a couple of days should be all he was decently required to do. His life had been disrupted enough already when he brought her here.

But he couldn't see any way around her dilemma.

"Then we make a copy and find out who we can trust," he said, moving from his chair.

She shook her head. "There's no *we* about it. This is bigger than I thought. I can't risk your life any more than I already have."

This would be a good time for him to agree with her and walk away. Tell her it was nice meeting her, they'd had a really good time together, and he was sorry it had to end.

He took in the stubborn set of her jaw. She would tackle her problem all by herself. Damn it, this was why he'd quit his job and moved back home. He didn't want chaos in his life again, but he was afraid that might be Fallon's middle name.

Great, this was just fucking great.

He took a deep breath so he could get the words out without stuttering. "The minute I brought you here I committed myself to helping. You're not in this alone."

Fallon was beautiful as she stood there, hands curled into fists, her fierce independence shining through. He sensed she felt it was okay if she got herself killed but hated like hell dragging anyone else into her problems.

"I can't risk your life," she told him, shaking her head.

"Let me worry about who's risking what." He closed the distance between them. Did Fallon realize what she did to him? Maybe it wouldn't be so very hard helping her. It wasn't like they'd be capturing this Cavenaugh all by themselves.

He ran his finger down the side of her silky smooth cheek, outlining her jaw. An ache began to build from somewhere deep inside him, but before he could capture her lips, she moved out of his reach and began to pace back and forth across the room.

"But I can't help worrying." She stopped and looked at him. "This isn't your battle."

"Maybe it's time I rejoined the war." Just this once, he promised himself, and only to find Cavenaugh . . . nothing more.

She shook her head. "Not here, not now, and not because of me." Her eyes pleaded with him to understand. "It's a war you might not win."

He took a step closer, but she held up her hand to stop him.

"Don't."

"Why not? What are you so afraid of?"

"Myself," she whispered before turning and leaving the room.

He didn't try to stop her. She needed time to think, but he knew what the outcome would be. She had no choice but to take his offer of help. The frustration that she had to accept anyone's assistance was clearly written on her face. But accept, she would.

A familiar spurt of adrenaline rushed through him like a potent drug, but he quickly tamped it down. He wasn't returning to his old life. That was in his past. He was quite content with his calmer existence.

Fallon returned to the kitchen, hoping Wade wouldn't follow. She wanted to go over in her mind what she should do next. Her hand trembled as she ran it through her hair.

She walked to the refrigerator and pulled out a beer. After twisting off the cap and hurtling it toward the trash can, she downed half the contents like someone who'd been without anything to drink for days. She only wished the alcohol would numb her mind. She didn't want to think about what could happen if Cavenaugh discovered her whereabouts.

What the hell was she getting herself into? With each passing minute, Wade became more involved with her problems. Maybe at one time he'd been undercover, but he didn't know Cavenaugh—or what the man was capable of doing. He was ruthless and didn't care who he eliminated if they stepped on his toes.

A scratching at the door made her jump.

"Damn, stupid cat. You might have nine lives, but I don't." She went to the back door and opened it. The cat scurried inside, out of the cold, and went straight to her food dish. The mangy beast didn't even look grateful.

"A purr of thanks would've been nice," she muttered. As she downed the last of her beer, realization smacked her between the eyes. "Great, now I'm talking to cats." The next thing she knew, she might even start to like Cleopatra. Or her owner.

Her hand stilled from dropping the empty beer bottle into the trash. The notion she might enjoy being around Wade was absolutely ludicrous. She didn't form attachments, least of all with a lover— no matter how delicious he looked.

She let go of the bottle. It thumped when it landed. Fallon wandered from the kitchen, her thoughts on what was happening between her and Wade.

He was an exceptionally good partner in bed— or on the carpet. That fact wasn't debatable. And he'd wanted her tonight as much as she'd wanted him.

She shut the door of her room behind her and began undressing, dropping the pajamas to the floor.

It had been a stupid mistake making love to him again, but even now her body craved his touch like a dieter craved food.

She ambled to the full-length mirror and stared at her naked body, remembering his hands on her . . . the way he'd stood behind her, caressing the most sensitive areas. A deep yearning wound its way through her. She bit her bottom lip to stifle her moan and climbed into bed, crawling beneath the sheets.

She had to leave, but where would she go? She had no money, Cavenaugh more than likely was looking for her, and toss into the mix a man she was beginning to feel comfortable around. Her situation was only getting worse by the minute.

Screw it. She was going back to sleep.

Dr. Canton frowned down at Fallon's wound as she lay on her side in bed. The pajamas she'd hastily pulled on covered all but her injury. She'd been right. He wasn't thrilled she'd busted a stitch.

"What'd you do, go chase criminals after I left?"

Before she could come up with a plausible excuse without shocking the old man into an early grave by telling him she'd had the best sex in her whole life, he began complaining again.

"Everybody thinks I have all the time in the world to just keep stitching them up, or taking a cast off." He filled a syringe. "Maybe I've got other plans. Like dropping a hook in a tank and catching a catfish. But no, every time I want to take a day off some fool gets himself"—his bushy brows furrowed and he tossed an unforgiving glower in her direction—"or *herself* busted up because they don't have the sense God gave a goat."

"Are you going to sew it up?" She propped her head on her fist and looked over her shoulder. "Or bellyache?"

"Now I guess I can do both," he huffed, but when he deadened the area he did so with a gentle hand.

She faced the other direction, gritting her teeth against the initial sting.

"Did you at least take the pills like I told you?"

She rolled her eyes. "Yes." She hadn't been interrogated this much since she joined the DEA. They'd turned her inside out, wanting to know every little detail of her background. It hadn't mattered that much to her at the time. After all, her past was only words on paper.

"Well, maybe you do have a smidgen of sense."

"I'm glad you noticed," she wryly commented.

Her skin tugged as he made the stitch, but she didn't even feel a twinge of pain.

"Is the man who did this goin' to come lookin' for you?"

"Probably." She hadn't realized before now the doctor could be in danger if Cavenaugh discovered her whereabouts. "Maybe you shouldn't come by anymore."

"So now you think I'm some old codger who can't take care of himself." He clipped the end of the stitch and patted her wound with a small, cotton square. "I'll have you know I made it through the war without a scratch. I might have a few years on me, but that doesn't mean I'm worn out. Not by a long shot."

"Don't stroke out on me, Doc. These men mean business. They shoot first, no matter who gets in their way. I just don't want you in the middle."

"You let me worry about that. I can take care of myself." He put ointment on her wound and covered it with a bandage. "You worry about not busting another stitch."

She hadn't meant to ruffle his feathers. The last thing she needed, though, was another person in Cavenaugh's way. She couldn't be responsible for everyone in this godforsaken town.

Hell, she would've been better off staying in Dallas. The missions were always taking in the homeless.

But it wouldn't have been nearly as enjoyable.

She hated when her conscience spoke the truth, but it was right. Wade was a damn good lay. She smiled. And he did have one hell of a sense of humor. And he was the only man who'd made her want to have sex with him again. Just the thought of lying in his arms brought a rush of excitement.

"I'm not going to tell you to stay in bed so you don't bust another stitch," Doc said, breaking into her not-so-nice thoughts.

"Thanks," she grumbled.

"Don't figure it would do me a bit of good anyway. But take those antibiotics or you'll end up with an infection that'll put you in bed whether you want to be or not."

"I told you I was taking them, didn't I?"

"Saying and doing are two different things."

Sheesh, what was it with him. He acted like he was her father or something. The sooner he realized she didn't need his, or anyone else's help, the better.

"Count them if you want. I'm taking the damn pills."

But when he didn't speak an unfamiliar wave of guilt washed over her. She peeked over her shoulder. He was busy putting his equipment back into the little black bag he'd carried into the room. He acted as if she hadn't just said something incredibly rude. She faced the other direction, chewing on her bottom lip.

The sound of his bag snapping shut echoed through the room.

"Hey, thanks for stitching me up, Doc." Her words sounded stiff to her ears. She didn't turn to look at him.

He sighed deeply. "I wish I could fix whatever's eating away on the inside. I 'spect only time will mend those wounds."

"Don't go digging, Doc. You might not like what you unearth."

"And maybe I would. It's about time you stopped hating yourself so much, don't you think?"

She pulled her pajama top down and rolled to the side of the bed. "Hate myself?" She came to her feet. "Why would I do that? I'm perfectly content with who I am."

When he didn't say a word, she continued.

"My job is dangerous, but I love it." She lightly touched her chest. "Maybe it's made me a little hardhearted, but hate myself?" She shook her head. "You're wrong there."

"If you say so." He picked up his bag and left.

She stood in the center of the room watching him walk away. Arguing would get her nowhere. He had it set in his mind that she needed help.

It wasn't herself that she hated. It was Cavenaugh. Revenge burned deep in her heart. His day would come.

Wade watched as Doc pulled away. His 1982 Chrysler bounced as the tire that was on the curb slid off. Doc had never liked driving, and it showed.

From the corner of his eye he saw Callie coming down the sidewalk. Trouble with a capital T, and dressed in painted-on jeans and a black, stretchy top that displayed more midriff than a fifteen-year-old should be showing, especially on such a cool day.

Deep down, Callie was a pretty good kid, just a little mixed up about some things. Once she gained a little confidence, she'd be okay.

The teen glanced up. "You're back early. I was supposed to take care of Cleo two more days. I've been doing a good job. You can ask old lady Johnson. She's always looking out her window so I know she saw me going inside your house."

"I'm sure you've been doing what I asked. Cleo certainly looks like she's put on a few pounds."

Callie relaxed and smiled. "Yeah, she likes to eat a lot." She nodded after the Doc's car, then gave him the once-over. "You sick?"

"Not that I know of." He didn't want to go into an explanation about Fallon. The fewer people who knew she was staying here, the better. "We had some business to discuss."

"Whatever."

"I'll get the money I owe you." He left the door open and went back inside. He always kept a few bills in the drawer of the hall table. Grabbing a ten, he turned around, but Callie had followed him inside.

"Thanks." She snatched the money and tucked it inside her top. "You didn't . . . uh . . . want change, did you?"

She tried for a seductive pose, but it came off rather immature. Another couple of years, and less cosmetics, and she'd have the boys running after her, though.

"I don't suppose there's another doctor in this town—one with manners," Fallon complained as she came around the corner. "I swear. . . ." her words trailed off as her gaze landed on Callie, then went to Wade. "A little young for you, isn't she?"

"Who's she?" Callie bristled.

"A friend." Wade didn't want to go into any more of an explanation. A few more minutes and he would have avoided the two of them even meeting.

"Wearing nightclothes?" Callie arched her eyebrows in obvious disbelief.

"I'm known for my unusual taste in clothes," Fallon sarcastically remarked, crossing her arms in front of her. "You got a problem with that?"

"Well . . . no."

Fallon's gaze wandered over the younger girl. "I really doubted you would."

"What's that supposed to mean?"

Wade decided to step in and avert the brewing argument. "She just means you have unusual taste in clothes, too. That's a compliment."

"Oh."

He ushered her toward the door. "I really appreciate you taking such good care of Cleo. I'll call your aunt when I need you again."

Callie shrugged. "Okay, whatever." She glanced up at him as she walked out the door. Her eyes reflected sincerity that he didn't often see in her. "Thanks, Mr. Tanner."

Before she went down the steps, Callie turned to Fallon. "Your taste in clothes sucks. They still look like pj's." She hurried down the steps before Fallon could comment.

"Little monster. If she doesn't watch out her *attire* will land her in juvey hall, or pregnant."

Wade shut the door. "She's a little rough around the edges, but she isn't a bad kid."

"That's your opinion," she scoffed.

"She's had a hard time. Lost her parents in a car accident and then moved here from California. She's living with her aunt. It's a lot to take in for a young kid."

Something on Fallon's face made him wonder what her childhood had been like, but her brief glimpse of pain vanished only to be replaced with a look of boredom.

"You know, if you're not careful the next stray you take in might scratch."

"I don't know. I'm pretty good about guessing their weaknesses." He ambled closer until he could smell her scent. A blend of musky woman, and heat.

"And what's my weakness, Tanner?"

Her words came from deep in her throat, sending an aching need washing over him. "You need to feel alive." He brushed his hand through her hair, stopping at her neck and lightly massaging.

She closed her eyes, giving in to his ministrations. He glanced down. Her nipples were hard little nubs poking at the material, begging him to come closer . . . to touch.

"I think you're a passionate woman and you want what I can give you," he whispered close to her ear.

She opened her eyes. "And I think you have one hell of an ego."

She whirled around to leave but he stopped her with a hand on her arm. "It's not ego. I know your body. And I want to feel myself buried deep inside you."

"No."

One word, but it lacked the conviction he knew

she wanted to convey. She could deny wanting him until this time next year, but he knew better.

"Are you sure you don't want to make love?" He ran his hand over the front of her top, grazing lightly against her tight nipple. "Are you positive?"

Chapter 8

"**D**amn you, Wade Tanner," she murmured before pressing her body against his. He was right. She wanted him. She wanted his hands on her body. She wanted him buried deep inside her. Damn it, she wanted him now.

Her fingers tangled in the back of his hair, pulling him closer still as her lips found his. He tasted hot and sexy. She inhaled a ragged breath and caught the scent of spicy aftershave. Her body trembled with need.

His mouth slid from hers, his lips burning a trail down her neck before returning to tease her earlobe with his teeth. She moaned and tilted her head so he had better access.

"You taste good . . . sweet," he murmured close to her ear just before his tongue delved inside.

"Ahh . . ." Her legs suddenly wouldn't hold her any longer. If he hadn't scooped her into his arms, Fallon knew she would have slithered to the floor, her body dissolving into a mindless puddle.

He carried her to his room, his thumb tracing

the outline of one taut nipple against the material of her pajama top, sending shivers of pleasure up and down her spine.

Through heavy-lidded eyes she vaguely noticed embers still glowing in the hearth of the stone fireplace, scenting the room with the sweet smell of oak. She could easily imagine them making love in front of it, but he laid her gently against the scattered pillows of his rumpled, four-poster bed, his eyes smoldering as he tugged off his shirt. She was hypnotized by the intensity of his gaze, unable to move.

He leisurely undid his jeans . . . one button at a time. Did he know the sweet torture he was putting her through? Probably, but she couldn't tear her gaze away as he shoved the material over his thighs and kicked them off.

Maybe he wanted her to go insane with desire. Or maybe he just wanted to prove her vow not to sleep with him again had been ridiculous. But he'd already done that. Whatever his game, it was working.

He hooked his thumbs in the waistband of his briefs. She held her breath when he slid them down, revealing himself. She slowly expelled her breath and drew in a deep, shuddering sigh.

Magnificent.

Unable to wait to feel him against her naked skin, she moved to her knees and unbuttoned her top. He stood captivated as she slipped it off her shoulders and let the soft material slide down her arms. Closing her eyes, she tilted her head back. Like a butterfly emerging from its cocoon, she reveled in her unfettered freedom.

"You're so damn beautiful," he muttered.

Ripples of pleasure washed over her. She opened

her eyes. *Beautiful?* She'd never paid that much attention to her looks. She knew she didn't have to wear a paper bag over her head during sex, but she'd never thought of herself as beautiful.

No! She tamped down the giddiness that bubbled inside her. This was only sex. Something they could both enjoy without recriminations. Her spine stiffened. She pushed her bottoms downward, watching him the whole time. He was no one to her. They were only two people who'd been thrown together by circumstances. She would enjoy her time with him—but when it was over, they would part company.

Before she could kick out of her bottoms, he grabbed the hem and slowly tugged them off. Instead of letting go of her ankle he slid his hand up her leg, caressing her thigh.

For a moment, she luxuriated in his touch. He was good, she had to admit that. When it was time to go, having sex with him would be the only thing she'd hate leaving.

She'd make sure of it.

His hand moved up her thigh and she forgot about everything except the sweet ache beginning to build inside her. He massaged her inner thighs, spreading her legs. But at the last moment, she grabbed his hand and shook her head.

"What?" he asked.

"My turn." She might as well take full advantage of their time together.

His brow furrowed.

She shrugged. "I'm not a bystander. I want to participate." Grabbing his hand, she pulled herself to a sitting position, legs hanging off the bed, mere inches from touching his body. When he leaned forward, she moved back. "Oh no you don't. I'm calling in our bet. One hour where you have to do whatever I want."

He grinned, and she almost forgot what she'd decided to do. The man had a way of making her lose her train of thought. She slipped out of bed, her body barely grazing his, but she felt his muscles tense.

"You're going to torture me, right? Look, but don't touch." He dropped onto the bed, lying against the pillows. "You're a cruel woman. Just shoot me right now and put me out of my misery."

She laughed. He did have a sense of humor. She rarely smiled, let alone laughed. What was it about him that could make her feel so damn good?

"You *are* going to torture me." He hung his head, but she noted he still watched her from the corner of his eye.

"Of course I wouldn't."

He brightened.

She pulled the case from one of his pillows and twirled it around and around. "I plan on covering your eyes so you won't be able to see me."

He groaned. "Not fair."

She motioned for him to sit on the side of the bed again, and was a little surprised when he did. Deftly, she tied the pillowcase at the back of his head, stifling a chuckle when her breasts brushed his arm and he groaned. "Now lie back on the pillows."

Her humor drained away as she looked her fill. The man truly was magnificent. And for the next hour, all hers, to do with as she wanted. She lightly scraped her fingernails over his chest, swirling around one nipple before continuing her downward trek. He inhaled deeply when she touched his stomach.

"You're killing me. Let me take off the blindfold."

"Nope. I won . . . remember." She trailed her fingers past his hard arousal. It quivered, as if begging her to touch . . . to taste. But she continued downward, lightly brushing his inner thigh.

"I hate to tell you, but if you keep this up, I won't last an hour."

His pained expression told her he might be telling the truth.

"I can always take my time in increments. Twenty minutes here, twenty minutes there."

"If you don't stop, that might be stretching it a little."

She stared at him. "Umm, I don't think it could get any bigger." Unable to resist, she encircled him, her thumb grazing across the pink tip. He arched his hips. She wanted to taste him—to know the essence that was him and only him.

This wasn't a temptation she could pass up . . . but not yet. She wanted him to know she could give, as well as take.

"Don't move," she cautioned.

"I couldn't if I wanted."

Her laughter floated past as she hurried from the room and went into the kitchen. Cleopatra was curled on a rug in front of the sink. She opened her good eye and yawned, but then went back to sleep. Did the cat do anything besides nap? She shook her head and opened a cabinet. Glasses and plates. A whole damn set. She didn't even have two that matched. *Amazing.* She shut the door and moved to the next one. Food supplies.

A man after her heart. She grabbed a bottle, glancing at the label as she brought it out. Virgin Olive Oil. Laughter bubbled out of her. Well, that would be a first. She retraced her steps.

Wade hadn't moved. Her gaze traveled lower. She wondered what thoughts had been crossing his mind. He was still very large, and very stiff.

He looked toward the doorway.

"Can you see me?" She thought the pillowcase was snug, but . . .

"Can't see a thing. I sensed your presence. And I could smell you."

She frowned and raised her arm, sniffing.

"You smell like wildflowers on a summer day," he continued.

"Good, I was afraid I just stunk. And your *flowery phrases* won't change things. I want you blind-folded."

"Come on, Fallon. I want to look at you. I want to taste you—all of you."

Halfway to the bed, she stumbled, but quickly regained her balance. The thought of his mouth on her, kissing . . . licking . . . brought a rush of heat spiraling over her. She could almost feel his tongue gliding down her body, touching her most sensi-tive areas. She bit back a groan.

He was good. Oh, he was real good. "It won't work. The blindfold stays on."

"You're killing me, woman," he groused.

"That certainly isn't my intention," she purred, twisting the cap off the oil and placing it on his bedside table. Raising the bottle high, she slowly let the liquid drizzle over him. Starting at his chest, she went down the center, veering off when she reached his erection. He arched his body and moaned, but she continued down his leg, then up the other one. She set the bottle on the floor, and straightened.

Her gaze wandered over him. Casting any lin-gering doubts to the back of her mind, she reached out and touched him. He drew in a sharp breath and jerked his hips upward. Unable to resist any longer, she lowered her head and ran her tongue over his penis.

"Ahhh . . . Fallon," he breathed.

She closed her eyes, tasting him, taking him into her mouth and gently sucking.

He massaged the back of her head with his hand while the other knotted the covers in his fist.

She rolled her tongue over the tip, capturing the salty flavor of his body as she drew him farther into her mouth.

"No"—he inhaled sharply—"no more, or I'll explode."

She straightened, licking her lips. "Now we wouldn't want that to happen, would we. Not when I'm just getting started," she murmured.

"Let me take off this damn blindfold."

He reached toward his face, but she grabbed his hand. "This is my hour. I can do whatever I want."

"Okay, you win, but remember, payback can be hell."

She smiled. "Didn't I tell you? I don't lose . . . ever."

Before he could comment, she ran the palms of her hands down his chest, smoothing the oil into the light sprinkling of hair, spreading the liquid over his skin.

"Just feel what I'm doing to you." Her voice was low, soothing. She could see him begin to relax. That was good. She wanted him ready for the next round. She concentrated on his shoulders, massaging his tense muscles. He sighed deeply as she moved down his arms, applying pressure to each finger, keeping her moves impersonal.

His face relaxed. This was good. He'd need his strength for later.

She worked her way back up his arm, slowly . . . methodically . . . before moving to his feet, kneading the soles with the tips of her fingers. The oil helped her hands glide along as she moved to his toes, then his legs, then his calves. She stayed there for a few minutes, letting him become completely absorbed in her relaxation techniques.

"Does that feel good?" she whispered.

"Umm . . . nice. Maybe I'll let you win again."

"Let, my ass."

She grinned before climbing on the bed and lying on top of him. He grunted but she didn't think it was from pain as her body slithered over his, the oil making her as slick as Wade. Sensations rocked through her as she slid up and down him, her breasts mashing against his chest. Each time she moved a little farther downward, until she rested her head against his erection. Turning slightly, she grazed her teeth across him before taking him in her mouth for a moment of pleasure and then releasing him.

Wade groaned. "You don't play fair."

"I know." She scooted upward and ran her tongue up the side of his neck, nipping his ear before moving to his mouth. His tongue was hot and moist against hers. It felt like she'd waited a lifetime for his kiss.

Not breaking the connection with his mouth, she positioned herself so that she could take him inside her. Damn, he felt hot and hard. She brought her knees up beside his waist and began rotating her hips. Catching his moan of pleasure, she sucked on his tongue and licked across his lips before slowly straightening.

Fallon closed her eyes, letting him fill her before moving her hips up and down. She tightened her muscles, her body closing snugly over him. From somewhere far away she could hear his ragged breathing mingle with hers. She rocked her hips faster and faster. He met each thrust until he gripped her hips, a low growl emanating from him just before he quivered inside her. She gasped as liquid fire filled her, mingling with the heat of her own juices as she came.

Struggling for each breath of air she drew into her body, she collapsed on top of him, resting her head on his chest. She could hear the beat of their hearts. Strange, but to her ears, it sounded as if they were one.

Wade kissed the top of her head as he pulled his blindfold off. "Are you witch . . . or woman?"

"Close. I know I've been called *bitch* a few times." She raised her head and met his gaze. God, he was handsome.

"That person was an idiot." He tenderly kissed her lips, nibbling on her lower one, before leaning slightly back and staring at her. "You taste like . . ."

"A virgin?"

He frowned. "Uh . . . well . . ."

She laughed. "It was the only oil I saw in your cabinet."

He relaxed. "I'll never look at a bottle of oil the same way again."

For just a moment she was caught in his smile: the way his eyes twinkled up at her. She knew she was in way over her head. She hadn't wanted the relationship to go this far—she hadn't wanted to like him so much. It was going to be damn hard to say goodbye. Damn hard.

Wade knew when she began closing herself off

from the feelings they'd just experienced. "Don't think about it, Fallon. Don't dissect what we have."

She rested her head on his chest, refusing to look him in the eye. "Hey, Tanner, it's no big deal. We have a lot of fun together. I'll hang around a few days, until I know the coast is clear, and then I'll go back to my job. No regrets."

"Are you sure?"

She hesitated before raising her head. "I'm sure," she spoke the words just above a whisper. Then, in a stronger voice, "Attachments don't seem to last very long in my life, and that might not be a bad thing; no one gets hurt."

"Who hurt you, Fallon? Who stole your dreams?"

Indecision crossed her face, but it was gone as quickly as it appeared and she grinned, although her smile wavered slightly. "This is just who I am. Don't read too much into what you see. There's nothing complex about me."

Yeah right, and pigs really can fly. But Wade knew when to back off and quit pressing. Sooner or later, she'd open up to him. Then maybe he could right the wrongs done to her. He had a feeling there were a lot of them.

"Hey"—she nudged his chin with her finger— "don't go playing psychiatrist. Can't we just have fun for what little time we have together?"

He smiled into her eyes. "Sure." He studied her face for a moment before slapping her on the butt.

"Ow. What'd you do that for?" She puckered her lips and rubbed her hand across her backside. The movement caused most of her weight to shift to the center of his body, and it responded.

"I couldn't resist. You have a very sweet ass, and your hour is up."

She jerked her head toward his bedside clock. "So it is. I guess I'll have to think of something else to wager on."

"I bet I can beat you into my shower."

"You're on."

She came to her feet and scurried into the bathroom, laughing as the lock clicked behind her. He smiled as he slowly came to his feet. He'd been meaning to fix the broken lock. He was certainly glad he hadn't gotten around to it.

Chapter 9

"You have to call King." Wade handed her the phone. "Maybe if you talk to him you'll be able to tell if he's the one who betrayed you."

Fallon knew what she *should* do, but that didn't mean she had to like Wade's idea. Instead of taking the phone, she stood and walked to the living room window. "He's an agency man." But how could she be a hundred percent positive he wasn't the one? That's why she hadn't contacted him.

"Something must've made you suspect him, or you would have gotten in touch with him."

She looked over her shoulder. "Gun-shy, I guess. I've seen good men turn bad when the stakes were right."

He came to his feet and ambled across the room to join her. Thoughts of Cavenaugh and the agency flew out of her head as she watched his slow, easy stride. Visions of the two of them in the shower filled her mind—how they'd made love again while the warm, gentle spray of water cascaded over their naked bodies.

Wade could've told her it wouldn't do any good to lock the bathroom door. Not that she'd minded when he'd joined her.

"Phone him," he said, breaking into her thoughts as he came to stand beside her. "At least see what he has to say." Once again, he handed her his cell phone.

She gripped it, their gazes locked. Wade was right. She punched in the number to King's private line.

The phone rang twice.

"Nathan King's office," his secretary answered.

Fallon closed her eyes for a moment. The other woman was more than King's secretary. Fallon had long suspected Linda would've liked Nathan to see her as more than someone who worked for him, but Nathan had blinders on when it came to his secretary.

She drew in a deep breath. "Linda, this is Fallon."

"Fallon, oh my God, girl. Mr. King has almost had a coronary trying to locate you. Where are you?"

Who to trust? Damn, she just didn't know anymore. "I . . . I'm safe."

"And Cavenaugh is nowhere to be found." The secretary paused, then whispered, "You're not still with him, are you?"

"No, I'm with . . . a friend. Is King in?"

"What am I thinking? Of course Mr. King is in. I'll put you through to him."

She waited to be connected. What if he'd been the one who'd blown her cover? Nathan King had taken her under his wing at a time when she'd needed a swift kick in the pants . . . and someone who cared.

Damn it, she just couldn't be sure.

"Nathan King," his deep voice rumbled across the connection.

"Were you the one? Did Cavenaugh get to you? Did you take a bribe?"

"Fallon?" A note of urgency crept into his voice. "Is that you?"

"It's me, damn it. Now answer my question." She gritted her teeth.

"Yeah, I'm rolling in money right now. That's why I'm still sitting behind this blasted desk worrying about one of my agents who I haven't heard from and who was *supposed* to check in three days ago. Where the hell are you?"

He sounded genuinely worried. Fallon distinctly heard the familiar rattle of a bottle and knew King had reached for his antacids. He consumed them like candy. Her grip on the phone loosened—just a little.

"First, answer my question."

"What the hell was it?" he yelled back. "You better have a damn good explanation. I've pulled a dozen men off cases just to look for you. Shit, I didn't know whether Cavenaugh had cemented your feet and dumped you in the nearest river or what."

She closed her eyes, wondering if she would know if he lied. "Did Cavenaugh get to you?"

"What the hell do you think?"

"I don't know anymore." She turned away from Wade, not wanting him to see her anxiety.

King's voice softened. "I made a promise to you a long time ago that I would always be here if you needed me. I've never gone back on my word, and I'm too damn old to start now."

She exhaled a long, ragged breath. Deep down

she'd known he'd never betray her. Money didn't matter to him. It never had. Maybe she just needed to hear him say it. Fallon hadn't wanted a repeat performance of her past.

"Where are you?" he asked.

She looked at Wade. She couldn't put his life in danger by taking a chance and giving her location. "I'm safe."

"Are you hurt?"

Again, she hesitated.

"Fallon?" Worry laced his question.

"I'll mend."

"What happened this time?"

"Someone blew my cover. I don't think Cavenaugh suspected until a couple of days ago that I was undercover. One minute I was filing papers, and the next I was on my way to Dallas to meet with a buyer— someone who wanted to purchase a large shipment of oriental rugs. Cavenaugh wanted me along to take notes—or so he said."

"Who was the person?"

She bit her bottom lip. "I don't think he was anyone—a stooge maybe. We met him at a large, crowded restaurant. I think so the informer could identify me."

"Son-of-a-bitch. From the agency?"

Before she could comment, he continued.

"Sounds like it. He wouldn't want you to recognize him. But who? Do you have any idea?"

"No." She ran a shaky hand through her hair. "I'm afraid to guess anymore." She cleared her throat. "I didn't really think it was you. It's just that . . ."

"You don't have to explain. I understand."

Yes, he would.

She straightened. "Okay, so what do we do now?"

"First, how bad are you hurt?"

"It was just a graze. I'll recover."

Silence.

"Nathan?"

"Sometimes I feel like your father," he grumbled. "If you weren't such a damn good agent, I'd make you quit. One of these days a bullet or a knife is going to find its intended mark."

She grinned. "Not likely. As you said, I'm too damn good at what I do."

"And too damn cocky. And you've got the balls to go with it." He cleared his throat. "Now, are you safe?"

"For the moment. I'm with a . . . a friend."

Silence again.

"I do have some, you know," she spoke wryly.

"Really? I always thought you were too damn prickly to let anyone get close—unless you were acting, that is."

She loved his confidence in her social skills, but enough of her personal life. "Do you think it'll be safe for me to come in?"

"No, stay where you are. I'll work from this end. If there's an informer here, I'll sniff him out." His bottle rattled again. "This traitor better not be someone on the inside. If it is, I'll make sure he never sees the light of day."

"Can you find out Cavenaugh's location, too? I don't want any surprise visits."

"That's a problem. He's lying low somewhere. When you didn't call in, we started looking for you. So far we haven't located him."

"That's not good."

"Tell me about it. But we'll find him."

Sudden anger burned inside her. "I was so damn close." She curled her hands into fists.

"Apparently too close. I shouldn't have put you

on the case. That was stupid of me, but I let you talk me in to it."

She glanced toward Wade. He looked absorbed in what went on outside his living room window. She returned her attention to the phone.

"You couldn't have stopped me. Not when I knew he'd resurfaced again."

His sigh was audible. "I know, but you have to realize sometimes it's best to let the past go."

"I can't. I won't."

"It's going to be your downfall someday."

"Not this time. I found a secret office behind a panel."

"And?"

"I downloaded a disk. It has everything we need to convict Cavenaugh. Money laundering, business listings . . ."

"He'll try to get to you, and if he does, he can't afford to let you live."

"I know. But it's the only way to stop him." And she planned to stop him any way she could. "Do you want me to call you in a couple of days?" she asked, changing the subject.

"Yeah, and don't forget this time. I'll see what I can uncover on this end. You just sit tight where you are, and stay low."

They said goodbye and she hung up. Relief washed over her as realization hit her once more. She'd known it couldn't be King who betrayed her. Deep in her heart, she'd known it.

From the corner of his eye, Wade watched the changing emotions that crossed Fallon's face. He'd probably learned more about her in the last few minutes than he had since he'd met her. Like the fact she obviously cared about Nathan King. Had he been her lover? Was he still her lover? Sudden anger swept over him.

"So, apparently you've ruled out your boss." He tried to keep the hostility from his voice but when she cast a bewildered look in his direction he knew he hadn't succeeded.

"I didn't really think he was the one, but I had to be sure."

"And a few words spoken cleared the misunderstanding? I thought you more cautious than that."

"King and I go back a long way."

"Is he your lover?" he blurted, then wondered why he'd asked. Hell, he had no claim on Fallon.

She chuckled. "Jealous?"

"Yeah, maybe I am." He could tell his answer took her by surprise.

"Wade, you know we're nothing to each other," she quietly told him, then continued. "King took me under his wing . . . sent me to college. He's been like a father to me."

Great. He'd certainly made a fool of himself. Damn it, why had he started acting so possessive all of a sudden? He turned back to the window.

"You're right," he told her, fighting for composure. "I guess I just got lost in the moment. Put it down to memories of old times. You know"—he glanced her way—"the rush of living in the fast lane again. I'd forgotten how it could pull you in."

"Are you sorry you decided to help me? I can always go to a motel. Bailey won't have to know. You can tell her I decided not to take the job after all."

His brow creased. "But I'd know. There's something I should tell you. I keep my promises."

"Not many people do."

"Why do you want Cavenaugh?" He switched

topics, watching her reaction and learning a little more. Deep pain filled her eyes, and on its heels came rage. The curtain on her emotions closed, leaving him wondering if he'd only imagined what he'd seen. He didn't think so.

She shrugged. "He's the bad guy."

"I think it's more than that." For a moment he thought the subject was closed, that she wouldn't let him inside.

She took a deep breath before speaking. "He destroyed my family."

Before he could probe deeper, she turned and strode toward her room, effectively shutting him out. He watched her go, not even trying to stop her. There'd been such a wealth of hurt in that one sentence. He couldn't push for more details.

She was right, though. He was starting to take the relationship more seriously than he'd intended. He had to remember she meant nothing to him. Strange, but he didn't quite believe that anymore. One thing he did know was that he wanted to help her at least locate Cavenaugh. The rest he'd leave up to her and the Drug Enforcement Agency.

He went to the kitchen so he wouldn't be overheard and punched in a number.

"Have you got anything?" Wade asked Josh after he answered, hoping his friend could shed some light on Cavenaugh and where the criminal might be right now.

"Not yet. I've had a couple of leads, but so far nothing has panned out. By the way, why do you want him? You told me you weren't going undercover again. What changed your mind?"

"I'm helping a friend."

"Female?"

He hesitated. "Yeah."

Josh chuckled. "Figures."

"It's not like that."

"Uh-huh."

"I'm serious. Just find out what you can."

"You got it, but remember I told you that you'd never be able to give up undercover work. Not when it gets in your blood. Besides, you were the best cop on the force."

"You mean except for that one time." Wade couldn't keep the sarcasm from his voice.

"We both know that wasn't your fault. If that kid had trusted you, he'd still be alive. He chose to go back to his gang, and it cost him."

Wade gripped the phone. "I'm not coming back. I like my life here, and I don't intend to give it up for anyone." His words didn't sound quite as sincere as when he'd first spoken them. No, he was meant to be sheriff of Two Creeks. Most of his family lived here, friends he'd grown up with. This was his life now.

"Just see what you can find on Cavenaugh." His words were harsher than he'd intended.

"You got it, pal."

They said goodbye and Wade put the phone back in the cradle. When he turned around, Fallon stood in the doorway. Her hands were drawn into fists, her knuckles white.

"I thought I told you not to call anyone."

"Josh isn't anyone. He's a cop."

"You just don't fucking get it. It doesn't matter that he's a cop. I should have known not to trust you." She turned on her heel and stormed out of the room, throwing over her shoulder, "I'll be out of here as soon as I get my disk."

Chapter 10

"Fallon, wait." Wade caught up to her and grabbed her arm.

She stopped, whirling around to face him. "I told you not to bring anyone else into this," she ground out. "You said you kept your promises"—her voice cracked and she looked away—"but apparently you don't."

Damn it, how the hell could he persuade her he'd called Josh to help, not to cause more problems? One look at her face, and he knew it wouldn't be easy convincing her of that fact.

"Josh and I go back a long way. He's like family."

She raised her chin and looked him in the eye. "Family has a way of betraying you."

"He wouldn't."

"How can you be so sure?"

He loosened his grip on her arm and looked into her eyes as he tried to ferret out the inner turmoil he saw reflected in them, but she'd locked it away so deep he wondered if it could ever be brought to the surface. It was the only way she would heal.

"Trust me on this, Fallon." He ran his finger down her jaw, feeling the tenseness.

She jerked away. "Trust isn't given—it's earned."

"Touché."

Fallon was right. If their positions were reversed, he'd think twice about putting all his faith in someone he'd only met a short time ago. But he had to try to convince her to stay. He drew in a deep breath. "Please don't go. Josh is a damn good cop. If anyone can find Cavenaugh, he can."

Anger flared in her eyes. "I don't need anyone's help. Least of all yours or your friend's. You don't know what the hell you're getting into." She whirled around and stormed off toward her room.

"You do want to know what hole he's crawled into, don't you?"

Her steps faltered.

"Josh can dig into some pretty deep places."

She looked over her shoulder. Indecision was written on her face. He'd dangled the carrot. She wanted Cavenaugh.

Her spine stiffened and she thrust out her chin. "And he can also end up dead. I can find Cavenaugh on my own."

"Can you?"

She leaned against the wall and rubbed her temples. He waited patiently until she finally spoke.

"Okay, I'll stay, for a while, but don't ever pull this kind of crap again."

"I won't," he promised.

She nodded and started to turn away, but stopped. "Has Josh found out anything?"

He shook his head. "Not yet, but he will." He could see the strain etched in the fine lines around her mouth and made a quick decision. "Come on, let's get out of the house for a while."

"And go where?"

His gaze trailed down her short top, over her bare midriff, past snug-fitting jeans, stopping at the white sneakers, the ones Bailey had kicked into a corner on his back porch and forgotten about. Odd how Fallon looked so damn sexy in his little sister's clothes while Bailey had just looked like his . . . well, like his kid sister.

"We could go shopping for clothes," he told her, his gaze meeting hers.

"I probably won't be here that long. What I have is all right." She hugged her middle.

"You can't very well wear that when you leave."

"I'm broke."

He wasn't about to give up as he tugged her toward the front door. She needed a break, and so did he. "I'll loan you a few bucks and you can pay me back later."

She dug her heels in.

He stopped and faced her. Their gazes locked. "I said I was sorry."

She looked away first. "Oh, all right, but I'm keeping every receipt."

"Are you always this stubborn?" He tossed her a windbreaker from the hall closet and grabbed a light jacket for himself before he opened the front door.

Her body relaxed as she slipped her arms into the sleeves. "You think this is stubbornness?"

He chuckled as they went out the door. When she let herself, Fallon had a pretty good sense of humor. Wade had a feeling it didn't come out very often.

"Where are we going?" she asked as she climbed into the passenger side of his vehicle. "I mean, I'd hate to run into Bailey. I *am* supposed to be suffering from a stomach virus, after all."

"I thought we'd go to Wichita Falls. It's not far, and we should be safe from prying eyes."

Safe wasn't a part of her vocabulary. But instead of saying anything, she nodded and turned her head toward the window knowing she was probably the biggest fool in the world right now. Wade had lied to her. He'd brought Josh in on the case. It didn't matter that his friend was also a cop. Hell, for all she knew it could've been someone in law enforcement who betrayed her.

Her shoulders slumped against the seat as Wade stopped at the intersection before pulling onto the highway and heading for Wichita Falls.

She scanned the passing scenery. Trees stripped of their leaves by a cold winter stood starkly against the gray background of an overcast sky. Why anyone would want to live in this area was beyond her. There were no swamps where moss draped from the trees like antique lace—just endless, bland, rolling plains.

"In a couple of weeks the scenery will drastically change," Wade told her, as if reading her mind.

Glancing in his direction, she arched a skeptical eyebrow.

He chuckled. "It's like going to bed and waking up to presents under the Christmas tree. The fruit trees start to bud. Before you know it, there'll be pink and white blossoms everywhere you look for at least a week or so. Then the bare limbs will be filled with leaves."

"Still doesn't make it any less flat," she spoke dryly.

"So where are you from?"

"Here, there, everywhere." She shrugged. "No place in particular." No place she wanted to remember.

"You had to be born somewhere."

She closed her eyes as sounds and scents drifted across her mind from a seemingly distant place— one she'd steered clear of over the passing years. She knew it wasn't that far away at all, but she could never get back what she'd lost.

"Louisiana." She spoke the name without thinking.

"It's a beautiful state. Lots of history. I've been there a couple of times."

"I don't remember a lot about it." Her stomach began to churn. She shifted in her seat.

"Do you ever think about going back?"

"Never. Do you always ask this many questions?"

"Sorry. Just making idle conversation. I didn't realize speaking about where you were born would make you so nervous."

She crossed her legs and folded her arms in front of her. "Who said it made me nervous? Did I say it made me nervous? No. I just don't think where I was born is relevant."

She glared at him, but his gaze was focused on the road in front of them. He seemed so damned relaxed it irritated her. And she wasn't nervous. "I was born in New Orleans."

"Fascinating city," he replied easily. "I've always wanted to go, but never made the trip."

"Yeah, well, send me a postcard when you do."

Instead of her ire pissing him off, he laughed. Most people would've backed away from her prickly attitude by now. It had always been a good defense in the past when someone started asking too many questions—prying a little too deep into an area she had no intention of discussing.

"Do you have any family? Should you call and let them know you're okay?" he asked.

She chose her words carefully. "There's no one that I'm close to, except maybe King, and he knows I'm safe."

"That's where we're different. Hell, I'm probably related to most of the people in Two Creeks."

She hadn't wanted to get pulled into a conversation about family, but her curiosity got the better of her. "Was that why you moved back?" Fallon couldn't imagine giving up her life and living in a town that only had a population of three thousand. Undercover work was dangerous, but it was also exhilarating and exciting.

"I came back for a lot of reasons," Wade hedged. "Family played a role, but only a minor one."

So, he had secrets, too. "And what was the major one?"

He shrugged. "Sometimes you lose whether you want to or not. People get hurt . . . or killed."

She hated the note of pain she heard in his voice. For a fraction of a second she wished she could soothe his hurt. She quickly shook off the unfamiliar feeling. "But in the long run, you're doing good. I mean, by putting the criminals behind bars you're making it safer for other people."

He shook his head. "Not to the exclusion of everything else. Not when you stop living when you're away from work. Not when you focus so much on a case it consumes you. Not when you give up your life." Abruptly, he looked at her. "When is the last time you did anything for yourself? Had fun?"

She thought for a moment. "I took down a petty thug not long ago. Knocked out three of his teeth. That was fun." Her adrenalin had been pumping that day. The guy had shoved a little old lady to the ground and stolen her purse. The woman had just cashed her social security check and was going to buy groceries. Taking down the creep had been a hell of a lot of fun.

"That's exactly what I'm saying. You've excluded everything from your life except work."

Her spine stiffened. Her life was her work. It had to be. "I live life exactly the way I want."

"Yeah, right."

"What's that supposed to mean?"

"Okay," he nodded. "Tell me the last thing you did and had fun doing it—besides work."

She thought for a moment. When had she actually done something for herself? She shifted in her seat. Her life consisted of TV dinners or a quick burger. And she liked it that way. She cut her own hair and grabbed clothes off the rack unless it was for an assignment. Only then would she take meticulous care in buying what she needed.

"Was the question that hard?" he asked, keeping his eyes on the road and his hands on the wheel.

"No, it wasn't that hard. I do a lot for myself. I was trying to think which time."

Wade didn't look convinced. And why should he? It was a bald-faced lie. "I don't give a rat's ass if you believe me or not."

"Who said I didn't believe you? You really need to learn to trust people."

"Trusting people can get you killed."

"Or they can watch your back."

She laughed without mirth. "Is that what you're doing, Wade? Keeping me safe? I've been taking care of myself for a long time, and I don't need anyone's help."

"So you've said." He flipped his blinker on and stopped for oncoming traffic. "We're here."

She hadn't even noticed when the barren scenery changed to businesses. Words on a gray marble stone proclaimed this as the Sikes Center Mall. They pulled through the entrance. Normally, she was very observant. Wade had made her forget Cavenaugh was still out there. He'd made her forget why she was here.

Her heart skipped a beat. What if something had happened? Could she have responded to the situation fast enough?

Damn it, for a brief time he'd made her forget what she had to do. Not again. She'd grab some clothes and get the hell out of there.

As soon as Wade stopped, she was out of the vehicle.

"Hey, what's your hurry?" he asked as he caught up to her.

Fallon glanced at him. "I don't like shopping. The sooner I get this over with, the better."

She paused when a pained expression crossed Wade's face and he grabbed his heart. She quickly put a hand on his arm as cold dread filled her. He hadn't told her he had a bad ticker. Good grief, he could've keeled over any time after the wild sex they'd had. All she needed was a corpse to go along with her other troubles.

"Are you okay?" She gripped his arm a little tighter.

A frown marred his features and his eyes were squinched shut. Fear raced through her veins. Crap, she didn't want him to die on her. Suddenly she realized how much she *did* care.

"A woman who doesn't like to shop," he gasped. "My heart can't take the shock." When he opened his eyes they twinkled down at her.

Hers narrowed dangerously. "I don't think that was at all funny." She spun on her heels and strode toward the glass doors, not really caring if he followed or not.

Damn it, she'd thought the jerk was dying.

"Fallon, come on." His footsteps sounded behind her as he hurried to catch up. "I was only joking. You know, you really need to learn to loosen up."

It only took a few strides for him to reach her. "Were you worried about me?" he asked.

"No, but if you died I'd have to buy my own clothes." She stopped and faced him, her stance rigid. "I'm not here to have fun. I'm going to get some clothes I don't particularly want, but it seems I need. The sooner we get this little adventure over with, the better."

He stared at her for a few minutes—long enough for her to grow uncomfortably warm. There was something in the way he looked at her. Like they were the only two people for miles around. She shifted from one foot to the other.

"God, you have to be the most beautiful woman I've ever met, but when you're angry"—he shook his head—"I don't know. There's just something so damn sexy about you."

Flattery wouldn't keep her from being ticked off at him for the stunt he'd just pulled. "Did anyone ever tell you that you're crazy?"

He grinned, and flutters of excitement raced around inside her belly.

"Only my siblings, and sometimes Josh."

"They're right." She absently fingered the ends of her cropped hair.

He stepped closer. His fingers intertwined with hers. "You're not Barbie-doll beautiful." He nodded toward a buxom blonde as she made her way inside the mall.

The girl looked up and gave him a come-hither smile that sent a burst of anger shooting through Fallon. *The bitch.* Anyone who wasn't blind could see Wade was with her. Not that she cared one way or the other, but she didn't like women who traipsed on another woman's territory.

"You're different," he continued. "Dark and mysterious. Your eyes are a haunting deep blue that makes me want to step closer to see if I could really get lost in them."

She held her breath—wanting him to step closer—but a group of women, laughing as they strolled by, broke the spell.

Damn it, he'd cast his line and reeled her into his fantasy again like she was an easy mark or something. She knew she wasn't ugly, but he made her out to be a madonna. Yeah, right.

"Whatever, Tanner. Now that you're through drooling all over my magnificence, can we get this shopping over with?"

He sighed and waved his arm toward the door. "Your wish is my command."

"Not a bad idea. You can buy me lunch then. I'm starved."

She took the lead and entered the mall, sensing he was studying her as she went inside. Or maybe dissecting her would be a better word. People had been doing that all her life: trying to discover what made her tick. So far, no one had figured her out. Hell, she sometimes wondered.

She stopped at a sign that told her what section she was in and offered a listing of all the stores.

"Okay, where to first?" She looked over her shoulder.

His grin was wicked. "Victoria's Secret?"

Sensuous thoughts drifted across her mind as

delicious tremors raced up and down her spine. When she glanced up, Wade's eyes mirrored her desire. What might have started out as teasing on his part had developed rapidly into something more.

Damn, she couldn't very well have sex with him in the middle of the mall. "You're not funny, Tanner. Not one damn bit, and I hope like hell you're hurting as much as I am."

"Actually, probably more," he grumbled, tugging at his pants.

Good! She strode past stores with displays meant to entice shoppers to come inside and look around. But she couldn't stop the smile that tugged at her lips. He was definitely full of it. And, if she were honest, he was the best fun she'd had in a hell of a long time. So maybe she would take the day off. Forget for a moment there even was a Cavenaugh and just have fun with this very intriguing man.

She glanced toward a flashy display window and stumbled to a grinding stop. The window artfully displayed red satin sheets draped over a plush mattress. She could envision Wade lying against the big, fluffy pillows, not a stitch of clothes on, beckoning her closer. She almost groaned out loud.

Fool! Fool! Fool! What could she have been thinking about? Wade made her forget who the hell she was.

Desperately she glanced around the mall. She needed space. Hell, what she needed was to get away from him for a while, but unless a guardian angel swooped down it looked like she might be stuck.

She glanced upward.

If you're there, then send me a diversion!

Chapter 11

Wade had to remember not to tease Fallon, not if it was going to cause him this much discomfort in his lower region. He shifted his gaze away from her as he tried to bring his salacious thoughts under control.

Not looking at her didn't help.

A simple display of red satin sheets had him salivating. He pictured Fallon's naked body draped across them, eyes half-closed as she wantonly invited him to strip and join her on the bed.

"Wade . . . Wade Tanner? What the dickens are you doing in Wichita? I thought you left for the big city."

His vision came to a screeching halt. *Damn!* What was Ben Carr doing in the mall today of all days? His gaze swiveled toward Fallon.

She looked relieved. His eyebrows drew together. He'd thought she would be pissed they'd run into someone he knew. She looked almost glad for the interruption.

Wade returned his attention to the old rancher,

covertly glancing around as he did. *Good.* He didn't see Ben's wife, Audrey. Maybe Ben just wanted to escape the small town of Two Creeks and people-watch while relaxing on one of the benches. Wade couldn't really envision that being the reason Ben was here.

The older man stood and ambled over to join them. His gait rocked side to side from years spent in a saddle. Wade shook hands with him before turning to Fallon. He made the introductions as quickly and painlessly as possible.

Ben gave Fallon a slow appraisal before turning to Wade with a speculative gleam in his eyes. He opened his mouth to speak, but was interrupted when his name echoed across the mall.

"Ben, dahlin'! Look what I found. And all on sale."

A slender woman, slightly younger than Ben, rushed toward them, a large bag hooked over each arm. Her mellow-yellow hair, which could only have come from a bottle, peeked from under a wide, black hat with red velvet flowers attached to the brim.

Wade inwardly groaned as Two Creeks biggest gossip plowed her way past other shoppers in her haste to show Ben the treasures she'd unearthed from the bottom of a sale bin. *What rotten luck.* He plastered a bright smile on his face, hoping he looked more sincere than he felt.

She skidded to a stop, but her packages still had enough forward momentum that she would've toppled over if Ben hadn't reached out a hand to steady her. Only her hat went askew.

"Oh dear, how clumsy of me." She shoved it back in place and blew a couple of corkscrew curls out of her eyes. "Why Wade Tanner, what are you doing. . . ." Her smile wavered when she caught sight of Fallon. "You have a lady friend. How nice." A grin as wide as the state of Texas slowly spread across her face. "How very, *very* nice."

Wade cleared his throat and looked at Fallon. She'd lowered one of her eyebrows. The other remained arched. He coughed and turned back to face Audrey. Again, he made introductions.

"I thought you went to Dallas on vacation," Audrey drawled, looking from him, to Fallon, then back again. Her eyes twinkled with mischief. "I do swear, Wade Tanner, you've always had a penchant for getting the best souvenirs. Your momma didn't say a word to me, either. But then, she's always been closedmouthed. I've often wondered if she was really born in the South. There's not a gossipy bone in her body."

"That's because you never let anyone get a word in edgewise," Ben scolded. "You're always the first person spreading news."

Instead of upsetting Audrey, she preened. "Yes, I always seem to be in the right place at the right time. But it's never malicious gossip, just"—she smiled like the cat who got the cream—"delicious facts."

Wade knew it wouldn't do a bit of good to ask Audrey to keep quiet about Fallon. It would probably have a reverse effect and only fuel her desire to get back to the small town even quicker and spread her new information.

"How do you do," Fallon said as she suddenly stepped forward. Her slight southern drawl became more pronounced. "I haven't had the pleasure of meeting Wade's mother . . . yet. I'm sure that's why she hasn't mentioned me. I'm Josh's cousin. You must remember how close Josh and Wade were growing up. You'd have thought they were brothers."

Ben and Audrey nodded.

"Actually, I'm Josh's cousin on his father's side," Fallon continued. "His Uncle Bob's daughter. That's twice removed, but Josh and I have always been close. Thank goodness for the telephone." She chuckled. "My father was in the Air Force, so we traveled a lot. I felt like a gypsy sometimes. It was simply dreadful," she simpered like a true southern belle.

"Oh, you poor dear. Living from base to base. It must have been excruciating." Audrey patted Fallon's arm. "Where are you staying now?"

Wade crossed his arms and watched Fallon's acting ability with amusement . . . and a touch of awe. He wondered how she'd sidestep the other woman's question. And he wondered why she was acting like Audrey was the best thing to ever walk into her life. He'd bet his last dollar there was a reason behind her friendliness.

"I'm staying with Wade," Fallon's words tripped easily across those beautiful, sexy lips. "I went to Dallas with Josh. Well, one thing led to another, and Wade offered me a job when he discovered I was looking for one." She rolled her eyes. "Then I came down with this dreadful stomach virus, but Dr. Canton was kind enough to make a house call."

Audrey clicked her tongue. "You poor, poor dear."

"Wade and I have corresponded on and off over the years—so often that he's practically like my own brother."

Wade coughed and sputtered as he attempted to cover his burst of laughter. Audrey turned concerned eyes toward him.

"You aren't getting her bug, are you?" Audrey asked.

"He's fine. I'm almost positive it was just a little old upset stomach."

Audrey nodded. "Ginger tea. That'll cure your ailment quicker than anything."

"Of course! My grandmother used it. I'll have to remember that next time."

"I thought we were going to eat," Ben grumbled. "You said after you finished that last sale we could get something. I didn't know you'd be in there for over an hour," he groused. "I'm so starved my belly's grown to my backbone."

Fallon smiled warmly. "We were just talking about where to go ourselves. Wade said he was getting a little hungry. Why don't we all sit down together?" Fallon tucked her arm inside Audrey's. "That way we can get to know one another."

Now what in the world was she up to? He knew Fallon didn't want to have lunch with the other couple any more than he did.

Just about the time he thought he had her figured out, she'd do something so outrageous he didn't know what to think. He shook his head and trailed along beside the other three, who seemed to be on their way to becoming lifelong friends.

Except he knew better.

But what the hell could she be up to? A couple strolling hand-in-hand caught his eye as they passed. He said something, and she laughed. He looked at Fallon and saw she stared at them, too. Her face paled before she swallowed hard and refocused on Audrey.

That was it. Fallon was afraid to be alone with him. He wondered why.

* * *

Two hours later, and Fallon knew it would take a pry bar to remove the smile from her face. If she were trying out for a toothpaste commercial, she'd have gotten the job hands down. *Good Lord, these people were boring.* They'd discussed the dropping price of cattle, some guy named Skip who'd been kicked by a horse and Dr. Canton had just removed his cast—the man's, not the animal's.

From what she'd gathered, the horse had been cursed to spend all of eternity in hell. And if that wasn't bad enough, Audrey was now talking fashion. Like Fallon cared.

Smile firmly in place, she tuned Audrey out and thought about what she should do next. If Cavenaugh had gone into hiding, then it might be months before he resurfaced. She couldn't very well stay with Wade for that length of time. She was already taking chances she normally wouldn't take.

And too many people knew she was in Two Creeks staying with the local sheriff. She had to be more careful. It might be wise if she didn't leave his house anymore; fake a relapse, or something. Yes, she absently nodded, that's what she'd do.

"Oh good, I'm so glad you agree," Audrey broke into Fallon's thoughts.

Her gaze swiveled to Wade. He kept a straight face but she could tell something amused him.

"Well," Ben beamed. "That lets me off the hook." He reached inside his pocket before handing his wife a set of keys. "I'll ride back with Wade and you two girls can shop to your hearts' content."

Shop? What had she missed?

Wade reached into his wallet and handed Fallon his credit card. "Have fun."

Absently she took the piece of black plastic with gold lettering. *Fake a relapse,* her mind screamed. She looked at her empty plate and knew Audrey wouldn't believe a sudden bout of queasiness. Not after the food she'd packed away without batting an eye.

Great, she was stuck.

Audrey smiled lovingly at Ben. "We won't be too late." Then before Audrey blinked again, she grabbed Fallon's arm and practically dragged her from the restaurant. "Come, dear. We don't want to miss the sale at the new store that's opened. And I hear they're running a special at the beauty salon: buy one facial, get a second one free. We can split the cost."

Fallon looked over her shoulder, but Wade only grinned as Ben bent to retrieve his wife's packages. So much for Wade watching her back. Surely he could've said something to keep her out of Audrey's clutches. A lot of help he was. Now she was stuck with this crazy woman for the rest of the afternoon instead of just lunch.

What the hell have I gotten myself into?

She'd thought that by befriending Audrey, there wouldn't be as much gossip for the other woman to spread and she'd be able to get her head on straight concerning Wade. Her little scheme backfired, though. And now she couldn't see any way out of her dilemma.

". . . and I saw this adorable little outfit at Sears that would be absolutely too cute on you." She ran a discerning gaze over Fallon's attire. "What you have on doesn't do a thing for you." She shook her head, sending her hat bobbing and the flowers bouncing. "In my day we used what we had, but young people today don't even try. My mother would've locked me in my room if I'd have come downstairs dressed like you."

Fallon had been up against hardened criminals and never batted an eye, but this woman left her speechless. What could she say to her, though? *You crazy old bat. I don't want to shop! And I damn sure don't care what you think about my style.*

But she couldn't say any of that. Not if she wanted to go unnoticed while in Two Creeks, and right now she had little choice of places to go. She was stuck until King thought it safe for her to return.

Audrey skidded to a halt outside the glass doors of the beauty salon. Her eyes took on a reverent glow. "We're here," she breathed.

I don't want to do this! I don't want to do this! I don't want to do this! But her feet trudged behind Audrey as if they had a will of their own.

"Can I help y'all?" The receptionist's sugary smile would've sent a diabetic into a coma.

Before she could do anything besides open her mouth, Audrey proclaimed in a loud voice they wanted the works and money was no object. Fallon groaned as heads swiveled toward them. It was a wonder the only two stylists not working didn't get whiplash.

Great! She didn't want *the works.* Damn it, she was an undercover agent with the United States government. And she never went to beauty salons. There was no way she'd let these overeager hair-teasers get anywhere near her.

"Just relax dear and let them do what they're trained to do," Audrey said as if she sensed Fallon's hesitancy.

"Come this way, please," one of the two hair-dressers said as they rushed forward.

"And I don't have unlimited funds," Fallon frantically whispered.

"It doesn't matter," Audrey whispered back. "They can only charge what's listed, and I've been here before. They're reasonable. Somehow it always makes them jump when you tell them money isn't an issue. Don't ask me why. Mind over matter, I guess."

Reluctantly, Fallon followed them behind a curtain. The younger of the two motioned for Fallon to sit.

Well hell, she might as well get this day over with. But she'd bet her last dollar, if she'd had one, that Wade was laughing his ass off right now.

"Back we go," the hairdresser spoke in a bubble-gum voice.

Fallon grabbed the arms of the chair when the grinning girl tilted the seat back. She didn't stop there, but nudged Fallon's shoulder until her neck was braced against hard plastic. Fallon gritted her teeth. Ready for whatever the girl dished out.

But the hairdresser only began spraying warm, soothing water over Fallon's hair. Okay, so maybe this wasn't so bad after all. It felt rather nice and . . . relaxing. She closed her eyes. Sounds began to filter into her brain. She lost herself in the meditative music coming from speakers hidden somewhere above her head.

Methodically, the woman applied shampoo before massaging gently with her fingers. Fallon could feel all the bones in her body dissolving into a puddle of mush.

A cream rinse followed—a tropical scent that

made her dream of sandy beaches, a tall pina colada in her hand, and Wade stripped naked lying on a towel beside her. She sighed.

She almost hated when the girl stopped, but then she began to apply a cool cream to Fallon's face. *Heavenly*. Fifteen minutes later and feeling somewhat like a limp dishrag, Fallon let the hairdresser lead the way to the other room.

Tammy, as Fallon learned the girl's name was, suggested colors for her makeup. Like Fallon really cared at this point. Letting the girl choose, Fallon closed her eyes and wallowed in total relaxation. This was almost better than sex.

Her experience didn't stop with makeup. Tammy began to trim the uneven ends of Fallon's hair, hypnotically running the comb through the short strands.

Fallon had never known what she was missing. She glanced toward Audrey. The older woman winked and tossed her a saucy grin. In the short space separating them they shared a moment in time, a bonding of two women enjoying one of the pleasures that life had to offer.

She'd never experienced a connection with another female, had never really felt the need—in fact, avoided it. An odd feeling swept over her. She couldn't really explain it, but maybe it wasn't so awful . . . having a friendship. And maybe it was time she did something for herself. She'd let Cavenaugh consume her every waking moment for as long as she could remember. She wanted to let go . . . but only for a little while. She'd sworn to get revenge, and she would.

Any tense muscles that were left inside vanished as she completely gave in to the hairdresser's ministrations. *Yes, this was nice.* A deep sigh escaped her. She let herself be swept away as Tammy began fluffing and drying her hair. Then her nails were manicured and lotion massaged into her arms and hands. Fallon knew today she'd been given a little bit of heaven.

"You haven't fully lived life until you've been pampered," Audrey said as they were leaving the salon. She glanced at Fallon. "And that fingernail polish looks very pretty on you."

Fallon stretched her arms in front of her and turned her hand to the left, then the right. "I don't know." She'd always filed her fingernails, keeping them well trimmed and neat. She only wore polish if it lent credence to her undercover assignment.

"It's a very sexy shade."

Fallon looked at Audrey. The woman had to be at least sixty-five.

"What?" Audrey asked. "You don't think I know what it's like to feel sexy? I'm not that decrepit, dear. And if you play your cards right, you're never too old for sex. It's a state of mind. You're only as old as you feel, and as long as you don't hurt other people, then what's the harm?" She smiled. "I do believe I've shocked you."

No words came to Fallon. "I . . . I . . ." Her mouth snapped shut. She looked at the other woman and burst out laughing. "Audrey, I like your attitude."

"Yes, I thought you'd see it my way. Everyone thinks we discuss the new way to cook a pot roast at our little quilting bees. They'd never guess what we *really* talk about. Someday I'll bring you along to a delicious little party I go to a couple times a year. They have the most scrumptious little sex toys. It beats those other in-home parties by a country mile."

Nice, older women were not supposed to talk like this—were they?

When she was just a teen, she'd begun watching people: looking past their smiles and seeing the real person beneath the façade. But she'd really screwed up with Audrey. She wasn't a simpering, older southern lady. She was a woman who apparently knew what she wanted and didn't hesitate to go after it.

Fallon decided she liked her.

"Here we are." Audrey beamed. "Let's see if we can change Wade's outlook. Brotherly love, my foot. Not when he has you under his roof. I swear I don't know what the younger crowd would do without us older generation pushing them in the right direction."

Maybe it was time she burst Audrey's bubble. "I don't need a man in my life to make me happy. I'm content on my own."

Audrey's laughter trilled across aisles stuffed with racks of clothing. "Honey, I'm not trying to marry you off. Please tell me you're not one of those frigid women who hates sex? If so, you're missing out on the best years of your life."

"But I thought . . ."

"You want to make the experience pleasurable for the both of you. And if you're worried about Wade thinking of you as a sister, then don't." She grinned. "The man certainly wasn't looking at you like he does Bailey."

"I . . . I . . ."

Audrey patted her hand. "Ben says I owned a brothel in a previous life. I think he might be right."

As did Fallon. The woman was certainly straight-forward. She could almost imagine Audrey in her younger day giving all the men, young and old, a run for their money. Hell, she had no doubt Ben still panted after her.

"Here we are," Audrey proclaimed, bringing a hanger off the rack. "The perfect dress."

"That's a dress? I thought it was a scarf," Fallon commented dryly but couldn't stop the flutter of excitement that skidded down her backbone when she thought of Wade's expression if he saw her wearing the slinky scrap of black material.

"Want to try it on?"

Audrey swung the hanger back and forth in front of Fallon. The woman had issued an unspoken challenge.

"Give it here." Fallon grabbed the dress and dashed toward the dressing room, Audrey's knowing laughter following her all the way.

This, of course, was totally ridiculous. Wade would just as soon have her without a stitch on. She went inside one of the booths and pulled off her clothes. She wasn't wearing a bra, but it didn't matter. The dress was so snug it made it impossible to wear undergarments.

She slipped it over her head and tugged it downward. When she raised her head a stranger stared back. This wasn't the same Fallon who'd left Wade's house earlier today. *Nope.* Her gaze trailed downward before she raised her head once more.

Not even close.

A slow grin spread across her face. So maybe she wouldn't let Wade get too close to her inner feelings, but it damn sure didn't mean they couldn't have wild nights filled with hot sex.

And this was just the dress to inspire such thoughts.

Chapter 12

Audrey insisted that Fallon wear a sleek, black leather suit home: pants that fit her like a glove, a form-fitting turtleneck top she thought might be made of spandex the way it hugged each curve, and a short black leather jacket. *Look out Rambo— Rambina has arrived.* Okay, maybe she was being difficult. She guessed the suit was fine. Besides, she blended in better.

But the boots Audrey had chosen were her nemesis. The heels were blocked and at least two inches high. They were sheer torture. If she could only kick them off for a few minutes everything would be fine, but then she really would look out of place. Damn, she was beat.

Audrey, the shopaholic, had dragged her into every store in the mall. Some twice. In the beginning, it had been rather fun—a novel experience. After the first couple of stores, shopping ceased to entertain her. Somehow Audrey had maneuvered her until saying no wasn't an option. King could really use the woman's tactical skills.

"It looks like we're through." Audrey sighed. "I think I'm getting close to my credit card limit."

Fallon shifted one of four bags that cut into her arm. "It's about time."

"I believe it's five o'clock," Audrey absently muttered as she slowed her steps, mesmerized by a store display they had to have passed at least three times today. "What about that blue hat?"

"Don't you think it's a little old for you? I mean, you dress so chic and it looks a little dowdy." She held her breath, hoping Audrey would think the same thing. She wanted to get out of this mall. The longer they were here, the more crowded it became.

"Maybe you're right." Audrey nibbled her bottom lip, but then pointed toward a long hallway. "Oh, but there's the bathroom. Do you mind watching my packages? I'll just be a minute."

How many times had she heard that today as Audrey tried on one more hat or one more dress? "Sure, go ahead." Just so they could leave in the next ten minutes, before her façade slipped and she killed the woman.

As Audrey hurried away, Fallon propped her packages against the wall.

Okay, so maybe she wasn't *that* upset. Just beat. Her side ached and she didn't think she was quite caught up on her sleep. How could she be, with Wade around?

Sensuous tingles made a beeline for the juncture between her legs. She had a feeling her suit wouldn't stay on long after she got home. Not that she would mind.

Maybe this enforced time off from the agency wasn't so bad after all. She could think of worse things to do while she waited for Cavenaugh to resurface. Having Wade around was a bennie she hadn't counted on. She closed her eyes as sweet visions filled her mind. His slow striptease the other day—one layer of clothes at a time. Her mouth watered. She could almost feel the heat of his. . . .

"Looks like you've changed your style." Sarcasm dripped from Callie's words. "If I didn't know better, I'd think you were trying to catch a man. Anyone I know?" She snickered.

That kid could sure fuck up a good wet dream. Fallon opened her eyes. Sheesh, what'd Callie do, buy stock in one of the cosmetic companies? She had on so much makeup the kid would have to use a hammer and chisel to get the cosmetics off. "Aren't you supposed to be in school or something?"

One side of Callie's mouth turned down. "Uh, hell-oo, it's five o'clock."

School had lasted a lot longer when she was going—or so it seemed. Something caught Fallon's attention out of the corner of her eye, and she shifted her gaze from the bratty kid.

A man swaggered toward them like God had put him on earth to impress women.

She wasn't.

He wore jeans that looked like they'd been put through a shredder and a shirt unbuttoned almost to the waist. Even though he couldn't be more than twenty-one or two, everything about him made her insides crawl. His stride was a little too slithering and his hair a lot too greasy. She'd seen his type too many times.

Fallon could tell he was bad news even before he noticed her. When he gave her a long, slow appraisal she knew her instincts were right.

He sidled up to Callie and put his arm around her. Fallon almost groaned. What the hell was the girl thinking about when she'd hooked up with this loser?

A rush of memories came back to haunt her, and the years fell away. For a moment she could almost feel this jerk's arm around *her*. But his name had been Danny back then. She probably should warn Callie, but knew the other girl would only dig her heels in deeper.

Callie flinched when the guy pulled her closer. *Or maybe not.* The kid didn't look quite so enamoured with him as she'd like to pretend.

"Who's your friend, baby?" Mr. Slicker-than-a-sidewalk-magician asked.

His scratchy voice scraped down her spine like coarse sandpaper. She started to turn away in disgust but thought about where she'd be if someone hadn't come along and knocked some sense into her fool head.

Damn it. Why now, and why this kid? She hadn't cared for her from the moment they'd met. Callie had a mouth on her that needed to be washed out with a bar of strong soap. Besides, she didn't have time for this.

"She's not my friend," Callie grumbled.

That makes two of us.

He trailed dirty fingers up and down Callie's arm. The girl raised her chin in defiance, as if daring Fallon to say anything. Fallon arched an eyebrow. Callie's bravado wavered and she looked down at her feet.

So maybe Callie didn't like this dirtbag as much as she pretended, at least not enough to fight for him. Fallon should walk away. Right now. Not get involved.

Hell!

This wasn't going to be easy, but she'd give it

her best shot. She lowered her eyelids seductively while her stomach threatened to heave. Callie concentrated on looking anywhere but at her so she didn't notice Fallon's flagrant come-on. "Yes, introduce us, Callie."

"I'm Steve," he said, not waiting.

"He's my boyfriend," Callie muttered.

Fallon looked pointedly at Steve.

"Hey, baby, why don't you run and get us a couple of drinks from over there." He motioned toward a place not far away that sold soft drinks.

Callie raised questioning eyes. "Aren't you comin'?"

He cast a glare in the kid's direction, his hand squeezing her arm. The girl flinched. Fallon clenched her fists. She couldn't afford to draw attention to herself or she'd floor the jerk.

"I can't ask you to do one thing for me." Steve swore under his breath. "If you don't want to make me happy we might as well leave right now."

"No . . . no, I'll do it. I just thought you might want to come with me, that's all. Don't get mad, okay?" When he let go she hurried away to do his bidding.

"Your place or mine." Steve looked pointedly at her breasts before returning his gaze to her face. "I'll have you screaming before the night's over."

She sauntered closer and leaned toward him. In case someone was actually watching, they would only see a woman whispering something to a young man. When she was near enough, she grabbed him by the nuts and applied enough pressure that his eyes began to bulge.

"Bet I can make you scream right now," she whispered, keeping a smile on her face. "I'm going to say this slowly and clearly because I don't want you to misunderstand me. That's a fifteen-year-old girl's head you're fucking with, junior."

Steve's words were garbled.

"By the way, I'm a drug enforcement agent. What's say I call a couple of friends of mine and maybe we'll drop by for a visit."

She twisted her hand a fraction. Steve yelped.

"Listen, lady, I didn't mean no harm or anything."

"Then you won't argue if I suggest you end this relationship, will you?"

He shook his head. "Could you please let go of my balls, lady?"

The smile she bestowed on him didn't reach her eyes. "I'm glad we understand each other."

When she took a step back he raised his fist.

"Oh, we understand each other, bitch."

She dodged his blow and rammed the heel of her hand into his gut. He grunted and doubled over. She flinched at the pull in her side before quickly glancing around. Good, no one noticed anything out of the ordinary, and Callie was just getting the drinks and starting back.

"Callie's coming. You just be a good little boy and tell her you have other plans." She twisted his thumb until he straightened, noting the color of his skin was a little green.

He sucked in a deep, ragged breath.

"Smile."

His grin looked a little sickly. *Good.* Fallon detested bullies.

Audrey and Callie arrived at the same time.

"Here's your drink." Callie handed him the soda.

"Aren't you the little girl who's come to stay with Beth?" Audrey gushed.

"I'm almost sixteen."

Audrey continued as if Callie hadn't spoken. "Beth is such a sweet young woman. Always doing so much for others." The smile left her face. "And who are you?" She turned cold gray eyes toward Steve.

"I've gotta go." Steve shoved his drink into Callie's hand.

"Good." Callie started to follow, but Steve stopped her.

"No, you stay. I've got some business I . . . uh . . . forgot about." He nodded toward Fallon. "Get them to take you back."

"But . . ."

Steve hurried away.

"Call me!"

"Yeah, sure."

"Well, won't this be a nice drive home." Audrey tucked her arm inside Callie's. "Kids always make me feel younger. Imagine how good I'd feel if I went to work in a day care." Her laughter trilled behind her as she aimed the girl toward the exit opposite the one Steve had taken.

Fifteen minutes later they were inside Audrey's Lincoln and headed for Two Creeks. The ride home seemed endless. Callie didn't say more than two words, Audrey chattered endlessly, and Fallon's side ached. She only hoped she hadn't busted another stitch. All she needed was Doc jumping down her throat.

Finally they let Callie out at her aunt's house and waited until she went inside before Audrey pulled away from the curb.

"That boy was trouble," Audrey stated.

"I think that fact is plain to everyone except Callie. She needs a lot of supervision."

"Oh, Beth does her best, but it hurt to lose her

only sister, and she has three teens of her own, too. Still, she gives the girl a lot of love. Problem is, Callie's angry. Only time will heal her wounds."

Time? No, sometimes it didn't heal wounds, it only made them fester.

"But it was a good thing you were there," Audrey said, breaking into her thoughts.

"How's that?"

She pulled next to the curb in front of Wade's home and came to a stop before turning her gaze toward Fallon. "Why, by taking that scumbag down a notch." A fiery spark entered the woman's eyes. "I loved it when you grabbed him by the gonads and twisted." She doubled her fist and turned it.

"You saw?"

"Oh, yes. I thought you were a goner when he raised his fist, but you slammed the heel of your hand into his belly." Again she made the motion. "Does my old heart good to see a woman kick-ass. Now, go inside and have a wonderful evening with your young man. Goodbye, dear, and thank you for an enjoyable day."

Fallon frowned, but opened the door. For someone undercover, a lot of people were finding out way too much about her. And Wade had said Audrey was the biggest gossip in town. *Great.* This was just damned dandy.

"Don't forget your packages, dear."

Fallon opened the door and leaned into the back-seat, grabbed her four bags, then shut the door.

Audrey pushed the button and lowered the window on the passenger side. "Oh, and don't worry. I won't tell a soul I saw you kick-ass."

She was an odd woman. Fallon wasn't sure she could trust her. At least she didn't know she was undercover with the DEA. She watched until Audrey was out of sight.

A drop of rain landed on her nose. She glanced at the sky. Dark clouds hovered close to the ground, making it seem more like night than day. A storm was brewing. She turned and hurried inside, shutting the door firmly behind her. The house was dark and uninviting, reminding her of another time, another place.

Every nerve inside her tingled as her senses came alive. She set her packages carefully on the floor and cautiously made her way into the living room. Damn it, she needed a weapon. Tomorrow she was getting bullets for the gun she'd taken from George.

As she went through the living area a streak of lightning lit the room for a moment. Someone stood by the window. Her heart pounded.

"I was beginning to worry," Wade spoke softly from across the room.

Her pulse returned to normal. "Do you always stand in the dark?" He could've warned her sooner.

"I like storms. You can see them better if you leave the lights off."

She heard him moving about before he switched on a lamp, softly illuminating the room. It took a moment for her to grow accustomed to the light. When she did, her eyes filled with the sight of him. Her heart fluttered inside her chest. She wondered if he'd missed her as much as she had him.

The realization that she had almost floored her. She didn't want to care about this man. Damn it, why had she let herself get involved? It was only going to be that much harder when she left. And she *would* leave. Wade had already said his life was here—in this small town. She couldn't survive in Two Creeks. She'd suffocate.

"You look sexy." He ambled closer to her.

She stiffened her spine. "I didn't do it for you."

He smiled. "I didn't say you did." He stopped in front of her. "But it doesn't keep me from wanting to make love to you."

She drew in a sharp breath. "We have an impossible relationship," she murmured. "Nothing can come of our time together. We're two very different people."

"Say the word, and I'll back off." He ran his knuckles down the side of her cheek before fingering the ends of her hair.

She sighed, liking the way the heat from his hand warmed her cool skin. *Just say the word?* She couldn't. Not when she wanted more than anything to make love to him.

He slid his hand to the back of her neck and began to massage—a slow, sensuous movement that left her breathless. She shifted her feet to ease the ache that had begun to build inside her. The movement sent a spasm up her leg.

"Ugh!" She grimaced and grabbed her thigh, hoping to stop the cramp.

"Your side?"

"My feet." At least, more than her side. "Audrey insisted I wear this outfit home but she didn't say we had four hours of shopping left. My feet are killing me." She frowned. "And it's all your fault."

"Mine?" He chuckled. "You're the one who wanted to become best friends with her." He led her to the sofa so she could sit.

"No, I didn't." She eased to the cushions. "I knew if she realized just how boring her gossip about me would be then maybe she wouldn't want to spread it. I didn't know I'd have to spend all afternoon shopping."

"I tried to warn you." He sat beside her and pulled her feet onto his lap.

Her brow furrowed. "No, you didn't." She shifted into a more comfortable position.

He paused while removing her boots, his expression quizzical. "I didn't? I meant to."

"Yeah, right. You threw me to the wolves." When he began massaging her feet, thoughts of her day at the mall disappeared. "Umm, that feels good." Her eyes drifted closed.

Wade knew the minute she fell asleep. But he couldn't stop rubbing her feet. He wasn't ready to break the contact between them just yet.

What hold did she have over him? He stared at the beauty lying on his couch. He hadn't lied; she looked sexy as hell. The black leather pants hugged every delicious curve, as did the black turtleneck. And she'd had her hair styled. It suited her. But there was more to it than her looks.

Something inexplicable—hard to define—drew him ever closer. But she was right; theirs was an impossible relationship. He couldn't go back to her way of life, and he knew she wouldn't be happy in his. Yet, he was beginning to care . . . more than he wanted to admit.

Chapter 13

Wade really hated leaving a naked woman in his bed, especially when he hadn't just made love to her. He sighed and pulled up the covers Fallon had kicked off. It was a shame to hide that sexy bottom from his view, but he didn't want her getting cold.

He grabbed some clothes and went to the guest bathroom. His deputy would have a pot of coffee on by the time he arrived, so he only bothered with a quick shower, then dressed. When he peeked in, Fallon continued to sleep soundly. He let himself out the front door and climbed into his vehicle.

Five minutes later he parked in front of the sheriff's office and went inside.

"It's about time you came back to work," Andy smiled.

"I didn't think you'd miss me that much, or I would've come back sooner." He grinned at his deputy. Andy was worth his weight in gold. Not that he weighed a whole hell of a lot—even dripping wet. His wiry frame had fooled more than one person, though. Andy had a black belt in karate and wasn't afraid of anything . . . except maybe spiders.

"Course we missed you. I've had to take out the trash every night this week, and it's your turn."

"Your welcome-home brings tears to my eyes."

Andy chuckled. "Yeah, I kind of thought it would."

The deputy followed him down the hall into a small break room. Wade went straight to the coffee and poured a cup, adding a couple of packets of sugar.

It felt good to be home. Doc was right; the city was no place for him to go. Fallon suddenly flashed across his mind—wild and free, able to travel to different places, not knowing what awaited her around the next corner. A twinge of longing for that old life tugged at him. He thoughtfully stirred his coffee before taking a big drink.

Wade forgot about what might have been as he coughed and looked accusingly at Andy. "I told you, it's half a can of coffee to a pot, not a full one."

"Ha-ha. Hell, yours would stop a bullet. They could make second-chance vests out of what you brew."

Wade furrowed his brow. "You think I should patent it?"

"Funny." Andy poured himself a cup. "So I heard you brought something back from your little vacation." The deputy didn't look his way as he dumped cream and sugar into his coffee.

Before Wade could comment, the night dispatcher, who was just going off duty, and one of the secretaries entered laughing. Both women stopped when they saw the two men.

"Hi, Wade . . . Andy," they spoke in unison.

The men nodded.

"Let's go to my office. You can catch me up on what's been happening while I was away."

"And you can tell me about the extra piece of luggage you collected."

The two women chortled, but sobered when Wade scowled in their direction. The two men left the room and headed down a narrow hallway and entered his office. As soon as he shut the door, Wade turned to Andy. "How the hell did you know about Fallon?"

"Bailey."

"Figures," Wade grumbled and went to the chair behind his desk. He sank into the black leather, realizing how at home he felt. Even with his background in law enforcement, it never failed to amaze him that he'd been elected sheriff of Two Creeks. He'd always said small-town life wasn't for him. But that was before he'd realized he couldn't fix the world, only keep this small portion safe.

"She said you were going to hire Fallon for the records position," Andy mentioned.

Wade looked up. "Who said?"

The deputy slumped in the chair across from Wade's desk. "Bailey, your sister. Remember. Tall, leggy blonde with the most beautiful pair of—"

Wade frowned. "Don't even go there."

"—eyes. I was going to say eyes. Hell, Wade, you know I'd never disrespect your little sister."

He relaxed back in his chair again. "Good."

"So, who is this Fallon?"

"Josh's cousin." He picked up a pencil and began tapping the eraser against the desktop. "She was looking for a job, so I offered her the one in records."

"I thought you were giving that to Mary."

"We can give Mary another position. Besides, I don't think Fallon will be here long, but I couldn't say no to an old friend." He looked up to gauge the other man's reaction.

Andy nodded. "Not bad."

"What's not bad?"

"The story you just told me. I mean, if I were someone off the street it would sound plausible enough." He shifted to a more comfortable position and sighed deeply. "But you're yankin' my chain, buddy."

Wade opened his mouth, then snapped it closed. What the hell could he say?

"If you met this girl in Dallas, and couldn't get enough of her, hey, who am I to judge?" He looked thoughtful for a moment. "Just not sure I would've brought her home unless you're planning on marrying the gal."

And the hole got deeper. Wade silently groaned. He opened his mouth to refute Andy's words, but stopped. Fallon would go ballistic if she knew another person had discovered her true identity.

Instead, Wade winked conspiratorially. "Yeah, but if you met Fallon you'd understand why I took a chance and brought her home. She's one fine lady." And he had the strangest feeling he'd just signed his own death warrant. Fallon would kill him if she knew Andy thought she was just a piece of fluff. How in the hell did he get into these messes? Maybe he should just concentrate on work.

As Fallon dragged herself from the depths of sleep she vaguely remembered someone helping her remove her clothes the night before. Lord, she'd been dead to the world. She opened her eyes. Not her room. Not her bed. A lazy smile curved her lips. She was in Wade's plush, luxurious bed.

What a delicious way to wake up in the morning, and she knew exactly who was snoring softly next to her. There was nothing more sensual than making love early in the morning—before that first cup of hot coffee, before anything. One good orgasm, and you knew the day was going to be a winner.

When she moved to turn over, an annoying ache poked at her side. Reaching under the covers, she ran her fingers along the line of stitches. She must be healing. They were still intact. A morning quickie shouldn't pop one loose, either. She turned over with visions of wild sex filling her mind.

Instead of Wade, Cleo raised her head. The animal opened her mouth to yawn and the space between them filled with the smell of a whorehouse in the summertime.

Fallon curled her lip. She really hated the smell of tuna.

"Ugh! Get out of here you mangy, one-eyed beast."

Damn. She was horny, and the only thing in her bed was a foul-smelling cat. Where the hell was Wade? Shoving the covers aside, she climbed out of bed.

The sound of a vacuum running drew her attention. She was naked, in his bed, and he decides to clean house? She'd certainly pegged him wrong.

And if he thought she'd come to him, then he'd better think again. He'd had his chance . . . and blown it.

She rummaged through his drawers before grabbing a pajama top and plunging her arms into the sleeves. Too damn long. She rolled the material above her elbows, then yanked the bottoms over her hips. Never in her life had a man left her bed. She was always the one who'd leave first, often sneaking out in the middle of the night. She nabbed a plaid robe and jerked it on. Hell, she didn't even smell coffee brewing. What kind of host was he?

She jerked the loose cords dangling from the waistband and knotted them before stomping into the other room . . . and skidded to a halt at the entryway into the living room. It wasn't Wade running the vacuum, but Callie. Great, this made two strikes against him. She certainly didn't want to put up with the bratty kid this morning—or the sound of a vacuum. Reaching over, she pulled the plug from the wall and the vacuum stopped.

Callie frowned and stepped on the upright's power button with her foot. She stomped it a couple more times before turning—and screaming.

"Boo," Fallon spoke dryly. She dangled the cord from her hand like a bullwhip, sorely tempted to use it for just that purpose.

"You scared me," Callie accused.

"When you screamed like a banshee, I gathered as much. Do you mind telling me exactly what you're doing?"

The girl stiffened her spine. "I thought that would be obvious—even for you. I'm cleaning. On second thought, I didn't see any calluses on your hands so maybe you didn't know what I was doing." She pointed to the vacuum. "This is a vacuum. You clean carpets with it."

She really disliked this kid. "Where's Wade?"

The girl brightened. "Don't you know?" Mischief sparkled in her eyes. "I think he had a hot date."

Fallon lightly twirled the end of the cord. "I used to have a fascination with whips. I got so good I could actually flick a fly off a fence from ten feet away."

"He went to the sheriff's office," Callie grumbled, eyeing the cord with trepidation.

"Thank you." *For nothing.* She dropped the cord and started to turn away, but remembered something. "What *are* you doing here?"

Callie curled her lip. "I'm . . ."

"The truth," Fallon demanded.

"I clean Wade's house once a week," she replied in a surly voice.

"Keep the noise down." She headed toward the kitchen. Maybe she wouldn't have to put up with Callie's attitude long. Really, what did she actually need to do? The house looked pretty clean to her.

Once in the kitchen, she began opening cabinets. Three doors later she found the filters. Another twenty seconds and she discovered the coffee in another cabinet. A few minutes later the intoxicating aroma of the early morning brew filled the air. She leaned against the counter and inhaled.

Her father had always had the coffee going first thing in the morning, before her mother even woke up. Fallon closed her eyes and could picture him leaning against the counter.

"You fix enough for two?" Callie asked.

Fallon reluctantly let go of her memory and turned. Callie stood in the doorway, not looking directly at her. Why did this kid remind her so much of herself? But maybe she already knew the answer.

"Grab another cup."

Callie visibly relaxed and went to the cabinet.

"I've been here a couple of hours. I could've dropped a bomb, and I don't think you'd have heard it."

One of her faults. She died when she went to sleep, if she ever got comfortable. A criminal could slit her throat and she'd never know it. But she didn't tell Callie all that. Instead, she only said, "I was tired."

Fallon poured her coffee and went to the table, letting Callie wait on herself. She couldn't help noticing from the corner of her eye that she put more milk in her cup than anything.

"Don't you even want to know why I'm cleaning Wade's house?" she asked, bringing her heavily diluted coffee to the table with her and sitting across from Fallon.

"Nope." She blew on her coffee before taking a drink. God, this tasted good.

"Community service."

Fallon paused before slowly setting her cup down. "Come again?"

Callie ran her finger over the rim of her cup and didn't meet Fallon's eyes. "Well, sort of. I got into trouble, but instead of throwing me in jail, or making me do community service at some church, Wade offered me a job. I guess you could say it's sort of a community service."

"What the hell did you find in this speck on the map that would get you into trouble?"

She shrugged. "When I first moved in with Aunt Beth I started sneaking out at night. I hitched a ride with the first guy who stopped. It was Steve, and we went to Wichita Falls."

The teen watched closely, as if she wanted to shock Fallon. The kid was going to be sorely disappointed. In Fallon's line of work, she'd seen too much. Hell, in her own life she'd seen too much. "Maybe you should've waited for the second car. Your boyfriend's a loser."

The girl raised her chin. "He loves me."

"Ha! He loves controlling you. And you let him. I thought you had more backbone than that. Do you actually enjoy panting after him like an obedient puppy, ready to jump off a cliff if he asked?"

Her brow wrinkled. "No . . . I mean he wouldn't ask me to do anything I didn't want to do."

Fallon took another drink. The coffee suddenly tasted bitter. She set her cup back on the table. "Hasn't he already? Not literally, but has he wanted you to do something you wouldn't normally do? Are you going to jump? Or play it smart and dump him?" She watched the warring emotions crossing Callie's face.

The kid nibbled her bottom lip. "You don't understand. He loves me."

Damn it, she didn't want to play mother—especially to an emotionally troubled teen. She leaned back in her chair and took a deep breath. "Let me see if I can figure this out, and when I'm through, you tell me if I'm right. You're really pissed off because your parents are dead and that makes you feel guilty. Then along comes Steve. Mr. Slick himself. He's probably told you he'll make it all better. That he won't ever leave you. Open your eyes, kid. He only wants what he can get." She stood, taking her cup to the sink and dumping what was left of her coffee. She looked out the window and saw herself as a young girl, pissed off and angry at the world. She rapidly blinked away the past. "At first he'll have you doing petty crimes, telling you that if you really loved him you'd do this one little thing."

"It's not like that. . . ."

Fallon turned, her eyes narrowing on Callie. "Isn't it? Has he asked you to shoplift for him yet?"

Callie's face turned bright red, and Fallon had her answer.

"Next he'll want you to pick up a package but he won't tell you it's drugs. And when you get caught, and mark my words you will get caught, he'll say he doesn't even know you. And you'll feel that emptiness again—just like when your parents died."

Tears began to run down Callie's face. "Steve wouldn't do that!"

Fallon heard another voice from long ago, and her words softened. "It's not your fault they're dead. Stop blaming yourself."

Callie jumped to her feet, her chair toppling over. "Screw you. Steve loves me." She raced from the room.

Fallon crossed her arms in front of her as she watched Callie storm off. "Well, hell," she muttered. "It worked when King talked to me. Hmm, damn good thing I didn't become a counselor."

Turning back around, she reached for the pot, but changed her mind and headed for the shower instead. Maybe standing under the cold spray would wake her up and get these notions out of her head that she needed to set Callie's feet on the right track.

Chapter 14

Wade opened the door of his vehicle as Callie came running out of the house. "Callie?" Damn, he'd forgotten this was her day to clean.

She skidded to a stop. "I hate her."

"Who?" he asked as he climbed out and shut the door. Wade had a sneaking suspicion he already knew the answer.

"Fallon," she spat out the name.

Figures. "Why don't we go inside and talk about it. I'm sure we can work everything out. It's probably just a misunderstanding." For some reason he doubted Callie had taken anything the wrong way. Fallon didn't have a lot of tact when it came to the teen. Hell, she didn't have a lot of tact, period.

"As long as she's in your house, you can find someone else to clean it." She whirled around and fled down the street.

Wade shook his head, watching until she rounded the corner. Callie had a lot of problems. But then, he suspected Fallon did as well. He turned toward the house.

The house was quiet when he entered, except for the distant sound of the shower. A slow smile curved his lips. He pushed Callie's problems to the side and locked his front door—there were just times when it was best, and this was one of them.

He sauntered down the hall and slipped into the bathroom. Crossing his arms, he leaned against the countertop and closed his eyes, listening to the spray splash against the curtain. He pictured Fallon running the bar of soap over her slick body . . . right down to the little bubbles left behind. He was so lost in his fantasy, he didn't hear the shower curtain slide open.

The soggy washcloth slapped him in the face with a resounding splat before he had time to react.

"Damn it, Tanner! What the hell are you doing in here? If I'd had a gun you'd be dead right now."

He tossed the dripping washcloth into the sink and grabbed a hand towel. "Thanks for the bath, but I showered earlier." He wiped the water off his face.

"Quit sneaking up on me then."

Wade opened his mouth to fire back but for the life of him he couldn't remember what the hell he was going to say. He could only stare as she stepped out of the shower. Unconcerned and without a stitch on—except for the ones Doc had put in her, and the tattoo of a tiger on her left butt cheek.

Jeez, she was making him crazy . . . and horny! But he couldn't drag his gaze away as she grabbed a fluffy blue towel and began drying her hair. God, she was beautiful, and sexy as hell.

His gaze lingered on her lush breasts before moving down past tapered hips to the thatch of wet, curling hair at the vee of her legs.

"Put your eyeballs back inside your head, Tanner."

"I want to make love to you."

She stopped drying her hair and let the towel drop to the floor. His expectations rose, not to mention a prominent part of his anatomy, as visions of the two of them making love filled his mind—until she reached for another towel and wrapped it around her damp body, covering it from his view.

"If you had wanted sex you should have hung around this morning instead of sneaking out."

So that was her problem. She was pissed because he hadn't woke her before he'd left this morning. And when she'd gotten up, Callie would've been cleaning. Not a good way to start the day.

As she swept past, he reached out and touched her shoulder. She stopped, but didn't look at him.

"I thought you needed the sleep, and I forgot about Callie coming to clean this morning." He lightly stroked her arm, enjoying the silky feel of her skin. And when he inhaled, he caught the scent of peaches. She must have bought some shampoo or soap when she'd shopped with Audrey. He liked the fresh smell.

"The kid is obnoxious and doesn't have any manners—even when someone is only trying to help her."

He couldn't quite see Fallon guiding Callie gently down the right path. It would be much easier to picture her shoving, whether the teen wanted to go or not.

"She has problems," he compromised. He lightly turned Fallon so she faced him. "You smell good."

She arched an eyebrow. "Flattery will get you nowhere."

He ignored her. "I want to taste you."

Fallon stiffened her spine. She wouldn't be swayed. Let him suffer. She certainly had when she'd rolled over this morning only to come face-to-face with his smelly, one-eyed cat. Before starting out the door, she glanced down, a measure of satisfaction filled her. From the bulge of his pants, she knew he would ache for quite some time.

Before she'd taken more than a couple of steps, he tugged the towel from around her. Let him keep it; she didn't care.

"I want to taste all of you. Every . . . naked . . . inch." His words caressed her body, sending shivers of excitement up and down her spine.

She hesitated, visualizing exactly where he would put his mouth. The dampness between her legs wasn't because she hadn't completely dried off.

"I want to taste your neck . . . suck on your earlobe." His voice was low and husky as he seduced her with his words.

She closed her eyes and tilted her head. She could almost feel his hot breath on her neck. She moaned.

He moved closer, and then she *could* feel his breath on her neck as he stood behind her. "I want to suck your nipples. Graze my teeth across the swollen nubs."

She drew in a sharp breath. Her nipples tightened, aching to feel his mouth on them, but he didn't touch. She moved her hand away from the doorknob. She wanted him to finish telling her what he would do—if she said yes.

As if guessing her thoughts, he continued. "I'd glide my wet tongue over your stomach. Down each hip . . . but I wouldn't go any farther."

He moved to stand in front of her. She opened her eyes. His were glazed with passion. His gaze moved from hers and slowly drifted over her naked body. She arched toward him, but still he didn't make a move to get closer.

"I'd lick down your leg and come back up on the inside of one thigh." His words were thick with desire. "Then down the other one and up the inside of that thigh. Coming closer and closer."

She closed her eyes, moaning with frustration and heightened sexual awareness.

"Then I would lick where you would get the most pleasure."

"Ahhh." She gripped her thighs.

"My tongue would delve into you, then I'd nibble and suck." He drew in a deep breath. "But you don't want to make love, do you?"

"Fuck you, Tanner." She grabbed his shirt when he started to turn away.

"I don't mind if you do." He faced her with a devilish grin and pulled her into his arms. He lowered his mouth to hers, sucking first on her lower lip before plunging his tongue inside her mouth. His hands kneaded the firm flesh of her buttocks, tugging her closer. Her body melted against his. The scrape of his zipper against her slit sent spasms of pleasure sweeping over her.

"You taste good," he told her, his mouth sliding to her ear.

He nibbled on the tender lobe before circling his tongue along the outer edge. She leaned her head so he could get to the area better. When his wet tongue slipped inside she closed her eyes and bit her bottom lip.

"Ahh, Wade, please. I can't stand it anymore."

"But I haven't finished—remember what I told you I wanted to do?"

How could she forget? Her whole body screamed in remembrance.

He picked her up, putting her bottom firmly on the counter top. "I haven't even started." He dipped his head down and began to suck at her breast.

She grabbed his hair and pulled him closer. Her legs automatically opened wide.

"You don't want me to stop this soon, do you? Not when I haven't tasted all of you."

"Noooo. . . ."

His tongue circled the aureole of her other breast, his teeth grazing the tight nub before sucking her into his mouth. As he suckled her breast, his hands brought her hips forward until she was on the very edge. His fingers began to massage the inside of her thighs, causing an almost unbearable friction. She gritted her teeth, wanting his mouth against her.

The ache inside built to a crescendo of pleasure and pain as his tongue dipped downward, circling over her stomach, down her leg and up her thigh. She gripped the counter as he trailed his tongue down her other leg and slowly up her thigh. His breath was hot against her skin, fanning the flames of her desire.

And when his mouth finally covered her, naughty sensations rocked through her body like small earthquakes. Her hands tangled in his hair, pulling him closer as he tugged with his teeth and sucked her into his mouth. He rubbed his tongue against her hardened nub. Back and forth, back and forth, until her juices were released, and she cried out.

Before she could slump into nothingness, he unzipped his pants and kicked out of them, his underwear followed. Pulling her against him, he entered her, filling her, causing another wave of sensual delight to flood her body.

She grabbed his shoulders. As if he mentally willed her to, she opened her eyes and stared into his. Their gazes locked. She couldn't look away even if she'd wanted. His body arched and shuddered when he came.

She tightened her hold on him as spasms shot through her body, wrapping her in a sensual haze of colors and heat. Fallon knew he'd felt the same thing.

What an odd sensation, to know she'd given him this much satisfaction. She looked away, but he raised her chin and dropped a light kiss on her lips. She studied his face and wondered what was going through his mind.

"Don't worry too much on it." He ran his hand over her damp hair and along her jaw.

"What?"

"The fact what we have is more than just sex."

"It'll make it harder to leave," she warned.

"I know."

She nodded. A silent understanding passed between them. They would take each day as it came. No promises, no future. Just right now.

"I really don't think going to the sheriff's office will help," Fallon complained as she climbed into his vehicle. She was in a foul mood, and she knew it. And furthermore, she didn't care.

"You can't hide in the house while you wait to hear from King. Besides, being around law en-

forcement might jog your memory about who betrayed you."

"I doubt the DEA offices would like being compared to a small-town sheriff's office."

He ignored her slur and gave her a quick once-
over. "You look nice, by the way."

She opened her mouth, then snapped it shut.
What the hell was he trying to pull?

"That's a compliment, Fallon. You're not required to say anything except thank you."

He was making fun of her. "Fuck you, Tanner."

"I would have thought yesterday afternoon, last
night, and early this morning would be enough to
satisfy your sexual appetite." A pained expression
crossed his face as he started the vehicle. "I'm not
sure I'm capable of going another round."

She laughed, then quickly covered it with a
cough. "You're full of it." She turned her gaze out
the window so he wouldn't see her smile as he
backed out of the driveway.

"And you look very nice," he repeated.

She opened her mouth, then closed it. "Thank
you."

"You're welcome."

They were quiet as he drove the short distance
across town and pulled into his parking space,
shutting the engine off.

"Kind of small, isn't it?" she remarked as she got
out.

He shrugged. "We're a small town."

As they walked to the entrance, she glanced
around. Someone had planted little blue flowers
leading to the door. It looked pretty—and boring.

"Do you actually like your job?" She turned quizzical eyes in his direction. "I mean, after working

undercover, how could you come back here?" She swung her arm in a wide arc.

"It suits me."

"But what about the adrenaline rush? That burst of energy that flows through your blood when you're chasing a criminal? What kind of excitement can you get sitting behind a desk?"

"We have our share of bad guys," he defended as he opened the glass door.

"What? Kids papering houses at Halloween?"

"We've had cases a little more substantial than that." His eyebrows drew together, forming one line.

"Yeah, if you say so, Tanner."

They walked into the building. Fallon glanced around, realizing it looked just as quaint as the outside. God, she'd stepped back in time to the fifties.

"Hi, Wade." An older woman behind a glass partition smiled and waved.

"This is Nelda, our daytime dispatcher," he told her. "She holds the fort down."

"You must be Fallon." Nelda beamed. "I've heard a lot about you."

Fallon quirked an eyebrow in his direction.

Wade cleared his throat. "Anything pressing?"

"Well," Nelda thumbed through some papers. "Andy's on a call right now. Possible burglary and kidnapping."

Wade straightened. "Does he need backup?"

"Oh, no." She looked up after retrieving the call sheet, her smile stretched across her face. "Amy Bishop called it in."

"Wanda's daughter?"

Nelda's smile beamed brighter. "Yes, her five-year-old. It seems the little boy next door broke into her playhouse, vandalized the place, and stole her baby doll." Nelda chuckled. "She dialed 911."

Fallon burst out laughing. "Call out the helicopter! You might want to gather a search party, Tanner. This is really big."

Nelda chuckled along with Fallon.

"Maybe you *should* back him up." Fallon tried for a straight face, but knew she failed miserably. "I mean, the kidnapper could be a hardened felon, for all we know. This might not be his first offense."

"Hardened felon!" Nelda's laughter filled her small cubicle.

"I'll be in my office." Wade turned on his heels.

Fallon followed, not even attempting to stop her snickers. "You're right, I really underestimated the seriousness of your job here in Two Rivers."

"Two Creeks," he flung over his shoulder, and pushed open the door to his office.

She followed him inside. Her laughter died as she glanced around at all the awards and family pictures that hung on one wall and graced his desk.

Wade must've been a hell of an undercover cop. "Pretty impressive," she said, looking at him with admiration.

He shrugged. "Bailey and my mother insisted on hanging them on my wall."

"Are these all family members?" She walked closer to the pictures.

He drew next to her. "That's Bailey and my two younger brothers. Mike is away at college and Riley is out of town. That's my mother and father"—he pointed toward an older couple—"Dad passed away a couple of years ago." He pointed to another picture. "And that's Josh."

She stared at the blond, ruggedly built man. "Not bad." When she looked at Wade, a frown marred his features. "Don't worry, I don't want to jump his bones."

"Did anyone ever tell you that you have a way with words."

"I've been told I have a way with my mouth, too." She fingered the buttons on his shirt before trailing one manicured nail down to his belt.

"Jeez, woman." He jerked her into his arms and lowered his mouth to hers.

The heat from his kiss sent delicious tremors up and down her spine. She hadn't even come close to wearing him out. The man was rock hard. She wondered if he'd ever had sex in his office. A burning ache began to build as she envisioned them naked and on top of his uncluttered desk.

A knock sounded on the door just before it opened. "Nelda told me you were in your office. . . ."

Fallon slowly pulled out of Wade's arms and looked at the thin man who stood in the doorway, shifting from one foot to the other.

"Uh . . . sorry about barging in. I'll come back later."

"Your deputy?" She nodded toward the stranger.

Wade frowned. "My soon-to-be ex-deputy." To Andy he said, "You might as well stay." He made the introductions and took his chair.

Fallon propped herself on a corner of the desk and slowly looked Andy over. "Did you catch your criminal?"

"Criminal?" He looked from her to Wade.

"The kidnapper?" she explained.

He grinned sheepishly. "Oh, you mean little Joey Anderson. Caught him red-handed about to decapitate Amy's doll. It seems Amy didn't want to play with him, so he was seeking revenge."

"Temperamental woman." Wade grinned and leaned back in his chair.

"Stubborn man." Fallon crossed her legs.

Andy cleared his throat. "While I was out and about I saw Callie, though. We may have a problem. Did you know that Steve guy is back in town?"

She jumped off the corner of Wade's desk. "I told that sleazy, no-account what I'd do if he didn't stop sniffing around the kid."

As soon as the words were out, Fallon realized what she'd said. Andy thought she was going to work in records, not warn off unsuitable male suitors away from the troubled teen. And she'd failed to mention anything about her run-in with Steve to Wade. She hadn't thought he needed to know.

"And exactly how do you know Callie's boyfriend?" Wade's penetrating gaze captured hers. He made looking away impossible. What the hell did he do when he was undercover? Interrogations?

"I warned him off." She finally shrugged nonchalantly.

Andy looked from Wade to Fallon. "But I thought you were Wade's mistress. Why would you threaten anyone?" As if suddenly realizing his blunder, he looked down, shifting from one foot to the other. "I mean . . . uh. Crap, sorry about that, Wade."

Mistress? She looked at Wade. His guilty expression told her everything she needed to know. *Mistress!* Her eyes narrowed and her hands balled into fists.

"I'm your mistress now, am I. First I'm an office worker, and now I'm an . . . another notch on your bedpost. Is there anything else you'd like to add to my resume?"

He came to his feet. "Damn it, what did you want me to tell Andy? The real story? I didn't have a choice."

"Maybe one of you would like to tell me the truth?" Andy drawled and took a chair, stretching his long legs out in front of him.

Chapter 15

Wade and Fallon turned simultaneously toward Andy. Fallon had forgotten he was there, as apparently had Wade. They looked at each other. What the hell were they supposed to do now?

"Whenever you're ready. I have all the time in the world now that I've warned little Joey Anderson if he decapitates Amy's doll I'll have to throw him in the slammer. I don't think he'll commit anymore crimes in the near future, or at least before he turns six. So, take your time."

"Why, of course I'm going to work in records." Fallon batted her blue eyes at Andy. "I'm just a little upset Wade brought our"—She downed her head; when she raised it a few seconds later, she felt about as innocent as a death row inmate—"our intimate relationship out in the open. I'm understandably embarrassed."

Andy slowly clapped his hands. "She isn't bad," he told Wade.

Fallon curled her lip. "And you'd have bought it if Wade would've stuck with the original story."

She cast a frown in his direction. "I thought you said you used to work undercover. Weren't you taught the art of deception?"

"I was sick that day."

"So what *is* the truth?" Andy asked.

Oh hell, what difference did it make if one more person knew her identity? At least Andy was in law enforcement and Wade seemed to trust him. "I'm an undercover agent with the DEA, but my cover was blown. I ran into Wade in Dallas and he offered to help."

Andy doubled over with laughter. "Oh God, that's the best one yet. An under . . . undercover . . . agent."

And why wasn't that believable? She socked her fists on her hips and glared at Wade. It was his fault.

"You have to admit, it does sound a little far-fetched when you think about it." He snickered.

Andy's laughter died. "You mean that's the truth? You're with the DEA?" He still didn't look convinced.

"I don't happen to have any identification with me, but yes, I'm with the DEA." Why hadn't he believed her? She'd always thought of herself as lean and mean. What was happening? Was she going soft? Had she absorbed the small-town atmosphere through osmosis? If she wasn't careful, the next thing she knew she'd be baking brownies, cleaning house, or some other equally nauseating task.

Andy's gaze swept over her appreciatively. "You definitely don't look like any cop I went through the academy with."

She wasn't sure if that was an offhanded compliment or not.

"Don't let her looks fool you, she's pretty tough,"

Wade said. "She narrowly escaped being killed. Fallon evaded two men ordered to take her out, and then got the drop on me."

At his words of praise a warm glow circled around the inside of her stomach then fluttered into the region of her heart. Before his compliments had time to do any more damage, she shook off the odd feeling. Crap, the town *was* soaking into her bloodstream. She needed a transfusion of the real world ASAP.

"You caught Wade by surprise. Well, I'll be damned. I never thought I'd see the day." Andy sat a tad straighter. "If Wade says you're an agent, then that's good enough for me."

She crossed her arms in front of her. "Oh good, I'm so glad you believe me," she spoke wryly. "It would've broke my fucking heart if you hadn't."

"I forgot to tell you that she also has a vocabulary that would make a convict blush." Wade looked at Fallon. "But I'm more curious about what you did to Callie's boyfriend."

She shrugged, ambled over to the other chair, and made herself comfortable before she spoke. "Steve's a control freak. He and Callie showed up at the mall. I just advised him it might be a good idea if he didn't see the kid again." She glanced at her fingernail polish, noting it still looked good. Audrey had been right; it hadn't cost much, and they'd done good work.

"You just talked to him?"

"Sort of." She rested her elbows on the arms of the chair.

"Sort of?"

"Yeah, pretty much." She nodded. "Callie went to get them something to drink and I sort of grabbed him by the balls and squeezed before I told him to quit fucking with the kid's head. Yeah, that's about it."

Andy chuckled but stifled his laughter when Wade glared at him.

"Apparently he didn't listen, since Andy saw the two of them together."

"She's rebelling."

"Rebelling?"

"That usually happens when you tell a teenager someone isn't good for them. They feel they have to prove you wrong."

"And why would Callie think that?"

"Yesterday morning I told her Steve was bad news. She wasn't very receptive." She frowned. "The guy is a total jerk. I can't understand why she doesn't see the obvious."

Wade leaned forward in his chair. "Maybe it was the way you put it?"

She shook her head. "No, I don't think so. I didn't pay that much attention when I took psychology in college, but I thought I did rather well explaining the situation."

Fallon had a feeling his estimation of her might have dropped a notch or two. She could deal with the Steves of the world a whole hell of a lot better than she could the Callies.

She *knew* the Steves and the Cavenaughs. She knew the evil that oozed from their pores. She knew what they were capable of doing.

Her gut twisted as she fought back memories. They were coming more often now . . . and they were getting harder to ignore. But she wasn't ready to let them resurface—not completely. Not until she could destroy Cavenaugh. Only then would she let herself remember what her life had been like.

The intercom on Wade's phone buzzed, jarring her out of her reverie. He spoke a few seconds, then hung up and jumped to his feet.

"Ten-fifty major at the crossroads south of town."

Andy vaulted out of his chair. "Shit, I hate wrecks." His worried expression said it all. Was it someone he knew? How bad an accident was it? Was anyone dead?

"I'll ride with Andy." Wade fished his keys out of his pocket and tossed them toward her. She automatically caught them. "Take my vehicle and I'll be back at the house as soon as I can."

The two men were out the door before she had time to protest she wasn't just a bystander and she might actually be of some use. She stared at the keys in her hand for a moment. She could leave, go sit impatiently in his house while she waited for him to return with news of what had happened. That would probably be the best thing for her to do. Technically, she was out of her jurisdiction since she wasn't on a case.

But then, when had she ever played by the rules? She tossed the keys in the air and deftly caught them before heading out the door.

It wasn't hard to figure out what direction she should go. She just followed all the sirens and flashing lights of the fire trucks, but the closer she got, the more bottlenecked the traffic became.

A menacing plume of gray and black smoke curled and rose ahead of them. Traffic wasn't moving, not even at a crawl. Swearing softly under her breath, she grabbed the portable light between the seats, let her window down, and slapped it on the cab top before pulling completely off the road onto a narrow stretch of land fenced off by barbed wire. She barely had enough room between her and the stalled traffic to maneuver Wade's SUV.

As she approached the mangled cars, she could see why traffic wasn't moving. At least five vehicles were involved, completely blocking the road. One was upside down and another on its side. The other three were heavily damaged. *Not good.* She spotted Wade in the crowd as he took charge of the chaos and directed the rescue workers.

Only one ambulance was at the scene. The two paramedics had their hands full. The wail of another siren sounded in the distance, but with traffic jammed, it would take awhile before they arrived, and a box unit wouldn't be able to pull off as easily as she had.

She parked his vehicle and hurried forward, making her way through the crowd to Wade. The least she could do was help direct traffic. "Where do you need me?" she yelled above the noise.

Startled, Wade turned to look at her. His hesitation was brief. "Callie's in the front car. Go to her," he yelled back.

No! She couldn't. Her first aid was sketchy at best.

"Please," he mouthed.

Fallon drew in a deep breath before nodding and making her way across the carnage littering the highway. She worked her way around the broken cars, stepping over a twisted mass of metal she thought might have once been a bumper.

She dodged firemen as they dragged a hose from a pumper so they could put out the car fire. More firemen used the Jaws of Life to open a crushed door on another vehicle.

Fallon finally reached the car Wade had directed her to. It was turned crossways in the road, the passenger side crushed. She ran to the open door on the driver's side.

"Callie?" She leaned inside.

"Help me!" Callie sat facing the driver's side, huddled in the far corner on the passenger side.

"Everything's going to be okay, kid." She grabbed some paper from the floorboard and used it to brush bits of broken glass off the seat before scooting across the black vinyl.

Tears streaked Callie's face. "They said my leg might be broken. The fireman told me he'd come back but he hasn't," she babbled hysterically. "They left me, and I've been here by myself. I'm scared."

Fallon didn't want to play mother the other day, and she certainly didn't want to now. It seemed she had little choice, though. She moved closer to the girl to check her injuries.

"Just be still and let me see where exactly you're injured." She did a quick head-to-toe visual evaluation. Other than minor cuts and abrasions, Fallon didn't see anything major. "Which leg is hurt?" She moved so she could get a better look.

"This one." Callie pointed to her right leg.

"I'm going to touch it, okay."

"No, it'll hurt."

Their gazes locked. "I'll be careful. I promise if it hurts, I'll stop. Okay?"

Callie finally nodded, biting her lower lip and turning her head so she wouldn't see what Fallon was about to do.

Fallon ran her hand over the girl's knee and slowly down her leg. "Does that hurt?"

"A little."

At least there were no bones sticking out, only a swollen ankle. She didn't see any signs of deformity.

"Is it broken?" Callie whimpered.

Fallon scooted to her side of the seat. "Maybe just sprained."

Callie slumped. "Did anyone die?" she whispered, not meeting Fallon's eyes.

"I don't know," she answered honestly. "Can you tell me what happened?" Fallon waited for the girl to speak. She didn't rush her, but she sensed Callie needed to talk.

"I didn't really want to go with him."

"Who?" she asked, but she already knew the answer.

"Steve." Callie laid her head against the back of the seat. "Aunt Beth made me clean the bathroom. I guess I was mad at her because she let Sarah go to the mall. When Steve called, I agreed to meet him on the corner then sneaked out of the house. Aunt Beth is going to kill me," she mumbled.

"More than likely you'll only be grounded for the rest of your life."

"I deserve it."

No, it wasn't the vulnerable kid who needed punishing. "Where's Steve?"

Callie sucked in a sob. "He ran away. I thought he loved me." Her eyes were big and round when she raised her head. "You were right. He didn't really care about me. Steve said I'd better tell everyone I was driving, but I'm not going to. He left me here all by myself."

Fallon awkwardly patted the kid's hand, but the girl unexpectedly threw her arms around Fallon. "You were right, Steve only used me." She sobbed into Fallon's jacket. "I miss my mom and dad. I want it to be like it was."

How many times had she wished the same thing? How many times had she cried herself to sleep curled up in an alleyway with dirty rags pulled over her for warmth, hoping the people of the night would leave her alone. Sometimes they did . . . sometimes they didn't.

"I know, Callie, I know." She brushed the girl's hair away from her face.

Callie suddenly pushed out of her arms. "No, you don't. You're like all the rest. You don't know what it's like to lose your parents."

Fallon closed her eyes tight against the agony, and the vision that had haunted her for so many years. "I know only too well, Callie."

She opened her eyes and their gazes locked. Understanding dawned in the girl's eyes.

"How old were you?" Callie asked.

"I was young when my mother passed away. Fourteen when my father and . . ." She gritted her teeth. Pain enveloped her in its cruel clutches. She slowly let her breath out. "I was fourteen when my father passed away."

"Was it a car wreck like my parents?"

"No."

"I'm sorry I said you dressed funny."

Fallon relaxed. A tentative smile curved her lips. "They really were pj's."

Callie returned her smile. "Yeah, I know. Are you going to marry Wade?"

Hell, what could she tell the kid? *No, I don't want to marry the man. I'm only using him for sex.* Although she hadn't paid attention in psychology classes, she had a feeling that's not what someone would say to an impressionable fifteen-year-old.

She glanced out the window. A fireman hurried toward the car. Thankfully, they were about to be interrupted and she didn't have to answer Callie.

"Here comes a fireman." She nodded out the passenger window.

Callie grabbed her hand. "Please stay with me."

The oddest feeling washed over her. She heard another voice.

Please stay. Don't leave me.

Anguish ripped through her. She wanted the memories to let go.

"Please," Callie pleaded.

She drew in a ragged breath. "Sure, kid. I'll stay with you."

Wade studied Fallon. She hadn't left Callie's side. She'd ridden in the back of the ambulance all the way to the hospital. When they wheeled the stretcher into X ray, Fallon had let go of the teen's hand. Why the sudden change?

"I'm going for coffee." Fallon started to leave but hesitated at the last minute. "Want some?"

He shook his head.

Wade watched her walk away, until the crowd of people waiting to hear news about relatives or friends swallowed her up. For the life of him, he'd never understand women. Callie and Fallon acted as if they'd always been close. What had happened between the two of them while they waited in the wrecked car?

His cell phone rang, interrupting his thoughts. He pulled it from the leather case attached to his belt and flipped it open.

"Yeah?"

"Andy here. Thought you might want to know

the highway patrol just picked up Steve Gates trying to hitch a ride."

A grim smile lifted the corners of his mouth. "I didn't think he'd get far. He'll have a lot to answer for."

"At least he didn't kill anyone."

Wade thought about the mother who'd be in the hospital for quite a while recovering from a broken leg and a broken arm. And the two small children in one of the other cars who suffered from what would probably turn out to be concussions. And the elderly couple who wouldn't bounce back as fast.

"Yeah, at least he didn't kill anyone." They said goodbye and Wade replaced the phone as Callie's harried Aunt Beth rushed toward him. "The hospital called. Is she okay?"

"She's going to be fine. I spoke with Doc Canton earlier and he doesn't think anything is broken."

"Oh, thank goodness. I couldn't take another tragedy striking our family."

The woman was about ready to collapse, so Wade led her to one of the few remaining chairs and made her sit.

"First my sister and her husband." She opened her purse and rummaged inside until she came up with a wadded tissue and dabbed at the tears running down her face. "Then when the hospital called and told me Callie had been in a wreck, I thought the worst. I almost threw up."

"It's okay, Beth. Callie will be just fine."

"Are you sure?" She clung to his hand and squeezed until he thought his fingers might break.

"I'm sure." He gently untangled his hand from hers.

"Aunt Beth?" A timid voice spoke. "I'm okay."

Wade and Beth looked up at the same time. Callie was in a wheelchair, her right foot and ankle wrapped in an ACE bandage.

"Dr. Canton said it was only a bad sprain."

"Oh, thank God." Beth rushed to her niece.

Wade knew the scolding would come later, but for now they needed to reassure each other the love was there, probably as it had always been, only buried beneath all their pain and suffering.

Out of the corner of his eye Wade caught sight of Fallon. She stood not far away and watched the reunion between Callie and her aunt. She looked wistful, and sad. Wade realized he knew very little about this woman. She'd only spoke briefly about King. Where was her family? She had to have come from somewhere besides just New Orleans. Maybe it was time he asked a few questions.

The ringing of his cell phone interrupted his thoughts. What could Andy want now?

"Hello."

"Hey, buddy."

He relaxed. Only Josh. "Yeah, what's up."

"I think I found your man."

"Cavenaugh?"

"Remember our friend Fred?"

He snorted. "That slime-bag?"

Josh chuckled. "The one and only, but the best mole when you want to root out a rat."

"And you think he's found him?" *Good.* They could alert the agency and the man could be taken into custody. And Fallon would walk out of his life. Somehow that didn't make him feel like he once thought it would, although he knew it was bound to happen eventually. He squared his shoulders. "Where is he?"

"It's the best lead I've had so far, but you aren't going to like where Cavenaugh's located, buddy."

Dread filled him. He had a feeling he already knew. "Where?"

"He's hiding out at The Pit."

Cold chills ran up and down his spine. He'd thought he'd seen the last of that place. And he'd sworn never to go back. That's what he got for swearing.

"Still there?"

Wade drew in a shaky breath. "Yeah, I'm still here." But he suddenly wished he weren't. He'd gone so deep undercover last time that he'd started to blend in a little too well. He felt what they felt. He began to think like they thought. He let them get inside his head, and it nearly destroyed him.

"Hey, if this guy means so much, I'll go. You damn sure won't get the law across the border," Josh said, interrupting his thoughts.

He knew perfectly well what the law on this side would and wouldn't do. Damn it, he should pretend he never got this call, that Josh hadn't told him anything about Cavenaugh.

But his conscience wouldn't let him lie—even by omission. "No, I'll go. You almost got yourself killed last time."

"Only because I was saving your ugly ass. Hey, seriously, you're going to need help."

He looked up, watching Fallon saunter toward him. God, she was sexy and sinful as hell. "Actually, I think I have all the help I'll need."

Chapter 16

Fallon could tell something was up as she made her away across the crowded hospital. Wade stood a little too rigidly as he spoke on his cell phone, and when he snapped it closed and raised his head, his eyes were deadly serious. She knew the call had been from Josh without him having to say a word.

"Just how good of an agent are you?" he asked after moving her to a secluded corner, away from Callie and her aunt.

"Josh found Cavenaugh." Excitement, and fear, filled her.

"He thinks he has a lead."

Her heart pounded. The end was getting closer. She'd felt it for a long time. Cavenaugh would pay for his crimes the way it would hurt him the most. Death would be too easy. She wanted him behind bars for the rest of his life. She wanted his freedom.

She raised her chin. "I'm a damn good agent. When do we leave?"

He hesitated.

"What?"

"I need to know you'll do exactly as I say when we get there."

She opened her mouth, but he held up his hand before she could utter a sound of protest.

"No, this isn't debatable. I have to have your word you'll follow my orders precisely."

Did he think he was dealing with a rookie? No, she wouldn't bow to his authority.

As if sensing her thoughts, he continued, "You either agree, or this ends right here."

Her spine stiffened. Damn it, she didn't want to take orders from anyone. Cavenaugh was hers to capture and bring in. Her battle to fight. She didn't even want Wade's help.

Just as quickly, her anger faded. If she didn't agree, Cavenaugh might slip out of her reach again. Years could pass before he resurfaced.

"Okay, fine. I'll follow your lead."

"I'm serious, Fallon. You don't know this place like I do."

"And just where are we going?"

"The Pit."

A cold chill ran up and down her spine. The Pit. Everyone in law enforcement had heard of the place—most thought it was a figment of someone's twisted imagination used to scare the hell out of rookies. She often wondered herself if the place was real, even after Wade said he'd been there. Well, she'd find out soon enough.

They stopped by the house, gathered what they would need, and were on the road again in less time than it would have taken for them to brush their teeth.

"I need to call King to let him know what's going on."

Wade handed her his cell phone with one hand and kept the other one on the wheel. He looked deep in thought—almost like he was having second thoughts about bringing her along. He should know by now, he wouldn't have been able to stop her.

She punched in the familiar numbers. Her heart continued to race as she waited for King's secretary to pick up the phone.

"Nathan King's office," Linda answered.

"Fallon here. Is King in?"

"Are you okay?" Worry laced her words.

"I'm fine." A flutter of warmth wove its way around her heart that Linda would care so much for her safety.

"You were supposed to check in yesterday. Nathan has gone through a whole bottle of antacids. And Cavenaugh still hasn't come up for air. Please tell me you're safe."

"I'm fine, and this may all be over soon."

"You've discovered his whereabouts! That's great."

"It may be a wild goose chase."

"Just be careful, dear. I'll connect you to Nathan."

"Hello." His gruff words spoke volumes.

"I'm okay."

"Damn it, girl. You were supposed to call yesterday."

"I'm sorry."

The unmistakable rattle of a bottle told her he was downing more antacids. Guilt spread through her like wildfire during a drought. She'd probably given him most of his ulcers.

"I still haven't located Cavenaugh." He spoke while chewing. "None of our sources are talking, or they just don't know."

"We may have discovered where he's hiding. We're headed there now."

"I'm almost afraid to ask," he groaned.

"The Pit."

Silence.

"King?"

"That's somewhere in Mexico, out of our jurisdiction. If they find out you're a cop, they'll kill you."

"They won't. At least I don't think so. I wore a blond wig the last time Cavenaugh saw me. If I get close enough, he might recognize me. I'll just have to make sure if he does figure out who I am it'll be too late.

"I still don't like it. Let me send some agents."

"Too risky. Hell, I've been in some pretty rough places in the past. Don't write my eulogy yet."

She was surprised he even had an idea where it was. She'd always heard it was anywhere from Canada, everywhere in-between, or all the way down to Mexico.

"You just watch your back."

She glanced across the seat at Wade. "I don't have to . . . someone else will do it for me." She turned her gaze out the window. "I'll try to keep in touch."

"Stay safe."

"Always." She flipped the cell phone closed and laid it between the seats. "Tell me about The Pit. The facts, not the urban legends I've heard since I went into law enforcement." She might as well prepare herself.

Wade glanced across the seat as Fallon went through the motions of checking her gun. He almost wished he hadn't gotten her the bullets she'd asked for. He had a feeling he was making the biggest mistake of his life by bringing her along. But would she have stayed behind? Doubtful.

He shrugged. "It's like any pit—full of vipers. And they don't mind crawling through filth to commit their crimes."

"Then why haven't they been stopped?"

"You know as well as I do that if you get rid of one, ten more are waiting to take his place. Besides, no one can exactly pinpoint where The Pit is located. Just that it's somewhere in Mexico."

So, King was right. "But you know."

"Not exactly." He sensed her frustration and went on to explain. "We're not chasing shadows. The place does exist. It's across the border. We don't have jurisdiction there, and either the Mexican police are too afraid, or they've been bought. Probably a little of both. And if they do get a little close for comfort, The Pit can pack up and be gone before anyone can catch them. Like a MASH unit."

"And how are we supposed to find this place?"

"I know someone who will help us get inside— for a price."

"A price?"

He pointed with his thumb toward the back seat. "The green bag has the money we'll need."

Now she was even more indebted to him. "I'll pay you back."

He grinned. "I'll split the cost."

She nodded. "What about this man who's going to help us get inside? Can you trust him?"

"Probably not, but he's the only chance we have of finding Cavenaugh." He knew she wouldn't like what he was about to say, but he might as well open her eyes to the facts. "Fallon, you know if we do discover his whereabouts you might have to walk away . . . let him go. I won't have your life or mine placed in jeopardy."

Her shoulders stiffened.

"Any wrong move could get us killed," he warned.

Could she walk away? She wasn't sure. It had been hard enough those few months she'd worked undercover gathering information. She'd smiled and was pleasant to him—to the man she'd waited so long to destroy. She did it because she had to. Now there was plenty of evidence to put Cavenaugh away. She only had to bring him to trial.

"Fallon?"

Damn it, she didn't want to let him slink away one more time. Not when she was so close. She gripped the edge of the seat. It was past time to end it.

Her grip loosened. But she had no right to put Wade's life in danger. She drew in a deep breath. "Okay, I'll walk away if it comes down to it."

There was a long pause before Wade spoke. "What did this man do to you?"

Her gut twisted into a hard knot. "He's the bad guy."

"We both know it's more than that. You said once he destroyed your family. What did you mean?"

That had slipped out. She hadn't even told King about her past. Like Wade, King only knew she had to put Cavenaugh away.

Nathan King had been an undercover officer when he'd caught her delivering a package of drugs. She'd been fifteen and hadn't known what was inside. The boy who'd sworn to protect and love her for the rest of her life said it was nothing, a present for an old friend. She never saw him again.

King had taken her at face value, a runaway caught up in something beyond her control. His kid sister had died of an overdose, and fixing Fallon was his catharsis—a way he could cleanse himself of the guilt because he hadn't been able to save his sister.

That day she'd changed her name and become someone else.

Now Wade wanted to know why Cavenaugh was so important to her. She drew in a ragged breath. "Because he's the bad guy." She turned her face toward the window, but heard Wade's sigh.

"You have to learn to trust people. Not trusting can get you killed."

"As can trusting."

Fallon closed her eyes and dozed until it was time for her to relieve Wade and take the wheel.

He napped while she drove. Occasionally she watched the even rise and fall of his chest. In sleep, he looked more relaxed, more vulnerable.

If she told him about her past, what would she say? Her past had made her strong? She was a damn good agent because of it. She took very few chances, and trusted no one.

No, that wasn't true. She'd trusted King. And now she was putting her trust in Wade.

Maybe it was herself she trusted the least. Her past could also destroy her. Someday she would be ready to think about what her life had been like. She'd bring out all the good memories, and she would look at each one as if it were a picture. One she could cherish.

But until Cavenaugh was behind bars, those pictures were ugly and tainted.

But not for long. . . .

Wade stretched his arms and glanced around the small hotel room they'd rented. There wasn't much to it. A small desk with a straight-back chair in front of it, two twin beds covered with matching dull-brown bedspreads, an end table fit snugly between them, and a TV on a scarred dresser.

It wasn't The Ritz.

"I'm going for some ice and a soda. Want anything?"

She shook her head. Something was up with her. He just wasn't sure what. He grabbed the ice bucket and went down the hall to the ice machine. When he returned, she was sitting on the edge of the bed tapping her sneakered foot on the olive-green carpet.

"Josh said we're supposed to meet the contact person here." He placed the bucket on the bedside table, along with his soft drink.

"When?" She stood, removing her jacket and tossing it on the bed behind her.

He glanced at his watch. "Not for a while yet."

"I'm going to shower, then do you want to grab some real food?" She strode to the window and jerked the blinds closed.

"What's the matter?" She'd been acting jittery the last couple of hours.

She shrugged. "Nothing's the matter. Why would you think anything was the matter?"

"I don't know. Maybe the fact that you opened three packages of cheese crackers in the last hour . . ."

"I was hungry. Do you have a problem with that?"

". . . and didn't eat any of them." He closed the distance between them. "Now, do you want to tell me what's bothering you?"

"I don't know. I mean, I *really* don't know." She went to the chair in front of the small desk and collapsed onto the seat. "Maybe because once again

I'm getting close to Cavenaugh. Maybe because I'll be going into The Pit. You tell me what's wrong."

He came up behind her and began massaging her shoulders. "You're tense. Just relax."

"I can't." She rubbed her forehead. "Don't worry about me. I'll be okay. I always get a little edgy before I go on an assignment. Once we get there, I'll be fine. I won't mess anything up."

"I never thought you would." But he didn't want her jumping out of her skin, either. He knew exactly how he could help calm her frayed nerves. "Take off your shirt. I'll be right back."

He hurried to the bathroom. Good, there were a few amenities, though certainly nothing to brag about.

He went back into the bedroom. "You haven't taken off your shirt." In fact, she hadn't moved at all.

"Your brilliance never ceases to amaze me, Tanner."

"Come on." He set the lotion on the desk and tugged at the hem of her shirt. "This will relax you."

"Maybe I don't want to relax."

"Has anyone ever told you that you're stubborn?"

"Yeah, you."

He helped her to her feet. Wade had never met a more obstinate female in all his life. She wasn't going to help, either. One eyebrow quirked, as if proclaiming with that finely arched eyebrow that he couldn't change the way she felt.

Damn, he loved a challenge.

He unbuttoned her shirt, trying desperately not to look at the lacy cups of her bra—or imagining what was in them.

Clearing his throat, he turned her around and slipped her shirt off her shoulders. "Lie down on the bed."

She rolled her eyes but did as he asked. "This won't help. I've tried all sorts of relaxation methods in the past. Nothing works. After the first half-hour or so I'll be okay."

"What if we don't have thirty minutes?"

"I won't screw anything up. I haven't been killed yet, have I?"

"There's always a first time," he told her.

He unhooked her bra. She flinched.

"Close your eyes. Take a couple of deep breaths."

She did, but it was clear they hadn't helped. He opened the lotion and squeezed some on the palm of his hand.

"This might be a little cold." He rubbed his hands together to warm the cream. Starting at her shoulders, he began spreading lotion, working his way methodically down her back.

After five minutes or so, he could still feel how bunched her muscles were beneath his fingers. This wasn't working.

"Turn over."

He went to the bathroom and turned on the hot water then went back to the bedroom. At least she'd rolled to her back.

"I told you it wouldn't work," she said nonchalantly.

"I'm not through yet." He reached for the button at the waistband of her jeans and slipped it through the hole before sliding her zipper down. "Raise your hips."

Wade tugged her jeans over her hips and realized he was almost as tense as she was now, except for a very different reason. He had a hard-on that made him ache to plunge deep inside her velvety softness.

He slipped her panties off next. Her bra followed.

She raised up on her elbows. "Do you think sex is going to help? It might be man's cure-all to whatever problem comes along, but it isn't necessarily a woman's."

He chuckled, liking her sarcastic wit. "Who said we were going to have sex?"

She very pointedly looked at the front of his jeans.

"A minor inconvenience. Don't let it bother you."

"I hadn't planned on letting it bother me."

He pushed on her shoulders. "Lie down and shut up, please." He hurried into the bathroom and ran a washcloth under the hot water, tossing the cloth from hand to hand until he had most of the water out of it. Keeping it tightly cupped, he went back to the bedroom after turning the faucet off.

"Close your eyes."

She did and he placed the cloth on her breasts knowing it wouldn't burn but rather soothe the tension from her muscles. At least, he hoped it would.

Slowly he ran the cloth over her skin. His pants became tighter, more uncomfortable. He tried not to look at her naked body. Feeling . . . imagining was almost as bad.

Don't think about her lying naked . . . on the bed. He was doing this for her, not him. Sweat formed on his brow. He ran the cloth over one . . . full . . . breast, then the other. Her puckered nipples grew hard beneath his fingers. He tried desperately to empty his mind of his lascivious thoughts.

"Okay, I admit that does seem to help." Fallon squirmed down in the bed and sighed.

Moving around like she was, even slightly, caused her breasts to jiggle. Her nipples teasing him, almost begging him to lean down and suckle.

Quit thinking with your dick, Tanner.

He drew in a deep breath. He had to get her to relax the rest of the way. He didn't want her blowing their cover. *Blowing?* He gritted his teeth and moved the now-cooling rag.

This was some idea he'd had. She'd probably be nice and relaxed. He was as hot and horny as a three-dick dog. She wiggled again. Her breast begged him to touch . . . taste.

He stifled a groan and reached inside the ice bucket. Cupping a handful, he shoved it down the front of his jeans. He sucked in a deep breath, as did she when one of the small cubes landed on her stomach. They both sighed at the same time.

"Um, that feels sort of . . . nice," she said, her eyes still closed, but now a contented smile played around the corners of her mouth.

It damn sure hadn't helped him. Now his dick was cold—*and* hard. But if it helped *her,* then by all means, he wanted to continue. He wouldn't want *her* to be a bundle of nerves. Oh no, that wouldn't do!

He sat on the side of the bed and grabbed another handful of ice. But when he looked back down at her, some of his irritability diminished.

Ah, sweet torment. He cupped her breast. She gasped. He would've pulled back but there was also such an exquisite look of pleasure on her face.

Very slowly, he ran the cubes over her stomach, watching as the heat of her body melted the ice.

He discovered he was quite thirsty. Screw it. Leaning forward, he licked the water off while his hand caught one breast, teasing the nipple.

She moaned. He continued licking, tasting. His teeth scraped across her stomach, moving lower. Automatically, she opened her legs. He didn't disappoint her, or him. She arched toward him when he took her into his mouth and began sucking, running his tongue up and down her. She tasted musky and sweet. He inhaled her womanly fragrance as his hands gripped her buttocks, massaging, bringing her closer still.

She clutched his shoulders, gasping for air. "Jeez, now," she moaned.

He didn't need any more encouragement than that. He quickly stripped. When he entered her, hot, wet heat sucked him farther inside. Wade maneuvered their bodies until her legs were over his. Her breathing was ragged.

"Shh, just catch your breath." He held her close, her head resting on his shoulder. Slowly at first, he started a rocking motion. She went with his rhythm. The heat began building inside him. He picked up the tempo. She gasped, but matched his movements.

When she reached her orgasm, her juices were hot, cupping him in liquid heat. He jerked forward and cried out as he climaxed.

They clung to each other. Their ragged breathing filled the tiny room.

"I think I'm pretty relaxed now, Tanner."

"Good, good." He nodded, trying to catch his breath. "You did say something about taking a shower, didn't you? That'll relax you even more."

"I should make you wash my back."

"Baby, you don't have to make me do anything."

Wade didn't mind filling her request when they were in the shower a little later. In fact, he filled more than her request. Knowing he'd better leave the bathroom or he wouldn't be able to walk, he left her drying off and went into the other room.

He stretched out on the bed, wadded one of the pillows beneath his head, and grabbed the remote.

It didn't take long to discover there wasn't anything worth watching on the four channels, not that he could've paid attention to anything. He tossed the remote and closed his eyes. He must have dozed because the tapping on the door didn't quite filter into his brain until it got louder, and more persistent.

He came to his feet. The contact was early. He opened the door a crack, then all the way. "What the hell are you doing here?"

"Now, is that any way to greet an old friend? I happened to be an hour or so away and thought I'd drop by to see if you needed help."

Josh came inside. "I thought you'd be glad to see me. I know you said you were bringing some-one—" He looked pointedly toward the bathroom door. It was apparent someone moved about on the other side. "And I guess you did. Don't tell me you've brought Andy. He's pretty good, but he'd never last an hour in that hellhole."

"Andy is still in Two Creeks."

Josh stretched out on the bed, his body language looking anything but relaxed. "Damn, I'm beat. So, who'd you bring along? Please tell me he has a little experience and that I won't have to bail your ass out of trouble again."

Wade frowned. "Just make yourself at home."

"Don't mind if I do." Josh grinned.

Did Josh have so little faith in him? Wade hadn't forgotten what it was like going undercover. A twinge of uneasiness rippled down his spine. He quickly shook off the feeling. "What the hell *are* you doing here?"

"I thought I'd better keep you out of trouble." His features grew serious. "That place almost destroyed you. I'm surprised you're going back."

"Can we just drop it. Besides, it's different this time. We'll be in and out before they realize we're there. You might as well leave the way you came."

"Not until you tell me why Cavenaugh is so important to you."

The bathroom door opened and both men looked up. Fallon stepped out, her dark hair still damp. She wore jeans and a loose fitting sweatshirt and somehow managed to look sexy as hell. Wade's mouth watered even though they'd recently made love.

"Cavenaugh means nothing to Wade," she said. "It's me who wants him."

Josh slowly came to his feet. Wade could tell by the look on his friend's face that he was about to open his mouth and insert his foot. He thought about warning him . . . for all of two seconds, then decided against it.

"Surely this isn't who you're taking with you. You'll both be hung out to dry."

Fallon's eyes narrowed. She recognized Josh from the picture hanging on Wade's wall in his office. He was sexier in person. He had the look of a surfer: blond, tanned, muscled.

"So, this is your friend." She sauntered closer. "Not bad." She walked around him, blatantly looking him over. His jeans fit snugly, outlining every sinewy muscle. The jacket didn't hide much either, including the slight bulge of his holster and gun.

When she moved to stand in front of him she noted the gleam of doubt in his eye and knew he thought she was just a piece of fluff and Wade was about to make the biggest mistake of his career by taking her to The Pit. Time to burst his bubble. "Too bad he doesn't have any working brain cells."

Josh frowned. "What's that suppose to mean?"

Wade chuckled and pulled up a chair as if he were about to watch the Saturday-night fights and he had a ringside seat.

"Do you really believe Wade would take someone inexperienced? I mean, give him a little credit."

Josh planted his hands on his hips. "Don't tell me, you're a cop."

"Not exactly."

His brow furrowed. "Then what kind of training do you have?"

"DEA."

He snorted.

"Don't believe me?" She ran a manicured nail over each button on his shirt. Damn, her polish still looked good. She rather liked having them done. It made her feel almost . . . feminine.

"Can you give me a reason to believe you?"

Before he could blink, she snapped his gun loose and had the barrel planted snugly under his chin.

"Reason enough?" she purred.

From the corner of her eye she saw Wade grab his stomach. His laughter filled the room.

"Do you realize my gun is loaded?" Josh spoke carefully and distinctly.

"No shit. Unlike you, I do give Wade a little credit. I didn't think his friend would be as stupid as some people I've known in the past who *do* carry unloaded guns."

"Wade, you want to help me out here and call her off."

He shook his head. "No, you pretty well put both feet in. I figure you can get yourself out of this one."

"So," Fallon breathed. "Do you use one-hundred-and-fifty-eight grain, hollow-point bullets? I love a man who isn't afraid to make a statement. I mean, if you're going to do something—like, say, blow someone's head off, you might as well do it right. Don't you think?"

"Whatever you say, lady."

"The name is Fallon."

He swallowed hard. "Whatever you say, Fallon. Now, do you mind removing my gun from under my chin? I rather like my head all in one piece."

"And do you believe I'm with the DEA?"

"I'll believe anything you want."

She chuckled and moved the gun, twirling it a couple of times before slipping it back inside his holster. Wade was almost doubled with laughter. She arched an eyebrow in his direction. "I don't know what you find so damn amusing. He was a hell of a lot easier to convince than you."

"Jeez, where the hell did you find her?" Josh rubbed his chin as if to make sure it was still there before patting his holster.

"Actually, we sort of . . . bumped into each other." Fallon sat on a corner of the bed and crossed her legs.

"Yeah, she has this fetish for men and guns." Wade flipped his chair around and straddled it, resting his hands on the top.

"What can I say." Her voice dropped an octave,

becoming soft and sultry as she became the seductress in her mind's eye. "There's something about a man and a gun. Maybe it's the thought of all that explosive power packed in cold, hard steel." She closed her eyes and ran her tongue slowly across her lips.

When she opened her eyes, both men were slack-jawed. She inwardly smiled and sat a tad straighter, uncrossing her legs as she moved into another character.

"But of course, you would have to be careful one didn't go off accidentally." She innocently widened her eyes. "It would be horrible if someone actually got hurt." She delicately shuddered.

Josh looked at Wade. "Where the hell did you find her? The state hospital? DEA agent my ass; she's psycho. She has enough personalities she could star in her own movie."

Fallon thrust out her lower lip and became a French coquette. *"On t'a bercé trop près du mur?"*

"You got to admit, she's good—by the way, that was done rather well. The last was French, right?"

She smiled. "Very good."

"My French is a little rusty, but I think I caught some of it. He was hit on the head with a rock?"

Okay, he'd impressed her. She hadn't expected either one to know French. "The phrasing goes something like: when you were a baby, was your cradle rocked a little too close to the wall?"

"Very funny." Josh sat on the other corner of the bed. "I think the two of you can stop beating me up."

Wade chuckled, stood, and slapped his friend on the back. "Tell you what, I'll buy supper to make amends." He glanced at his watch. "Fred won't be here until closer to midnight. We have a couple of hours still. I don't know about you two, but I'm starving. The only thing we've eaten on the drive down were some stale cheese crackers and sodas when we filled up with gas."

"Okay, but I'm ordering the biggest steak they've got." Josh led the way out the door.

Fifteen minutes later they'd found a restaurant that boasted the largest steak in Texas. The way her stomach growled, Fallon figured she could put one away without much trouble.

As they went inside, Wade put her between himself and Josh. She shook her head. Did he think they would protect her if someone threatening came along? What the hell would he do when they crossed the border into Mexico? He still didn't realize she could take care of herself.

She covertly glanced from one man to the other. At five-foot, eight she didn't consider herself diminutive by any means, but they towered over her. She wasn't sure she enjoyed feeling like a pebble caught between two boulders. She stood straighter, but it didn't help much.

They went inside, and the waitress led them to a table at the back of the restaurant. After they were seated, she handed each a menu.

Wade ordered, then excused himself. An uncomfortable silence lingered between her and Josh. She had a feeling he wasn't crazy about her and Wade going undercover.

"We'll be careful," she finally spoke, then thought she sounded like a child reassuring a parent.

Josh took a drink from his water glass and set it down before speaking. "All the disguises in the world won't stop you from getting killed if you make one mistake. The people who hide out there relish the misery of others. They're not human."

"I know." She grew serious. "From what Wade has told me, they're the dregs of society. I only want one of them, though."

"Why?"

"So I can live again."

He nodded, as if he had his own demons to contend with. "Did Wade tell you he went undercover there once before?" When she nodded, he continued. "But did he tell you it was the final straw for him? That's why he moved home."

"He only said he was tired of fighting a losing battle." She leaned forward, waiting for Josh to continue.

"There's more to it than that." Josh picked up his knife, tested the edge, and set it beside his fork before raising his eyes to meet hers. "He'd been in deep cover a few months. Longer than he should've been. He wasn't thinking straight."

"Why?"

Josh shrugged. "Guilt, mostly. Back in the city, he'd been working with a young kid. Probably no more than seventeen. He thought the boy trusted him, but at the last minute the kid went back to his gang. He got caught in a drive-by and took a bullet. Wade blamed himself and grabbed the next assignment that came along. It just happened to be The Pit. It was deep undercover: if you get caught, we-don't-know-you kind of thing."

But yet he was returning—because of her. Fallon shifted in her seat, suddenly uncomfortable. "Why are you telling me this?"

"I just want you to be aware how seriously Wade is taking his job to help you find Cavenaugh. Don't let it destroy him."

She glanced up. Wade walked toward them. He didn't look like a man plagued by his past. In fact, he looked very self-assured.

What was it costing him to help her?

Chapter 17

They finished their meal and returned to the room, with Wade and Josh carrying most of the conversation. Once there, Josh left before the contact arrived. And for the hundredth time Fallon paced across the small space, lost in her own thoughts.

Damn it, she hadn't wanted to get pulled into his private life. Or know about the kid who went back to his gang or the fact The Pit had almost destroyed him. And she didn't like knowing he was returning because of her.

But she liked less the fact Cavenaugh was still a free man.

"What?" Wade blocked her path. "You've been acting funny ever since the restaurant."

She chose her words carefully. "Why are you going back when it almost killed you the last time?"

"Damn it, Josh should learn to keep his mouth shut." He whirled around and went to the window. "It's no big deal. Don't worry about it."

"I need to know. Why are you doing this for me?"

He faced her, grabbing her shoulders. "Because for some reason this man has hurt you so deeply you've let capturing him consume you. I want you to be able to move forward with your life."

"But you don't even know the reason."

"I don't need to know."

Damn it, she'd only wanted his help to get inside The Pit. The situation between them was getting too personal. She wished she could tell him why capturing Cavenaugh was so important to her. The words just wouldn't come, no matter how hard she struggled to say them.

"You don't have to tell me." His grip grew gentle.

"I'm sorry." God, why couldn't she open up? But she knew the answer. She was afraid of hearing the truth. She was afraid it would destroy her. "Maybe someday, but I can't right now."

"I understand."

"No, you don't. I'm not strong enough to bring it out in the open." There, she'd said it. She'd admitted her fear.

He pulled her into his arms. She knew her body was stiff and unyielding, but finally she began to relax and rested her head on his chest. Somehow Fallon knew she wasn't in this alone. An odd feeling of relief washed over her before she pushed out of his arms.

"Okay," she said, suddenly all business. "I don't want to screw up, so you'd better tell me more about this place. How many people stay there? Will I be able to blend in?" She glanced in the mirror above the scarred dresser. "If I keep a low profile, Cavenaugh shouldn't recognize me without the blond wig I wore when I was around him. What do you think?"

Wade sat on a corner of the bed, rested his fore-arms on his legs, and studied her. "If he's there, keep your distance just in case."

"And if he does recognize me?"

He shook his head. "He won't harm you. At least, not until he has the disk."

She still needed more information about The Pit, though. "What's the layout of the place?"

"It's been four years since I was there. It's bound to have changed, but there's always thirty or forty people. Some are like camp followers. They're used to living there and don't want to change. Watch them. They're the ones who will try to make money from any information they can get. But, on the other hand, they don't mind giving tips—for the right price."

"So, can anyone get inside?"

"Only if you have the money. I'll pay Fred, and he'll split with the other contact. Fred works both sides of the fence. He knows I'm a cop."

She'd worked with informers before, but it didn't mean she had to like it. They bothered her almost as much as the criminals. "Should I be worried?"

He shook his head. "He knows if he rats on us, he'll wind up in a gutter with his throat slit. He won't have to worry about jail time."

"And once we're there?"

"I have the money we'll need to pay Angelo. He's the top dog."

She chewed her bottom lip. "What's to keep Fred from taking all of the money and running?"

"He likes staying alive. And, by the way, he doesn't know my real name. I go by Johnny Taylor."

She chewed on her bottom lip. "Fallon is too recognizable. I haven't used Laura in a while."

A light tap on the door silenced them. Wade

drew in a deep breath. *The contact.* He went to the door and opened it a crack.

It had been a long time since he'd seen Fred, but the man still looked the same, except he'd added another twenty or so pounds to his already substantial girth. Other than that, everything looked familiar, right down to his greasy hair and the fact he probably hadn't bathed since Wade last met with him.

"Mr. Taylor." His Mexican accent was slight, making it obvious he'd crossed the border a few times. "It's been a long time, no?"

Not long enough. "Yes, a long time."

Fred looked around Wade. His eyes took on a feral gleam when he caught sight of Fallon. "You have a senorita. That is good." He pushed into the room.

"Laura, meet Fred." Wade really tried to keep the loathing out of his voice, but didn't quite manage. Greed motivated the path Fred walked. Whether it was for money, drugs . . . or a woman. He was loyal only to those who paid him the most. He'd sell out his own mother if he thought he could make an extra dollar or two.

"Hello, senorita." He licked his lips.

Fallon's slow appraisal would've sent any man with half a brain scurrying for cover. Unfortunately, Fred didn't have a brain.

"Cut the bullshit," Fallon growled. "Do you have information on Cavenaugh or not?"

This was the Fallon that Wade had first met: the one who didn't take crap from anyone. It damn sure wasn't in keeping with a low profile, not that it mattered. It wasn't likely Fallon would ever see Fred again.

Fred backed up a step. "This one has fire, amigo."

"I'd answer her," Wade warned. "You know how women are. They don't like to be kept waiting."

"Si, but the last one who complained too much"—his eyes narrowed—"I slit her throat." He made a motion across his neck with one finger.

Fallon planted her hands on her hips and glared at him. "Yeah, well, the last man who caused me a problem I cut his balls off and shoved them down his throat."

Fred guffawed. "This one I think you keep, amigo."

Wade was glad Fred approved. It made his day. "Do you have a lead on Cavenaugh or not?"

"Your man is jealous. That is good."

"We didn't come here for advice from the lovelorn. Do you have news or not?"

"My cousin told me he might still be at The Pit. His kind never stays too long in one place. At least there is a man who goes by the name Cavenaugh. It could be him . . . or not. He has men with him, though. It would not be good to get too close. They say he is fast to kill."

"How does he speak?" Fallon asked.

Fred looked between the two of them. "I do not understand."

She turned and strode toward the bathroom before abruptly turning on her heel. "Does he have an accent?"

Dawning showed in his eyes. "Ah, now I see. I do not know that, but my cousin calls him Frenchie." Fred's course laughter barreled out. "Just not to his face."

Wade looked at her for confirmation.

"That could be him. He's . . . Cajun. Part French. From Louisiana."

Where she was from. He had a feeling they went back a long way.

"We go see if he's the man you want." Fred grinned. "But first, you have something for me?"

Wade went to his bag, dug around inside, and tossed Fred a roll of bills, which the informant slipped into his pocket.

"What? Aren't you going to count them?" Wade asked.

"I trust you."

Yeah, right. He'd be fanning the greenbacks first chance he got. "Let's go."

Fallon and Wade grabbed their bags and climbed into Fred's lime-green Crown Victoria; it was much safer to take his vehicle.

The car looked like it came right out of the salvage yard, just before it was going to be crushed. Or, from the looks of it, maybe it had been crushed, then straightened out later.

The car was remarkably clean on the inside, though—surprising, seeing as how Fred could really use a bath. When Fallon climbed into the backseat, she lowered the window halfway.

"They've moved around since you were there last."

Fred started the car and turned on the headlights. Two warped beams of light illuminated the area in front of the car. It was a good thing there was a full moon tonight. Maybe they wouldn't run off into a ditch.

"I told my person on the other side you were bank robbers. The same as last time, except you have the girl." He chortled. "You can pretend you're

Bonnie and Clyde." He pulled into the flow of traffic. "It's maybe two or three hours to get where we're going, so you might as well relax."

Not likely. Wade didn't trust Fred any more than he had to. He'd keep his eyes open, at least until they met up with the other contact person. He still remembered the routine.

It was complicated, though. Even Fred didn't know the exact location. It kept the criminals safe, as much as a pit of vipers could be protected. The place had no law, except its own.

"I didn't think you'd ever go back inside. When you came out the last time you were a different man. You were a mean sucker. Like you became one of them." Fred shook his head. "That place is cursed. No matter how many times they move, the hex follows." He quickly crossed himself.

Wade shifted in his seat. "Stow the small talk." They weren't going to be there long enough that he would let the place effect him. He'd leave first . . . with or without knowing if Cavenaugh was there.

"Hey, I didn't mean nothin'." Fred took his eyes off the road long enough to glance across the seat.

"Then you won't mind shutting up." His muscles were as tight as a coiled spring. But there was something else, too. Excitement flowed through his veins. The Pit beat him last time. This was his chance to prove it couldn't beat him twice.

He settled back against the seat and waited.

The first point of their journey ended about three in the morning. Fred slowed the car and pulled into a roadside park. As they approached, headlights blinked twice in front of them.

Fallon reached into her bag and slipped her

gun into the waistband of her jeans, making sure the loose shirt concealed her weapon. As the car stopped, she slipped her arms into her jacket.

Her heart pounded. She'd put on a brave front, but she was as nervous as any rookie just hitting the streets. Shit, this wouldn't cut it. She'd get them both killed. Closing her eyes, she took a couple of deep breaths and rolled her head from side to side. Better.

Mentally, she prepared herself.

She was going after Cavenaugh. She pictured how she'd feel when she slapped a pair of handcuffs on his wrists. Satisfaction flooded her veins. This time, she'd get him.

"Are you ready, amigos? It is not too late to change your mind."

She opened her eyes and looked at Wade. Even with a full moon, the interior of the car was cast in shadow. She could only distinguish a shape, but she sensed his question, and that he waited for her to speak—to tell him what she wanted to do. It was her decision. "No turning back."

"We're ready." Wade opened his door and stepped out.

A touch of excitement laced his words, and she wondered if Josh really knew his friend as well as he thought. She had a feeling it might be time for Wade to settle an old debt of his own.

She climbed from the car. The other vehicle's headlights came on again, illuminating them in a circle of light. She felt for the gun tucked in her waistband, reassured it was firmly in place. A door slammed, then another.

There were at least two men.

With the bright light in their eyes, it was too dark to see if anyone came toward them. She glanced at

Wade. He looked relaxed, but she noticed the tell-tale signs of someone waiting to pounce: legs slightly bent, hands close to the gun he'd tucked inside his waistband. His eyes narrowed as he filtered out as much of the bright headlights as possible. He wasn't taking any chances.

Okay, she admitted she'd been a little nervous he might buckle on her. After what Josh had told her, she wasn't certain if his training would come back to him. You either use your skills or lose them.

"Hey, amigo." A thickly accented voice floated toward them from the darkness. "You have the money?"

Fred stood taller. "Of course. Do you think I'm a fool?" Fred pulled some money from his pocket, about half the amount Wade had given him.

"No, you would not be so crazy to cheat us." A slender, olive-skinned man stepped from the darkness into the light. There was no doubt in Fallon's mind the other one was still hidden in the shadows, probably with a gun pointed right at them. The tall man took the money from Fred. Unlike Fred, he counted it.

The man smiled. "So, how is my cousin?"

Fred shrugged. "How is any wife? She bitches all the time. I don't give her enough money. Then when I do she says she's too fat to buy clothes. Ah, amigo, women will drive you crazy."

The man's gaze strayed to Fallon. "Sometimes they can put fire in your blood."

Fred said something in Spanish, and both men laughed. His cousin-in-law answered back in his language. Unfortunately it was one Fallon didn't know, but apparently Wade did. His shoulders stiffened. He was posed to strike. Whatever they'd said, he hadn't liked it.

They'd come too far to walk away now.

"Can we go?" she interjected. "This family re-union is touching but you can do it on your time, not ours."

The contact stared at her. She stood taller, daring him to say anything. After a long minute he chuckled and nodded toward Fred. "When I saw you had brought a gringa, I thought you were crazy. But this one will do okay."

He glanced at Wade, his gaze moving over him. Recognition dawned in the man's eyes. He apparently realized Wade wasn't someone to take lightly, either.

"We go." He abruptly turned on his heels, leaving them to follow.

No names were exchanged. They got into the backseat. For the next hour, each person was lost in his own thoughts. The less they knew about their escorts, the better.

They eventually turned off the highway and onto a dirt road. Minutes ticked by. Finally, the driver slowed and pulled off the road.

"Out," Fred's cousin told them.

She wouldn't give two cents for their lives right now. She could almost smell the setup about to take place. Wade opened his door. She had no choice but to follow suit and open hers, but she damn well wouldn't die without taking someone with her. As she stepped from the car, she slipped her gun out of her waistband.

"Shut the door," the driver growled.

Son-of-a-bitch. She didn't like this. The hairs on the back of her neck stood up, but she slammed the door. They drove off in a choking cloud of dust. She glanced across the road toward Wade and breathed a sigh of relief. "Now what?" She slipped her gun back into the waistband of her jeans.

Wade brought out a small flashlight from his jacket pocket. "We wait," he told her. "The next person will pick us up here."

He shined the light around the area. Scraggly mesquite trees stretched their limbs toward them like the bony fingers of an old woman. She pulled her jacket snugly around her. His light moved over the area, stopping at an oak that had fallen and made a natural bench.

"We might as well get comfortable." He held out his hand and she took it. Hoping there were no snakes camouflaged in the thick underbrush, she cautiously made her way to the fallen tree. She hated the country. Gingerly, she sat on the rough surface, imagining every sort of bug crawling on the jagged bark. A shiver of revulsion swept over her.

"Cold?"

"No."

He didn't say anything.

The night wrapped around her. A few minutes passed in silence. Calm stole over her. She knew the darkness could be deceiving, and right now it wasn't all that dark, but she felt safe . . . and she owed Wade something.

"When I was fourteen I ran away from home," she hesitantly began. "Not the best thing to do when you live in New Orleans, but at the time it was the smartest thing for me to do. That first night I stayed in an alley and slept in a cardboard box. I could feel the bugs crawling on me. I hate insects." She drew in a deep, cleansing breath. She'd never spoken of that night.

He put his arm around her and drew her close. For just a moment she wished Cavenaugh was dead and she could stay wrapped in Wade's arms forever.

A flashlight flickered, then hit them in the face.

"Let's go," a gravelly voice came from the darkness.

She felt like a bug had just crawled across her. She had a bad feeling about this. A real bad feeling, and she didn't get them very often. But even while her brain screamed at her to grab Wade's hand and run the other way, she came to her feet and walked toward the beam of light.

Chapter 18

Wade wanted to tell the guy to forget the whole thing. He could say they'd decided not to go after all, but Fallon was already walking toward the next contact. Whatever Cavenaugh had done to her, it must've been pretty awful for her to want him so bad she'd follow him into The Pit.

Could he be the reason she ran away from home when she was only fourteen? His fingers curled into fists. He couldn't imagine a kid sleeping in an alley.

Memories of the kid he'd tried to help came flooding back. Ronnie had finally started opening up to him . . . or so Wade thought. But the kid hadn't listened in the end, and it cost him his life. Was the same thing happening again? Was Fallon saying she'd follow his orders so she could get Cavenaugh?

"Wait." He caught up with Fallon and put his hand on her arm.

She stopped.

"Are you sure you want to go through with this?"

She was silent for a moment. "It's not a choice anymore. That was taken out of my hands a long time ago."

He cupped her chin. "And you'll do exactly as I say once we get there?"

She squeezed his hand. "I'll do as you say. Don't worry."

"You coming or staying?" the man asked.

"We're right behind you," Wade told him. He just hoped like hell he wasn't making the biggest mistake of his life.

The man turned and began walking back the way he'd come. They trailed behind him, across the rough terrain, down a narrow, rocky path. Wade grabbed Fallon's elbow when she slipped. She murmured her thanks but didn't slow her pace.

Four years ago, it hadn't been this hard to enter. They were leery of newcomers . . . more cautious now, it seemed. He should've taken Josh up on his offer to come along with them. But then, it wasn't his friend's fight.

They came to level ground. The man with the light flashed it toward a boat that might have been painted light blue once but the color had faded and partially peeled. "Get in."

Wade and the man began rowing. It didn't take long to cross the river. They climbed out of the boat and made their way up the steep bank.

Wade stood on the small rise and reached his hand down to help Fallon the rest of the way, then looked around.

"How much farther?" Fallon asked.

In the distance he saw a fading beam of light. "I don't know. It would seem this escort has also departed." Wade hadn't even known when the man slipped away. His skills were rusty. If he wasn't more alert, he'd get them killed.

"And now we wait again," she said, frustration lacing her words.

"Someone else will come along."

"Or not."

"Or not." Hell, no one could be certain what would happen as each point man left and another appeared. They could kill them, and no one would ever be the wiser. Josh and Nathan King would know, but there'd be nothing they could do about it because they'd crossed the river into Mexico. That much Wade did know.

A rumble echoed across the open space. The noise became louder. Not thunder. A pickup, maybe?

Headlights came over the rise.

Their new contact.

"Take a deep breath. It gets tricky from here on out."

"You mean it hasn't been up to now?"

"That was nothing. Those men were only trying to make enough money to get by—ones you wouldn't look twice at if you passed them on the street. They probably have kids they bounce on their knees."

"Hmm, I just can't form that picture in my mind."

"Don't joke." He nodded toward the approaching truck. "We'll have to stay on guard. These men mean business. If they even get a hint we're the law, we won't live long enough to see another sunrise."

"I wasn't born yesterday, Tanner."

"Johnny. It's Johnny Taylor."

"I won't forget. Not when it counts."

"You got a bank robber personality in that re-pertoire of yours?" He certainly hoped she did.

"I think I might be able to come up with some-thing."

"Good, because the show is about to begin."

The pickup pulled to a stop beside them. From what little light the moon gave off, he could see it didn't look much better than Fred's car. He bet the motor was just as sound, though, and tuned to perfection.

His gaze scanned the vehicle. Dents, scrapes, and faded forest-green paint. An equally dented camper had been set on the bed. It looked like a pickup any hunter would be proud to call his own. There was nothing out of the ordinary . . . unless you looked close. The windows on the camper were blacked out so if you were inside you wouldn't be able to see out.

A flashlight shown in his face. He shielded his eyes. It moved to Fallon—and stayed longer than necessary. The hackles on the back of his neck rose.

"You got better taste in women now, Johnny-boy."

"Really?" Fallon spoke up.

Wade cringed. He should've told her it was bet-ter if she acted the silent type and let him handle everything.

"I've been told I have better taste in men now that I've hooked up with Johnny."

A burst of laughter came from the truck. "Sassy. Just the way I like them."

"Too bad she's already taken," Wade growled, hoping he wasn't going to be the one signing their death warrant.

"Same old Johnny. You never did like to share."

The voice sounded familiar.

When the pickup door opened the interior light came on and he could see a little better. His eyes narrowed. Yeah, he knew him all right. His jaw clenched. Angelo's second-in-command—Kinsey. The last time he was here Kinsey had thought he was vying for his position.

Kinsey stepped from the pickup. He was in his midfifties and had a penchant for Levi's, white western snap-down shirts, and white Stetsons.

He epitomized the clean-cut, older cowboy—except Wade knew better. Not only good guys wore white. And Kinsey was one of the exceptions to the rule. He not only bragged about how many men he'd killed, but just how he'd tortured them. And he enjoyed reliving every second.

"When they told me who was coming in, I thought I was hearing things," Kinsey interrupted Wade's grisly thoughts.

He drew in a deep breath before smiling. "Kinsey, I see they haven't bumped you off yet."

"I could say the same for you. Where you been keeping yourself?"

His question was asked casually enough, but Wade caught the slight edge. Kinsey wanted to know where he'd been and why he'd laid low for the last four years.

"You wouldn't believe me if I told you."

"Try me." He forced the issue.

"The Florida Keys."

Kinsey leaned against the pickup. Wade knew it would be days before he could check his story; even then, it wouldn't be easy. That's the last place Kinsey would ever go, so he probably didn't have any contacts there. Wade remembered him saying once he hated the ocean.

Kinsey's forehead puckered. "What the hell did you go there for?"

"Haven't you ever heard how soothing the sound of water can be?"

Kinsey snorted. "Yeah, until a shark decides he's hungry."

Wade could've told him there were plenty of sharks a hell of a lot more dangerous in The Pit, but he didn't.

"What exactly did you do while you were there? I didn't hear of any bank robberies."

Fallon knew why Kinsey questioned Wade. He wanted as much information as he could get. The wrong answer could get them killed, though. It was time to put a stop to the third degree.

"I know all this reminiscing is probably bringing a tear to your eyes, but my feet are killing me, I'm tired, and I'm hungry. Do you mind catching up later?" She crossed her arms in front of her like she was bored out of her skull.

Kinsey stepped closer. Her stomach knotted. One false move right now, and they were both dead meat. And the way Wade's hands curled into fists, she knew he was close to making that move.

"I might talk Johnny into swapping for the night. What do you think?" Kinsey drawled. "I'd feed you, and make all your aches and pains go away."

"You don't say," Fallon murmured. She moved closer to him. "Touch me and I'll blow you a new stomach." Kinsey hadn't noticed her slip the gun from her waistband. She nudged it against his gut.

Unconcerned, he ran his finger down her jaw. His eyes glittered dangerously. "I like a woman who fights back. It makes her screams all the more arousing when I'm fucking her."

Fallon had underestimated him. He didn't give

a shit if he lived or died. Death didn't frighten him. She swallowed past the lump in her throat. Cavenaugh was the only man who'd ever made her feel this kind of nauseating fear.

"I don't plan on letting you get to know her that well." Wade's words bit like an angry rattler.

She hadn't made things better; she'd made them worse.

Kinsey chuckled and stepped away. "Steady, Johnny-boy. What happened to your sense of humor?"

"I left it when I crossed the river into hell."

"Not hell, Johnny-boy. Just sanctuary for lost souls." He motioned toward the pickup. "You remember the routine. Get in and I'll take you to a place where you can rest in peace."

That was what she was afraid of . . . that they'd *Rest in Peace.* She only hoped it wouldn't be scrawled on a block of stone.

They climbed into the back of the pickup. A distinct click, and she knew they'd been locked inside the dark interior. The motor rumbled to life.

"Better find a seat. Kinsey drives like a maniac."

"It fits his personality," she mumbled.

He turned on his flashlight and shined it around the small, cramped space. A bench ran down one side. They grabbed a seat and hung on as Kinsey took off at an ungodly speed.

"Nice friend you have there." She said as they bumped across the rolling land.

"He's not a friend. More like a disrespected enemy. Be careful around him. The man isn't human. Angelo, the leader, keeps him under control as much as Kinsey can be controlled."

"Don't worry, I'll keep my distance." Once she had her balance, she grabbed onto anything that wouldn't move and made her way to the side window.

"They blackened it on the inside as well as the outside," he told her.

"Just thought I'd check."

"Been there, done that. Make yourself comfortable. It might be a long ride."

"Okay, tell me about Kinsey."

"He's power-hungry. We had a run-in the last time I was here. He's Angelo's second-in-command. Kinsey thought I was trying to usurp his position with the leader. Hell, I only wanted to get more information. One night he had his boys show me the error of my ways. Josh was there. He saved my life."

She gripped the bench. What the hell had she gotten them into? "Then why come back? Who's to say he won't kill you this time?"

"Because I won't let it happen."

No wonder Josh hadn't wanted him to return. *Damn, damn, damn!*

She drew in a deep breath.

Okay, they'd go in, see if Cavenaugh was there. Either way, they wouldn't hang around long. They'd find a way to get him to leave his safety net. She wouldn't let Wade come to harm.

She only hoped she wasn't lying to herself.

It couldn't have been more than a half-hour before the pickup stopped jouncing along the rough terrain and the door opened. The sun was just rising over the horizon.

"Grab the tarp from under the bench," Kinsey told Wade, then held his hand out to help her down.

There was enough light that she could see the tattoo of a scorpion on his forearm. She declined his offer and jumped to the ground. She despised bugs.

Once her feet were firmly on the ground, she

glanced around. Mountains surrounded them. Did they have active volcanoes in Mexico? A deep, reverberating sound seemed to come from deep inside.

Great, now she was hearing things.

They covered the truck with the beige canvas and when they finished it blended in with the landscape. No one would ever be able to trail them here. She thought about all the stories she'd heard about this place, and a shiver of apprehension ran up and down her spine as they started walking.

Damn it, she wasn't about to let Kinsey or The Pit get to her. Hell, she'd been raised around voodoo and the swamps all her life. This place was nothing compared to some of the stories her grandmother had told her.

She stumbled and quickly caught her balance. Jeez, she hadn't thought about her in years. The old woman had dabbled in voodoo, or had it been witchcraft? Both, for all she knew. It used to scare the hell out of her. Maybe Grandma's skills had passed down to her granddaughter? *Why not?* She squared her shoulders. She'd hex their asses if they messed with her.

When they rounded a corner, a large tent came into view. Music and raucous laughter spilled from the open flap.

Someone was certainly having fun.

Her gaze scanned the area. The large tent was flanked by rows of smaller, single-room tents. Set off by itself was one lone tent—probably where the leader of this nefarious group stayed.

They were all the same dull brown as the tarp on the pick-up. Wade had been right. It wouldn't be hard to pack up and move to another location if the cops got a little too nosey.

And now she knew where the rumbling noise came from. There was a generator somewhere. Of course, they'd need some form of power.

"Home sweet home." Kinsey waved his arm in front of him in a wide arc.

As the sun began to rise, an eerie play of light and shadow settled on the camp. "A regular Sodom and Gomorrah," she said.

A gleam of speculation sparked in Kinsey's eyes, as if he would enjoy an hour or so alone with her, teaching her all sorts of ways they could sin.

"Compared to this place, Sodom and Gomorrah were just small towns in the Bible belt."

Yeah, well she didn't plan to let him show her the difference.

"The same rules apply as before." He turned to Wade. "That there are no rules. Except if you kill someone you have to bury him . . . or her. Dead bodies tend to stink up the place."

"I'll remember that," Wade said and pulled Fallon closer to his side.

"No one stays free, though."

Kinsey deftly caught the money pouch Wade tossed him.

"You two can bunk in Troy's tent." He gestured toward the last one. "He had a . . . shall we say . . . an unfortunate accident and will no longer be needing it."

"And that tent." Wade nodded toward the one sitting away from the others. "Is that where Angelo stays?"

"Didn't I tell you? Angelo's dead. There's a new leader."

"Who?"

A cold chill slithered down her spine. Fallon had a feeling she wasn't going to like his answer.

"Me. But hey, no hard feelings. I've buried the past." Kinsey laughed as he strolled toward the lone tent.

"Yeah, no hard feelings," Wade muttered. "I just hope he doesn't want to bury us alongside Angelo. Damn, this throws a wrench in our plans."

Chapter 19

With a weary eye, Wade watched Kinsey stroll to his tent.

"This isn't good, is it," Fallon stated rather than asked.

"Let's just say I could've heard better news, but we won't be here that long." He turned his gaze away from Kinsey's retreating figure and looked at Fallon. "You ready?"

"Maybe we should just call it quits. I'm pretty good at hot-wiring a vehicle, and the pickup isn't that far away."

"You giving up on Cavenaugh?"

They'd come this far; could she turn around and walk away? But was staying worth the risk?

He squeezed her hand. "I wouldn't want to leave, either," he said, guessing her dilemma. "Not when we're this close. You ready to go inside and have a look around?"

She couldn't deny she'd like to get Cavenaugh. And they *had* come this far. They'd be fools to

leave without first checking the place out. "Let's
go." But she wouldn't linger—no matter what.

"Stay close. If Cavenaugh's in there, we don't want
to draw too much attention to you." He smiled.
"Do you have a quiet and unassuming character in
your bag of disguises?"

Her brow puckered. "That might be stretching
my talents a bit, but I'll see what I can come up
with."

Wade wished they had a hat she could pull down
low on her forehead, but then, maybe that would
draw attention toward her rather than away. Hell,
he just wanted to get this over with as soon as possible—even more so, now that he knew Kinsey was
in charge. That man made crazy people look sane.

Music vibrated the ground as they made their
way to the tent.

Like vampires, these people lived for the night-
time hours. When the sun began to climb, they'd
crawl into their tents.

He looked to the east. That time was near.

They stepped inside. Fallon stayed close to him
as promised. From the looks of things, the revelers
weren't ready to stop playing. The place was packed.

His eyes were already used to the darkness outside so it didn't take long to adjust to the dim interior. His glance swept the area in one swoop. Stale
cigarette smoke hung in the air like a heavy fog,
mingling with the sweeter odor of marijuana and
the stench of rotgut booze.

There were six poker tables, each chair filled.
Most of the noise came from the craps table, though.
The dice bounced across the green felt and the
winners cheered. He shook his head. Someone had
once called the camp Little Vegas. They weren't
far off the mark.

One of the poker players stood: a big burly man with a cigar clamped between his teeth.

"Mother fucker! You palmed that ace. It'll be the last time you ever cheat."

He pulled a knife, but the seated man was too fast. He didn't hesitate as he pulled the trigger. The derringer might have been small, but it was as deadly as a bigger gun. The cigar-chewer grabbed his chest and went down. The others at the table went back to their game.

Four years ago the place turned his stomach—until he got so used to the things that went on, he didn't even bat an eye. He wouldn't ever let that happen again.

Even as he told himself he was stronger, knots formed in his stomach.

"Johnny?" Fallon whispered, using his cover name. "You okay?"

He glanced down into her worried eyes. He'd lost himself in the past for a moment. He wouldn't let it happen again.

"Just checking the place out," he lied as he looked around. He focused his thoughts and shook off what was long over and done with.

He squared his shoulders and really looked this time. The place had grown. There were more people. And why not. Kinsey had supplied everything a disreputable person could ever want. Drugs, alcohol, and sex. All for a nice tidy sum to get in, and a hefty cut of any profits once you were there. And for that, he kept the law at bay.

Wade nuzzled Fallon's hair. "Do you see him?" For a moment he forgot where the hell he was as the fresh smell of peaches invaded his senses. This was real. Fallon would keep him sane in this place of insanity.

"No. He's not here."

"Let's get something to drink." They made their way to the bar. "Two beers," he spoke over the noise behind them.

The bartender acted like getting off his butt was more trouble than it was worth, but he finally managed with only a few grunts. He reached into a cooler and pulled out two bottles, placing them on a makeshift plywood counter held up by wooden barrels.

"That'll be five dollars . . . each," he grumbled.

"That's criminal."

The bartender had a dumbfounded expression on his face before he burst out laughing. "Ha! Criminal. That's funny."

Wade brought out a bill. "And this is a twenty. I don't want change—if you can give me a little information."

The man made a grab for the money, but Wade moved it just out of his reach.

"First the info. You heard of a man named Cavenaugh?"

The bartender's eyes narrowed. "Who wants to know?"

"Johnny Taylor. I heard he sells drugs, and I'm in a spending mood."

The bartender didn't look convinced. "Lots of people around here sell drugs. Why him?"

Wade shrugged. "He has the connections I'm looking for."

The bartender quickly eyed the room, probably to make sure he wouldn't be overheard. "He was here. Don't know if he still is, though. People come and go."

Wade handed the money to him, but kept his grip on it. "If you see him, let me know and I'll put some C-notes with this. And I'd rather it didn't get out that I'm asking questions."

The man wrested the money away and grinned a toothless smile. "Yeah, I'll let you know if I see him. You might want to check with the whore—Nicole. She has her own little business at the back." He jerked his head in the general direction.

A new owner. He wondered what happened to the last proprietor, Connie something or other. Wade grabbed the beers, handed one to Fallon, and they sauntered away.

"What if he's left?"

He inwardly cringed when he heard the dismal tone of her voice. It only told him how much she wanted Cavenaugh. "Then you'll get him another day." Or nature would take its course and someone would put a bullet in his head. "Besides, the bartender didn't say Cavenaugh left, only that he wasn't sure."

She squared her shoulders. "You're right."

Good, she wasn't going to let her disappointment take her down. He hadn't really thought she would.

They walked slowly to the back. Wade draped his arm around Fallon. Anyone watching would think they were lovers looking for a little more fun. The rear of the tent was the place to find that something extra.

Men and women could be purchased for the pleasure of whoever could afford them. Most of them were owned by one person or another at the camp, ready to be sold to the highest bidder—won or lost in a game of chance.

Cubicles were sectioned off, providing a minimal amount of privacy. They passed one cubicle, the opening only partially closed. A woman's wrists were chained, then drawn upwards, the chain looped over the top of a wooden T. Her clothes hung in shreds, her bare skin red where the whip landed on bare flesh.

Whether drug induced or the fact she was a masochist, the girl was in the throes of ecstasy. Her cries weren't from pain, but enjoyment of what the man did to her. They kept walking.

"Hey, baby." A naked blonde was lying on pillows inside her open cubicle, her legs open in invitation. "I can make you feel good." Slowly, she licked her lips. "Or I can make your woman feel good and you can watch."

"Not right now. Maybe later," he told her.

They continued to the back, to the darkest part of the tent, past more cubicles to an open area. Large pillows were scattered about on the floor. A couple of men and one partially clothed woman leaned against a grouping of them. As they approached, the woman opened her vacant, glassy eyes, smiled, and snuggled next to the man beside her. Wade didn't have to be told this was where you came for your next fix.

"You're new here." A sultry, feminine voice spoke from a shadowed corner.

Only a flickering candle illuminated the area. He couldn't pinpoint from which direction the feminine voice came from.

"We just got in," he cautiously told her.

She came toward them. Wade didn't know what to expect, but it wasn't the exotic beauty. She was like a delicate flower cast amongst the weeds. Until she turned and he saw the deep, jagged scar running down the side of her face from eyebrow to jaw. Fallon stiffened beside him. His reaction wasn't much better.

The woman smiled. "I know. I get that all the time."

"I'm sorry," they apologized in unison.

She shrugged. "It's not so bad anymore. Now you know why I'm here." She studied them. "It's you two who don't belong."

"Looks can be deceiving," Fallon spoke.

She chuckled. "Yes, they can. Are you going to tell me you're hardened criminals?" She waved her hand to encompass the entire tent. "Like this scum of the earth."

Fallon cocked an eyebrow. "Of course not. We're a hell of a lot better than they are."

The woman smiled, apparently liking her answer. "This is my portion of the establishment. Was there something, or someone, I could get you?" Her gaze trailed slowly over Fallon before she turned to Wade and gave him the same appraisal. "My name is Nicole. If you two ever want a little . . . company, let me know. I'll even bring my relatives."

Wade wasn't into threesomes or whatever the hell she had in mind.

"Relatives?" Fallon asked.

Apparently her curiosity got the better of her. He'd known she would never be able to play the silent type for very long.

"All the relatives. Aunt Hazel, Aunt Mary, Aunt Nora, and of course I would never forget Aunt Emma."

Laughter bubbled out of her. Wade didn't join in on her little joke. He knew the street names of her relatives—as well as the clinical: heroin, marijuana, cocaine, and opium.

"Maybe you know a friend of ours who supplies . . . your little family for you." Fallon spoke softly.

Wade knew Fallon understood exactly who the relatives were, too.

"His name is Cavenaugh," Fallon continued.

Nicole's eyes widened then narrowed. "I sell his drugs in this shithole, along with the meat market." She nodded toward the cubicles with a grimace of revulsion. "By the time he and Kinsey take their cut, there's barely anything left for me." She dropped to one of the pillows as if drained of all her energy. "I'm so damned tired. Go away. Find someone else to bother. I'm closed to newcomers for the night."

Fallon grabbed her arm. "Where's Cavenaugh?"

Nicole glanced up, staring into Fallon's face. Tears formed in her eyes. "I used to be pretty like you. Now I'm a hideous monster. Please, leave me alone."

Fallon's tone grew hard. "I need to find him."

"He's gone. But he'll be back, wanting more and more until there's nothing left to give. He and Kinsey were cut from the same ugly pattern."

Fallon let go of her.

"Come on." Wade grabbed Fallon's hand and led her away.

Once outside he took a deep breath, letting the clean, cool mountain air cleanse his polluted lungs.

"We came all this way for nothing," she ground out between clamped teeth and stormed away from the tents.

Wade caught up to her and grabbed her arm. "She's so steeped in misery, and who knows what else, she probably doesn't know what century this is, let alone if Cavenaugh is here or not. Why don't we get some sleep and see what happens after we've rested? One more day. Then, if he's not here, we'll leave. Unless you can tell me right now you don't want to find him."

She opened her mouth, then snapped it shut.

"It's okay. I understand."

She nodded. "We'll leave as soon as we find out for sure."

He squeezed her hand and only hoped it wouldn't be too late.

The tent Kinsey had said they could use was small and cramped, not much bigger than a pup tent. It didn't matter. They wouldn't be staying that long.

They lay down on top of the sleeping bags and curled against each other, her back against his chest. The closed flap shut out all but a sliver of light.

"Wade?"

He nuzzled her neck—not because he wanted to make love, but because he wanted to be closer to her.

"What?" he asked.

"Cavenaugh killed my father . . . and my sister. I'd gone to the store. Jody wanted to go with me, but she had a bad cold. When I wouldn't let her, she begged me to stay. Even though she was a little kid, she had these premonitions. I never paid them any mind. Cavenaugh would've killed me if I hadn't seen him leaving our house and hid in the brush."

He froze. "Why didn't you go to the police?"

"I did. I spoke with one of the officers. He put me in a room. I was there about a half-hour when I looked out the window and saw Cavenaugh. He and the officer were talking like they were the best of friends. I ran out of the police station, and eventually out of Louisiana. After all, who'd believe a snotty-nosed kid?"

"Didn't you have any relatives?"

"A crazy old grandmother, but she lived in the

swamps. I never would've been able to find her on my own, so I just left."

He gathered her close to him. "I'm sorry."

"Someday I want to go home. I want to put flowers where they've been laid to rest."

He kissed her shoulder and pulled her closer, knowing instinctively that she didn't need his words of condolence.

"I don't want to talk about it anymore."

"I know, baby."

She sighed deeply. A little later her respirations became even, and he knew she'd fallen asleep. He lay there for a long time, listening to the silence. He knew how deceiving it could be.

Fallon had trusted him with her past, maybe because they'd only catnapped the last twenty-four hours and she was more vulnerable. Or maybe she was beginning to trust him more. He didn't know. He only knew her battle had now become his battle. Together, they would get Cavenaugh and put him away for the rest of his life.

He only hoped Kinsey meant what he'd said about forgetting the past. Damn it, he'd be a fool if he actually believed the man. Wade had seen the excitement in his eyes. The games were about to begin. Kinsey loved toying with his prey—right before he killed them.

But they wouldn't be here that long.

He closed his eyes.

Now I lay me down to sleep. The Lord I pray my soul to keep. If I should die before I wake . . .

Chapter 20

"Good afternoon." Wade brushed the hair from Fallon's face. He loved the silky texture.

"How did you know I was awake?" Fallon rubbed the sleep from her eyes.

"I've been watching you. There was a subtle difference in the rhythm of your breathing."

Odd, how he could be so fascinated watching her. There was something about Fallon, especially when she slept: an innocence. He knew that was ludicrous, considering her line of work. She had to have seen as much, if not more, than he had.

"Why?" she asked.

"Why, what?"

"Why have you been watching me?"

That wouldn't be easy to explain, especially when he wasn't quite sure himself. "Because I like to." Because she'd become a part of him without him realizing it. Because he knew she was special. Maybe there was something to the words *soul mate*.

She took her time speaking, as if choosing her words with care. "I've lived most of my life trying to bring Cavenaugh to justice. I couldn't prove anything until I downloaded the disk." She absently stroked his hand. "I don't think I really know who I am anymore."

"I do. You're Fallon Hargis."

She snorted. "Don't you see? Even that's a lie. I stole that name from a grave the day after I ran away. There's nothing real about me."

He brought himself up on his elbow and turned her until only inches separated them. "I don't care about your name. What's on the inside is the only thing that matters."

She stiffened in his arms. "This isn't the place to have a discussion about who I am, besides the fact I don't want to stay any longer than you." She rolled away from him. "What time is it, anyway?"

She couldn't run away forever, but Fallon was right. There'd be plenty of time to talk when they returned to Two Creeks. He sat up and opened the flap so he could see. The afternoon sun came streaming inside. "Four o'clock. Hungry?"

"Starved."

They crawled from the tent. People were milling about, laughing and talking, like they were on vacation in a posh resort rather than on the run. Men, women, and he even saw a couple of kids.

A makeshift bathroom had been set up in the far corner of the enclosure. It afforded only the minimum of privacy: two sections roped off with blankets. He washed and met her out front again and they headed toward the main tent in search of something to eat . . . and Cavenaugh.

"I don't see him," Fallon stated once they were inside. Again, her gaze slowly scanned the immense interior.

"Are you sure?" He looked around. The only description she'd given him was medium height, five-ten or so, dark hair, and mustache. That could fit almost any man.

"No, he's not here."

"Let's get something to eat. Somewhere that we can keep an eye on the door." He started forward.

"You don't want to eat here," Kinsey spoke from behind them. "The food's terrible. Join me in my tent."

Wade stiffened. How much had he heard? There wasn't anything he could do about it now. "Sure," he spoke as casually as he could.

They followed Kinsey outside. Wade squeezed Fallon's hand to let her know this would only delay them for a while. They'd eat, then see exactly what Kinsey wanted.

"What do you think of our little hideout?" Kinsey waved his arm. "Angelo had us moving every few months before his . . . accident. He was always afraid the law would find us if we stayed in one place too long. The fool. If you give them enough money, they won't do a damn thing except look the other way."

Wade knew he wasn't expected to answer. Kinsey wanted to brag, let Wade know who was in charge, and what would happen if anyone got in his way.

Kinsey held open the flap to his tent, letting it drop back in place after they entered.

"Beautiful, isn't it?" His eyes glittered unnaturally.

Wade looked around. A sultan would've been proud to live here. Candles in tall sconces illuminated the room in a soft, warm glow. Silks and velvets draped the walls, hiding the fact this tent was just as dismal as the rest. Oriental rugs were scattered on the floor and a plush, king-size bed dominated the back wall.

Kinsey didn't sleep alone, either. Nicole snored softly, her arm flung across the scarred side of her face.

He continued his visual inspection. On the other side of the room a low table was surrounded by an abundance of silk-covered pillows in bright colors. The table was set with three plates.

He also noticed there was one way in, and one way out.

"It looks like you've done well for yourself." His gaze met Kinsey's. "I guess it was a good thing for you when Angelo had his . . . accident. Exactly how did he die?"

"Gunshot. Right between the eyes," Kinsey stated matter-of-factly.

"Suicide?" He wondered if Kinsey would catch the sarcasm in his voice. They both knew Kinsey had killed the former leader. "A shame, especially when he had so much to live for," he spoke dryly.

Kinsey stiffened. "Yes, a shame." He motioned toward the table. "Take a seat."

They walked over and sat on the cushions. Kinsey removed the lids from the silver bowls revealing fluffy, scrambled eggs, another with a creamy white sauce, and another with crisp bacon, sausage, and ham. A bowl filled with apples, oranges, and bananas was set in the center of the table, a gleaming knife for peeling placed next to it.

"I have an excellent cook. Please, help yourself." He uncorked a bottle of champagne and poured them each a glass.

"You're too generous," Wade said, knowing Kinsey

wouldn't show his hand until he was good and ready.

"A toast. To old friendships." Kinsey raised his glass.

They had no choice but to follow suit. Wade noticed Fallon only brought the glass to her lips, but didn't drink. Afraid he might have put their lives in jeopardy with his earlier remarks about Angelo's death, Wade emptied his glass and let Kinsey refill it.

"You still haven't introduced me to your lady friend."

"My name is Laura," Fallon told him as she took an orange and began to peel it.

"Did Johnny-boy tell you he and I became friends when he was here last time?"

Fallon looked between the two men. Innocence wouldn't work with him. Besides, she'd already shown him she wasn't afraid to stand on her own two feet.

She bit into a slice of her orange, chewed, and swallowed. "I think he left out the part about you two being friends."

Kinsey laughed. From the bed, Nicole moaned and turned on her other side.

"You're right," he admitted. "Johnny-boy wanted my job. I had to show him the error of his ways."

Wade rubbed his chin. "Yeah, well, I think you managed to do that."

Kinsey slapped him on the back. "I'm invincible, kid. No one can beat me."

Cold dread filled her. They should've left while they had the chance. Kinsey was too relaxed, too sure of himself. And too damn crazy.

The older man grabbed an apple from the bowl

and casually tossed it in the air a couple of times. "Tell me why you're looking for Cavenaugh." He bit into the fruit but kept his eyes on the two of them while he slowly chewed.

Wade shrugged. "There's money to be made in drugs. Less dangerous than robbing banks."

"I don't think so, Johnny-boy. There's more to it than you're telling me." Cold eyes stared at them from across the table. "Tell me why you dropped off the face of the earth. Then showed up here all of a sudden."

"I told you." Wade leaned against the cushion, taking his drink with him. He drained the glass before answering. "I'm looking to get into the drug trade."

"That's not what Fred told me—right before I killed him, that is."

Bile rose inside Fallon. Her gaze swiveled to Wade. He still looked calm and relaxed, but she knew better. His jaw twitched.

"Fred who?" Wade moved to set the empty glass on the table, but seemed to misjudge the distance. On the second attempt, he made it.

What was wrong with him? She glanced at her barely touched drink. Was it drugged? But she'd seen Kinsey uncork it.

"Good, I was hoping you'd play dumb about knowing Fred." Kinsey straightened from his relaxed position. "I'd hate for you to start blabbering away and telling me exactly why you're here. That would spoil all the fun."

"Listen," Fallon began, only to meet the full extent of Kinsey's fury as he turned blazing eyes in her direction.

"Shut up, bitch. When I want you to talk, I'll tell you."

Wade started to his feet, but fell forward instead. Fallon reached toward him, but Kinsey knocked her out of the way. She fell back against her pillow, pain burning down her arm where he'd shoved against her.

"Leave her alone," Wade's words were slurred. "Fuck, what'd you do?"

"I drugged the champagne. It's an easy thing to re-cork a bottle, but most people never think about it. Pretty ingenious, don't you think?"

Kinsey stood and dragged Wade to a chair. Fallon jerked the gun from her waistband and aimed it at him.

"Let him go, or take your last breath." Her words weren't a threat. They were a promise.

Kinsey only laughed, wrapped his arm around Wade's neck and pulled a knife from his pocket. When he pushed the button the blade jumped out, gleaming in the muted candlelight.

"Have you ever seen a chicken with its head cut off?" he asked. "Even though it's dead, the bird will flop around on the ground spewing blood everywhere until it finally lies still. I wonder how long Johnny-boy will flop?" He looked up and met her gaze across the room.

"Kill him," Wade told her. "For God's sake, kill him. You don't have to die, too."

"Go ahead, kill me. We can end it right here and now. You'll be free."

She didn't move. Everything she knew told her to shoot. Take a chance she could kill Kinsey before his knife touched Wade's throat.

"No? Then drop the gun, or Johnny-boy dies."

She looked at Wade. He was going to die. It hit her just how much she loved him. She squeezed her eyes closed. A hell of a time to figure that one out. Her arms went limp; the gun dropped from her hand.

"No!" Wade yelled, but it came across faint as Kinsey quickly tied Wade's hands behind him and strolled across the room toward her.

"I knew it from the very beginning, Johnny-boy. The bitch loves you." Even though he directed his comment at Wade, his gaze never wavered from her face. "Now isn't that sweet? I'll make sure I bury you two in the same hole. I know, I'm a sentimental fool."

Fallon raised her chin. "Fuck you."

He moved fast, his fist slamming into the side of her head.

Everything went black.

Chapter 21

Slowly, Fallon's world came into focus. Her jaw burned and her head pounded like someone beating on a set of bongo drums. She tried to move her hands, but Kinsey had tied them behind her and propped her in a chair. They didn't hurt. They were already numb.

Sounds filtered into her brain. Some instinctive sense of survival told her to keep her eyes closed.

"I thought you were a lot stronger, Johnny-boy. Hell, I doubt you'll last the night. I really had higher expectations. It's a damn shame I misjudged you."

"Bastard," Wade snarled.

She cringed.

What had they done to him? She was afraid to look, but not knowing was worse. Keeping her head down, she opened her eyes a fraction, then quickly closed them tight.

Ah, jeez. Her stomach clenched and the orange she'd eaten earlier burned her throat as it threatened to come back up.

There was a deep gash across his forehead. Blood

ran in a slow, steady trickle down the side of his face. One eye was almost swollen shut.

She gritted her teeth to keep from raging at the lunatic who'd done this. Slowly, she drew in a deep breath. *Remember your training. Survey the situation and try to get control of the scene.* Covertly, she scanned the area. They were alone—just the three of them. Nicole was no longer in bed.

"Ah, sleeping beauty is awake." Kinsey turned in her direction.

She opened her eyes, wondering how he'd guessed. The bastard grinned from ear to ear. He enjoyed torturing Wade.

Even Cavenaugh hadn't made her feel this much hatred. She wanted to kill Kinsey in a way he'd suffer a long time before he died.

She wrestled with the ropes that bound her hands, but it was no use.

He chuckled. "I can see you're not happy with me for messing up his face. Don't worry, there aren't any lasting scars. Not that he'll mind, where he's going."

Looking down at the knife he held, Kinsey ran his thumb across the sharp edge, leaving a thin line of blood. "You know pain can be quite an exquisite sensation." He glanced up, their gazes locking. "I once watched a man hang himself while masturbating. Did you know you can take yourself to the very edge and experience an unbelievable orgasm?"

"I've heard about it," she warily stated.

He nodded. "I rather thought you had. You don't look like you've led a sheltered life. Me, either. Now Johnny-boy"— he cast Wade a look of disgust, then returned his gaze to her—"I bet he was raised by loving parents. It's the little things you catch. Know what I mean?"

"Yeah, I know. Where the hell is this going? If you're planning on killing us, then just do it."

He jerked a chair forward, placing it directly across from hers, before straddling it. He still gripped the knife, occasionally looking at it as if to make sure it was still there.

"Not so fast, sweetheart. I want to savor the moment."

"Leave her alone," Wade warned. "She has nothing to do with what's between us."

"Doesn't she, Johnny-boy?" He ran the dull side of the knife down her face.

She held her breath, keeping perfectly still.

"She's got guts," he finally said, withdrawing the blade. "I'm curious how long it will take before she's screaming and begging me to kill her."

She spit in his face. Anger contorted his features into an angry mask. He jerked his hand above his head. The blade glittered in the candlelight.

"No," Wade yelled.

Kinsey slowly lowered his arm, wiping off his face with the back of his sleeve. "You're right. I don't want to end the fun before I get started."

Leaning forward, he grabbed the neck of her sweatshirt so hard he almost toppled her chair. He began sawing across the material, right down the middle.

"I hope you're enjoying yourself," she ground out.

"Actually, I am." When he finished cutting her shirt, he pushed back each side, exposing her breasts. "Like I said, Johnny-boy, your taste in women has improved."

He cupped one breast, squeezing her nipple.

She clamped her lips, but didn't cry out. He finally let go and sat down again. "I knew the moment I saw you it would be like this between us. We're a lot alike, you and me."

"I'm nothing like you."

"Maybe I'll keep you around just to prove you wrong. A year in this place, and you'll do anything to survive."

"I'd kill myself first."

He ran the handle of the knife down the middle of her chest. "You just think you would. The human spirit is something of an enigma. The mind can die, but the body has an innate will to survive—doing almost anything for one more hour, one more minute of life."

"Touch her again, and you won't want to live. In fact, you'll beg *me* to kill *you,*" Wade hissed.

Kinsey grinned as he stood, kicking his chair out of the way. "What's the matter Johnny-boy? Jealous?"

"She hasn't done anything to you. Why not let her go? It's me you want."

"But I already have you. And I have her." He jerked Wade's hair, forcing him to look up. "I think I want to keep you both. Until I get bored. Then I might put you out of your misery."

He moved the blade to Wade's neck.

"Don't! For God's sake. Leave him alone." She struggled against the ropes that bound her, but they didn't give.

Slowly, Kinsey moved the knife to Wade's arm and sliced across the muscle, opening the skin enough that it left a bleeding gash. Wade gritted his teeth, sweat dotted his upper lip.

"You know, it takes a long time for someone to

bleed to death when you don't cut too deeply." Kinsey strolled to the table and picked up the saltshaker.

Fallon's stomach turned.

"Even longer if you stop the bleeding." He removed the cap and poured salt into the wound.

"You son-of-a . . . aghhh!"

"What's the matter?" Kinsey innocently asked. "Don't you appreciate a friend's attempt to save your life?"

He rubbed the salt into the wound. Wade sucked in gulps of air as he tried to fight the pain.

Fallon turned her head. She couldn't watch. They should've left. Why the hell had she stuck around? And why had Wade stayed after he discovered Kinsey was in charge?

Cavenaugh. It all came back to him.

"Look, your little girlfriend can't stand the sight of blood."

"Go to hell," she spat.

"Probably." Kinsey laughed.

The flap to the tent opened and a bear of a man poked his head inside. "Hey, boss. He's here. In the big tent."

"Invite him over."

"Him and his boys are unloading some boxes at Nicole's, but I'll tell him."

"No, I'll go over. I want to see exactly what he's brought. My profit seems to shrink each month." He turned to Wade. "Now don't run off, Johnny-boy. Fred told me some interesting facts before I gutted him. It'll be fascinating discovering if he told the truth or not." His laughter followed him out the tent.

"I'm sorry," Fallon told Wade when they were alone.

Wade raised his head as if it cost him most of his energy. "For what?"

"This."

He shrugged, then grimaced from the movement. "Hell, who'd have thought Kinsey would be in charge. Even knowing that, I thought we'd have a little time. I guess we both used poor judgment."

She looked toward the top of the tent as she tried to keep the moisture forming in her eyes from trickling down her face. "I love you," she whispered.

"Now's a hell of a time to mention it."

He was supposed to tell her he loved her, too. He acted like her declaration pissed him off. She frowned at him. "I didn't know I loved you until a little while ago. Since it doesn't look like we're going to be leaving, I thought this was as good a time as any to tell you how I felt. Excuse me if my timing was off."

"It's not that."

"Then what is it, Tanner?"

"I love you, too."

"Oh."

Now wasn't this fucking romantic. Tied to chairs, bruised, her shirt ripped down the middle. In those rare moments when she pictured herself falling in love, it hadn't been quite like this. "A lot of good it's going to do us now. We'll be dead by morning."

"Not if you hurry," Nicole stepped from the back of the tent and rushed toward them. "I knew Kinsey was up to something. As soon as he left, I slipped around back and came in through a slit."

Taking the knife from the fruit bowl, she began cutting Wade's ropes.

"Why are you helping us?" he asked.

"I want to go with you. I'm tired of splitting the

damn profits. Hell, I've even been thinking about going legit." She looked at him as if he might not believe her. "I'm a damn good business woman."

"I'm glad you're letting your conscience be your guide," he told her.

Nicole freed Wade and they hurried to Fallon. Wade took the knife and began slicing across the rope.

"It wasn't exactly my conscience that bothered me. I owe Kinsey. He's the one who cut me." Fallon's and Nicole's gazes met and held. "I didn't want the same thing happening to you."

"Then let's get the hell out of here." Fallon shook her hands to return the feeling and they hurried to the back of the tent. She jerked a pillowcase loose as she went past the bed. They'd need some kind of bandage for Wade's arm before they went very far, and they couldn't afford to be picky.

Nicole stepped through the opening, but turned after they were on the outside. "Go, I'll catch up."

"No," Wade said. "If he returns, he'll kill you."

"I have to get something, I'll only be a minute." She shoved the light into his hand. "Go," she hissed.

"We're wasting time. Come on." Whatever Nicole wanted to retrieve, it must've been important to risk her life. She only hoped she'd find it soon and catch up to them. They hurried down the uneven path toward the pickup.

Dusk had settled over the place, giving them ample coverage in their flight. When they were far enough away, Wade turned the flashlight on, lighting the way for them.

They made it to the pickup and jerked the tarp off. Fallon got in and pulled a couple of wires while Wade held the flashlight.

"Hurry," Nicole frantically whispered as she ran stumbling down the path toward them. She dropped a small black satchel, and quickly bent to retrieve it. "It won't take Cavenaugh and his men long to unload the boxes, and Kinsey will return to the tent."

Fallon's hands stilled. "Cavenaugh? He's there?" She turned to look back. He was this close again?

"Fallon?" Wade grabbed her arm.

She looked at him and saw the question in his eyes. She knew he'd follow her to the ends of the earth if that's what it took.

When had she fallen in love with him? The first time they met? She lightly caressed his swollen face before abruptly turning back to her task. "Let's go home."

"Johnny-boy!" Kinsey's voice echoed across the evening air.

"Damn!" Nicole whirled to look back up the path. "Move faster!"

Fallon saw his hesitation. She touched his hand. "Sometimes you have to let go of the past."

He squeezed her fingers. "You're right. Let's get the hell out of here."

Her hot-wiring techniques were getting rusty; she didn't get the pickup started until her third try. They scrambled inside. Familiar with the land, Nicole jumped behind the wheel and drove at break-neck speed. An explosion lit the sky behind them.

"What the hell was that?" Fallon glanced in the side mirror. Yellow flames shot to the sky.

Nicole chuckled. "The barrel of gunpowder I put inside Kinsey's tent—right before I lit a nice long fuse. I've had it hidden in the back for months, waiting for the right time. I hope he went back inside before it blew. I'd like to think he was blown to smithereens. The bastard."

"We should be so lucky." Wade shifted in the seat.

Fallon glanced in his direction. It was too dark to see his expression, but he had to be hurting. "We'll be at the river soon and we can wash the salt out of your wound."

"Kinsey will expect us to cross there. We'll head east," Nicole told her.

"East?" Wade asked. "The border?"

"He won't go there. He might pay them off, but he isn't stupid. He doesn't take chances."

"What about you?" Fallon asked.

She patted the black bag beside her feet. "Give them enough money, and they'll look the other way in a heartbeat. I figured Kinsey owed me a new start."

"East it is, then."

Nicole found the road, not much more than a rough, wagon path, and turned east when she came to the first crossroads.

And then it hit Fallon. They'd escaped Kinsey . . . they'd escaped death. For the first time in her life, she also felt free of Cavenaugh. Someday he would be brought to justice and made to pay for his crimes, but revenge didn't seem to matter that much anymore.

Someone else had become more important.

It didn't take much to bribe the border officials to let them through without more than a cursory glance at the disreputable pickup or the fact they resembled refugees from a war-torn country.

Nicole took the pickup when they reached the hotel where they'd left Wade's vehicle. Without a backward glance, she headed for Houston and a new start.

"We can't stay here," Wade told Fallon. "I don't know how much Fred told Kinsey."

"Your arm's bleeding again. We can at least clean it before we leave."

But when she would've gone inside the hotel room, he put an arm out to stop her. "Are you sure you're okay about walking away from Cavenaugh?"

She went into his arms, feeling the warmth of his body wrapping around her like a shield protecting her from the injustice man inflicted upon humanity.

"Yeah, I'm okay about it." She hugged him before stepping back and letting him open the door.

A short time later they were on the road. They took turns driving—downing caffeine, and talking about everything except the fact they'd admitted they loved each other.

Wade knew she might have spoken because of the strain they were under. And that she might now regret what she'd told him.

"Why'd you leave the city?" she asked, interrupting his thoughts. "The truth this time—all of it."

He shifted into a more comfortable position. His arm didn't hurt as much. It had eased to a dull ache. It was a good thing Kinsey had wanted to drag things out, or he might have cut deeper.

So why had he left and moved home? "Neverending cycle?"

She shook her head. "I think it was more than that." She hesitated. "Josh said you got caught up in The Pit once before. What exactly did he mean?"

Wade closed his eyes, not wanting to relive that

time, but he owed her an explanation. Would it sicken her as much as it did him? "I was almost as bad as Kinsey," he finally admitted.

She kept her eyes on the road. "I don't believe that."

"I looked the other way." His glance fell outside the window. Trees lost in the dark of the night swept past like shadowy ghosts. "That makes me just as guilty."

"Sometimes we have to wait until the time is right. In the end, all we can do is our best. We're only human."

Her voice was soothing. Wade felt himself relax. He knew she was right, but it didn't stop his feelings of failure. "The Pit is still there."

"But, like you said, if you don't get them, someone else will."

She was right. It was time to let go. Weariness washed over him.

"Sleep," she told him, reaching across and squeezing his hand.

Fallon glanced at the clock. King would be in his office, and probably worried sick. She pulled into a restaurant parking space as Wade stretched and yawned.

"I'd better let King know where we are."

He nodded. "I want to wash, so I'll meet you inside. I feel like I haven't eaten in days."

She nodded and reached for his cell phone. Linda answered on the second ring.

"Is King in?"

"Fallon, I'm so glad you called. No, King isn't here. He went to Mexico."

Her heart skipped a beat. "Mexico?"

"He rang right before you. He took a team with him. They raided The Pit and captured Cavenaugh."

Her hand began to shake. "But it was out of our jurisdiction," she whispered.

"One of his favorite agents needed help. You know King. He strong-armed the Mexican and American government into helping."

"Where can I reach him?"

"Sorry kid, you can't. He's going to meet with some officials and see who gets extradited and who spends the rest of their lives in a Mexican prison. He called to see, as he put it, where the hell his agent was and if you'd checked in." Her soft chuckle came across the line.

Fallon couldn't stop her smile. That sounded exactly like something King would say. "I'm on my way to Two Creeks. I'm staying with the sheriff, Wade Tanner. And Linda . . ."

"Yes?"

"Have him call me as soon as he can." She rattled off the number of Wade's cell phone and hung up. Her limbs suddenly felt like rubber. She rested her head against the steering wheel and drew in a deep breath.

It was over. Her body began to shake. The driver's door opened and Wade pulled her close. "I saw you from the window. What's going on?"

"King and some agents raided The Pit. He got Cavenaugh. It's really finished."

Wade's breath whooshed out. "For both of us."

"I feel like I could eat everything on the menu." She hugged him around the neck.

* * *

Fallon absently scratched Cleo behind her ear. "I don't care what you say, I'm not calling Dr. Canton back and telling him not to come. He needs to look at that arm, and your forehead." She frowned. "Although your forehead doesn't look that bad."

She scooted Cleo off the sofa and leaned across to get a better look. Before she could react, Wade pulled her onto his lap. And nuzzled her neck.

"I can think of a lot better things I'd rather do than have that old codger look at my wounds. I've had a hell of a lot worse than this."

She closed her eyes and let the heat of his lips wash over her. "Ahh, that's nice." She almost wished she hadn't called the doctor. It seemed like forever since they'd made love. Her body screamed for release that only Wade could provide.

"Tell me, did you mean it when you said you loved me, or were you just saying that because you thought we were going to die?"

It took a few seconds for his words to sink into her muddled brain. When they did, she stilled. Slowly, she pulled from his embrace. What if he hadn't meant what he'd said?

"Uh . . ."

He raised his eyebrows. "Cat got your tongue?"

The doorbell chimed.

He chuckled. "Saved by the bell."

Wade started to stand, but she motioned for him to keep his seat. "I'll get it. And after Dr. Canton leaves I might tell you, and I might not." She stuck her nose in the air and waltzed toward the front door. She smiled as she opened it.

The color drained from her face.

"*Chère*, you've been a very bad girl."

Chapter 22

Fallon tried to slam the door, but Cavenaugh's flunkies jumped forward and shoved against it at the same time. Jack grabbed one arm and George the other. She tried to twist free, but their grip only tightened. She opened her mouth to warn Wade, but Jack clamped his hand over her face.

This isn't happening! It couldn't be. King had Cavenaugh in custody. She strained against their hold, but her efforts were useless.

"*Chère,* do not struggle so. You might hurt yourself," Cavenaugh told her.

"What the hell!" Wade came around the corner, but before he could do anything, Cavenaugh raised his gun and pointed it directly at him.

She stilled, holding her breath. George let go, but Jack tightened his hold.

"I think it's time you invited us inside. We wouldn't want to cause alarm from your neighbors." Cavenaugh looked around, saw that all was peaceful in the early morning hours, and came inside. George shut the door behind them.

Jack shoved Fallon forward. She stumbled, but Wade caught her before she fell. "King captured you," she snapped. "How'd you get away?"

She straightened, shoving the hair out of her eyes. *Damn it, what went wrong?* All the rage and hatred she'd thought was in the past came to the surface like a volcano about to erupt.

She took a step forward, but Wade caught her by the wrist before she could put her angry thoughts into action.

"So many questions, and we've only just arrived. Is that any way to treat company?" Cavenaugh motioned with his hand. "Shall we go into the other room?" Then to Jack. "Look around. Make sure we're alone."

Jack rubbed the side of his face, casting a look filled with hatred at Fallon, then went in the opposite direction while George stayed close to Cavenaugh.

She spun on her heel and marched into the living room. "How did you find me? Even King doesn't know where I'm staying."

He motioned for Wade and Fallon to sit on the sofa. She scooted Cleo out of the way, and they sat down.

Cavenaugh smiled. "But you made the mistake of telling his secretary. Didn't you learn anything in the time you worked for me? I can buy anyone I want."

"You bought Linda?" She suddenly wanted to throw up.

"It was an easy thing. A spurned lover—you did know she and King had a brief affair before he ended it. No? It doesn't matter. Then top it off with a job that doesn't pay for all the baubles you women seem to like. Actually, she was quite easy to buy, and went rather cheap."

Fallon raised her chin. "You haven't been able to buy everyone."

"You're wrong, *chère*. Money will buy anything, including you. Not that we'll ever know for sure."

"It wouldn't buy Philip." Her insides twisted. She closed her eyes, then opened them, staring at the man she'd almost forgotten to hate.

His eyes narrowed. "What do you know about my half-brother?"

"That you forgot to kill his other daughter."

Wade's body stiffened next to hers. She wondered briefly what he was thinking, and that she shouldn't care about him so much. Love had made her less cautious. And now they were both paying for it.

"That explains a lot." He laughed. "A family reunion. How wonderful." His eyes turned cold. "At least, until I kill you. And I'll make sure the job is done right this time."

She ignored his threat. "Why did you kill them?" she asked.

"Ah, so that's why you've been hunting me. Curiosity killed the cat."

"And, like I said before, cats have nine lives, and I haven't even begun to use all of mine."

"Yes, I can see where I misjudged you. I think maybe we are more alike. Philip was a spineless creature. I could've made him rich, but he discovered I'd hidden drugs in his house and he destroyed them. The fool. Thousands of dollars flushed down the toilet."

"And Jody?"

"An unfortunate accident." He shrugged. "She got in the way and caught a bullet."

"Damn you," she started up, but Wade grabbed her arm at the same time Cavenaugh raised his gun.

"Take his advice and keep your seat, *chère*. You might live a little longer if you do." He stared at Wade for a long moment before grinning and addressing Fallon. "Your man doesn't care for me, I think. Introduce us. I always like to know the person I'm going to kill."

"I'm Wade Tanner and until you pull that trigger, I'm not dead."

Cavenaugh sat in the chair opposite the couch and crossed his legs. "Maybe you have nine lives, too, eh?"

"Want me to plug him, boss." George guffawed. "Then we can see if he comes back to life."

"You talk too much, George," Cavenaugh said without taking his eyes off them. "Yes, Linda mentioned you. You're the sheriff of this town?"

"Yeah, I'm the sheriff."

"But apparently not a very good one, since I have you held at gunpoint."

"Lay down the gun, and I'll show you what I can do."

"That would not be wise on my part." He chuckled.

Fallon knew that although he looked relaxed sitting in Wade's chair, he would kill them if either one made a wrong move.

Wade squeezed her hand to reassure her, but she couldn't help wondering if they might not get so lucky this time. Damn it, she didn't want Cavenaugh to win again. He had to pay for what he did.

"We have two ways we can do this. Easy, or hard. Give me the disk." He leaned back in the chair. "Imagine my surprise when I returned home to find someone had downloaded from my computer. I'd hate for the disk to get in the wrong hands."

"Wouldn't that be a damn shame." Maybe she could buy them some time. She scanned the room. There wasn't a fresh brewed pot of hot coffee for her to throw like she had the last time. There wasn't much of anything she could use as a weapon.

"A worse shame if I were to shoot your friend," Cavenaugh motioned with his gun toward Wade. "Maybe then you wouldn't mind telling me?"

"Put up your hands," Doc growled.

All heads swiveled toward the entryway into the living room. Fallon's eyes widened. *Oh, no!* Doc stood there with a rusty shotgun older than he was pointed right at Cavenaugh.

"You deaf or something? Drop the guns before I blow a hole clean through you."

Seemingly unconcerned, Cavenaugh quirked an eyebrow and pointed his gun at Wade, but spoke to Dr. Canton. "And who would you be?"

"Not that it's any of your business, but I'm the doctor of this town and I don't plan on stitching up any more of my friends 'cause you took a notion to shoot them."

Fallon gripped the edge of the sofa. Jeez, why the hell hadn't Doc called for help instead of trying to save the day all by himself?

"Drop the gun, old man," Jack said as he came up behind Dr. Canton.

Doc lowered the gun slightly. "Who the hell are you?" He turned to face Jack.

"The grim reaper."

"Well, go to hell," he growled, raising the gun and firing.

Jack screamed and grabbed his arm. The kick from the gun landed Doc on the floor. Cavenaugh jumped to his feet, but so did Wade and Fallon.

Wade clipped George under the chin at the same time Fallon kicked the gun from Cavenaugh's hand. It flew across the room.

"Okay, you bastard, it's time to pay the fucking piper." She raised her fist and punched him in the face. He staggered back a few steps but quickly regained his footing. She dodged to the left when he tried to hit her and came back with a jab to his gut.

From the corner of her eye, she saw that Wade was quickly dispatching George. Jack was incapacitated and Doc didn't look that bad off from his fall. She focused all her attention on Cavenaugh.

"So," he gasped. "We end it here, eh, *chère?* You think you can take your uncle?"

She whipped her body around and kicked him in the side of his face. He went to the ground spitting blood.

"You son-of-a-bitch, you're not my uncle."

He swiped his hand across his face and laughed. "Ah, but you can't change who you are. We *are* related. Sometimes you have to take the bad with the good."

"I don't have to take a damn thing."

She raised her foot to kick again but misjudged the speed with which he could recover. He grabbed her foot and twisted, taking her to the ground. Before she could stand, he'd lunged for the gun she'd kicked from his hand earlier.

"I think now is a good time to end this." Cavenaugh raised the gun.

An explosion reverberated through the house.

Pieces of Cavenaugh's gun flew from his hand. He screamed and clutched his bleeding fingers.

"You're right, now is a good time to end this," Andy stated from the doorway. "Doc, you okay?" he asked, keeping his eye on Cavenaugh.

"Took you long enough to get here. I think I cracked my damn tailbone."

"I was out in the county on a call." Andy stuck his free hand toward the doctor and helped him to his feet, keeping his eye on Cavenaugh.

"Blasted gun didn't used to kick like that." Doc rubbed his backside, then went to Jack who moaned as he lay slumped in the floor. He glanced at the man's wound. "You'll live—if you don't bleed to death. Wouldn't that be a loss for society," he grumbled, going in the direction of the bathroom.

"Fallon? You okay?"

She looked at her hands and frowned. "I broke a damn nail."

Andy tossed Wade his handcuffs. Wade caught them and cuffed Cavenaugh. "Like I said, I'm not dead until you pull the trigger."

Doc came back and used a towel to stem the bleeding from Jack's wound.

"And I was going fishing this afternoon. Looks like I'll be in surgery instead." He glared down at Jack. "Ever had a pissed off doctor operating on you?"

"You took an oath."

"Why the hell does everyone think taking some oath makes me perfect?"

Wade grabbed his handcuffs, and although George didn't look like he would cause any more problems, he cuffed him.

Fallon looked around. It was truly over now. Cavenaugh would go to prison for the rest of his life.

Her gaze met Wade's across the room. King would laugh his ass off when she told him she'd fallen in love. Her, the tough agent with ice water running through her veins. What the hell would happen next in her life?

* * *

"You did a damn fine job, Fallon." King leaned back in the chair across from Wade's desk and stretched his legs in front of him. "You, too, Tanner."

"Thanks." Wade tapped the pencil's eraser lightly on the desktop and watched Fallon. She looked comfortable and relaxed sitting in a chair next to King. She and Wade really hadn't had a chance to talk. King had shown up not long after they'd put Cavenaugh and George in jail.

Now that Cavenaugh was incarcerated, would Fallon return to her job?

"What will happen now?" he asked.

"The Pit has been shut down . . . at least for a while. Kinsey will be sitting in a Mexican jail for some time. Louisiana will want to extradite Cavenaugh, I'm sure. He left the state the same day Fallon went to the cops. Guess he was afraid he couldn't buy everyone. And . . ."

"I don't care about that." Wade looked directly at Fallon, his tapping picked up tempo. "What are you going to do?"

"She'll get a commendation, of course," King spoke before Fallon had a chance to say anything. "I'm going to be busy looking for another secretary, since mine is in jail," he frowned. "But I have a case I want Fallon to start on . . ."

"No." Fallon met and held Wade's gaze. "I'm going to take a vacation."

"But . . ."

"No." She looked at King. "You owe me the time, and I'm taking it."

King sat forward in his chair. "And just where are you going that's so damned important."

"I'm not going anywhere. I want to explore Two Creeks a little more."

A slow, lazy smile lifted the corners of Wade's mouth.

King snorted. "That'll take all of two minutes."

Fallon stood, sauntering toward Wade. "Nope, it'll take a lot longer than that because I plan on doing a thorough investigation."

"Oh." His eyes widened. "Ohhhhh."

Wade came to his feet, wrapping his arms around Fallon just before tasting the sweetness of her lips.

Now this was pure southern comfort that no man would be willing to pass up.

The last thing Wade heard was the closing of the door as King let himself out.

Fallon moaned softly against his lips. "Ever made love in your office?"

Epilogue

"No," Fallon corrected Audrey. "You lean to the right and kick left so you can keep your balance." She moved the woman to the center of Wade's living room, trying not to laugh.

Audrey had arrived wearing lime-green sweats, sneakers, and a wild purple bandana. She wanted to be shown some of the defensive moves Fallon had used in the mall.

"Cleo, move before you get hurt." Fallon gently shooed the cat back.

"Come here, Cleopatra," Callie said, patting the sofa beside her, keeping her feet out of the way so no one would accidentally bump her sprained ankle. "Let's watch Miss Audrey kick ass."

"Ass?" Bailey repeated with raised eyebrow.

"Butt?" Callie's brow furrowed in concentration.

Fallon really tried to keep a straight face, but she couldn't help herself. She sat on the floor and began laughing. The other three looked at each other before breaking down and joining in.

When their laughter was spent, Fallon leaned

back on her hands and looked at the three women. She'd been here only a week, but she felt like she'd known them all her life.

"So Fallon," Bailey innocently asked. "Are you and my brother going to make it legal?"

Fallon tossed a pillow toward Wade's sister, who caught it and used it to cushion her elbow.

"None of your business." She straightened, crossing her legs in front of her. Not meeting their eyes, she became intent on examining her freshly painted nails. "And my name isn't really Fallon Hargis. I took that off a tomb before I left New Orleans."

"Tell us your real name," Audrey asked softly, giving Fallon's hand a gentle squeeze.

"Brigitte Dupree." She looked up then.

"I like that name." Bailey smiled. The other two nodded.

The front door opened and all heads turned.

"Is this a private party, or can anyone join?" Wade asked.

"Come in," Audrey sang out. "You're always welcome—especially in your own home. Besides, I have to be going. Ben will be wondering where I am."

"Me, too," Callie chimed in, wiggling off the sofa and grabbing her crutches. "Some of the girls from class are coming over tonight and we're having a slumber party."

"I'll drive you home," Bailey offered.

Fallon took Wade's hand and came to her feet. They walked them to the door and then went back to the living room.

"Do you think they knew we wanted to be by ourselves?" Fallon asked.

He nuzzled the side of her neck. Warm tingles ran up and down her spine.

"Maybe." He drew in a deep breath and moved away from her.

"Have I lost my ability to arouse you so soon?"

When he grinned all she could think about was grabbing his hand and dragging him into the bedroom. She didn't think she'd ever get her fill of this man.

"Just the opposite," he told her. "I can't say what I need to say with your body pressed against mine."

His expression grew serious, enough so a tremor of fear swept over her.

"What?"

"I've located the cemetery where your father's entombed."

She clasped her hands together and walked to the window, her steps heavy. Leaning her head against the pane, she drew in a shaky breath as memories assaulted her.

Her father's laughter. The way he'd hugged her, and Jody, close to him. Ah, Jody. She'd only been seven.

"I . . . I want to go home, Wade. I want to say goodbye to them."

"Fallon . . ."

Something in his voice made her turn and look at him.

"Your sister isn't dead."

"What?" The room began to spin. Strong arms circled her, bringing her close until the world was once more in focus. "I saw her. There was blood."

"Trust me, sweetheart, she's alive. She's a cop in New Orleans. I've already made arrangements to leave as soon as you can throw some things into a suitcase."

"Jody's alive." Tears she'd never let herself cry

ran down her face. "I love you, Wade Tanner." She threw her arms around his neck and kissed him long and hard. For once in her life, something good had happened.

And all because she held a sexy man at gunpoint and ordered him to strip.

We don't think you will want to miss
SOUTHERN EXPOSURE
by Karen Kelley,
coming in April 2005 from Brava.
Here's a sneak peek.

The captain looked toward the glass door. "Here he is now." Standing, he offered a welcoming smile. The door behind her opened as she came to her feet.

"Good, you made it. Logan Hart, I'd like to introduce you to your partner for the next month, Jody Dupree."

Oh crap, this wasn't happening. She could feel the color draining from her face. Please, let there be more than one Logan Hart. The doughnut she'd eaten earlier threatened to come up.

Surely there had to be another Logan Hart. She hadn't felt anything. Not one little tingle that something would happen. But just in case, she sent a quick prayer upward. Please, please, please let it be a middle-aged man with thick glasses, three kids, and a wife.

Slowly, she turned. Her heart clunked to her feet, but shot right back up on a flutter of excitement that she couldn't ignore. Right on excitement's heels came irritation.

What the hell was a reporter doing stripping in a club? Had he been moonlighting? No wait, the captain had mentioned a series of articles. His stripping had only been another story to him. Damn, damn, damn!

Logan watched the changing expressions on her face. Surprise, disbelief, and right now she didn't look at all happy. He wasn't exactly pleased himself. When he'd opened his eyes the next morning to find her gone, he couldn't have felt more used than if she'd left money on the nightstand.

A couple of the male strippers had warned him most of the women only wanted the fantasy to become real for one night. After that, they'd sneak home to their unsuspecting husbands. The men at the club told him it worked out well for everyone concerned.

It hadn't worked well for him. Hell, he hadn't been able to get her or the incredible sex they'd shared out of his mind. But it'd been more than that. He'd felt something deep inside him. Something he'd wanted to explore. But she'd left.

How do you look for someone when you only know her first name?

"Mr. Hart."

She held out her hand. He didn't hesitate as he took her hand in his. Hers felt small and warm, the palm a little moist. Was she nervous? She should be. She returned his grip with a solid shake of her own.

Okay, so she wanted to pretend she didn't know him. That was fine with him,. Two could play that game. "Let's not be so formal. You can call me Logan. And I hope it's not presumptuous of me if I call you Jody. Or would you prefer I use your *last* name?"

"Jody is fine." Her jaw twitched.

Suddenly, he saw the humor in the situation and smiled. "It will be a pleasure spending the month with you. *I'm sure* you'll show me a lot I hadn't planned on seeing."

Her smile could've chipped ice. "*I'm sure* you've seen more than I will ever show you."

She didn't have to add—*again.* He easily filled in the blank. "I don't know. I can be pretty persuasive I'm told. I want to know everything . . . about law enforcement and the city, that is."

"And Jody will be the perfect guide. She knows this town forward and backward. And she's a damn fine cop." The captain looked quite pleased with himself.

Logan grinned as he followed Jody out of the room and to the parking garage. She never said a word, not that he minded. He liked the sway of her hips. But the enticing movement didn't fool him. Her back was rigid and her shoulders squared. She didn't want him within ten feet of her.

The other strippers were right, she'd only gone to the club for a one night fantasy. He should be angry, feel used, but how could he when he'd never spent a sweeter night? Having her arms tangled with his, her legs wedged between his, had been as close to heaven as he would ever get in this lifetime.

And he didn't intend for it to be the last. She'd enjoyed their night together as much as he had.

She stopped next to a blue and white patrol car and whirled around to face him. Whatever she'd been about to say must have gotten hung in her throat. She stared at him without speaking until some officers walked past talking and laughing.

"Don't look at me like that." She frowned. "What happened between us is over."

A lazy grin lifted the corners of his mouth. "You enjoyed it as much as I did."

She jerked her keys from her pocket, almost dropping them as she strode to the driver's side and unlocked the door. "Did I say it hadn't been enjoyable?" she met his gaze across the top of the car. "I said there wouldn't be a repeat performance."

As she climbed in and unlocked his door, his smile grew wider.

Discover the Thrill of Romance With
Kat Martin

Desert Heat   0-8217-7381-X   **$6.99**US/**$9.99**CAN
For Ph.D candidate Patience Sinclair, leaving the ivy-covered campus of
Boston University for the wide, open spaces of Texas means a chance to
stop looking over her shoulder at every turn. Traveling incognito with the
Triple C Rodeo will help her finish her dissertation on the American
West while hiding in plain sight. But she can't hide from Dallas King-
man. The champion rider makes it clear that he's watching her...and he
likes what he sees.

Midnight Sun   0-8217-7380-1   **$6.99**US/**$9.99**CAN
Call Hawkins just wants to be left alone and leave the past where it
belongs. The bleak beauty of Dead Horse Creek is a perfect place to get
away from the world...a place where nothing exists to remind him of
everything he's lost. His isolation is complete—until Charity Sinclair
arrives from New York City. Stunningly beautiful and stubbornly
independent, she's shamefully ignorant of the untamed wilderness...and
the very real dangers she'll face if Call doesn't teach her a thing or two.

Hot Rain   0-8217-6935-9   **$6.99**US/**$8.99**CAN
Allie Parker is in the wrong place—at the worst possible time...Her only
ally is mysterious Jake Dawson, who warns her that she must play the
role of his reluctant bedmate...if she wants to stay alive. Now, as Allie
places her trust—and herself—in the hands of a total stranger, she
wonders if this desperate gamble will be her last...

The Secret   0-8217-6798-4   **$6.99**US/**$8.99**CAN
Kat Rollins moved to Montana looking to change her life, not find
another man like Chance McLain, with a sexy smile of empty heart.
Chance can't ignore the desire he feels for her—or the suspicion that
somebody wants her to leave Lost Peak...

The Dream   0-8217-6568-X   **$6.99**US/**$8.99**CAN
Genny Austin is convinced that her nightmares are visions of another
life she lived long ago. Jack Brennan is having nightmares, too, but his
are real. In the shadows of dreams lurks a terrible truth, and only by
unlocking the past will Genny be free to love at last...

Available Wherever Books Are Sold!

Visit our website at www.kensingtonbooks.com.